ZIA

TERRY LOVETT

For Information: http://terrylovett.blogspot.com

Book Design by WKL

Cover Photo by Дмитрий Байрачный

Zia-Book 1

ISBN-13: 978-1461127642
ISBN-10: 1461127645

To Sarah,

Hope you
enjoy the book!

Best
Wishes,
Jerry

CONTENTS

ACKNOWLEDGMENTS

Special thanks to...

My wonderful parents, Bob and Frankie Anderson, for a lifetime of love and support.

My two beautiful children, Scotty and Whitney, for teaching me the meaning of unconditional love.

The three best friends anyone could ever ask for: Pam, my best Texas friend; Jaime, my best Florida friend; and Hallie, my best Always and Forever friend.

Everyone in Celebration, Florida for giving me the best seven years of my life.

The Walt Disney Company, for designing, planning and building a community like Celebration – the *real* Happiest Place on Earth!

CHAPTER 1
THE SQUEEZLE

Zia stepped cautiously as she crossed the grass by the water's edge. It was soft and moist from the morning dew. Each blade of blue grass glistened with a drop of diamond colored water. The moisture had softened the leaves and twigs in her path, making them less brittle and prone to snap underfoot. Slowly, Zia placed one bare foot in front of the other and proceeded away from the river and toward the Baobab tree just ahead.

She glanced down occasionally to make sure each step fell silently on the mossy grass. Tiny gold rings encircled each of her toes.

Zia turned her head from side to side, determining her location before continuing. Her long blond hair swayed across the back of her thulian pink gossamer gown. The ends of her hair stopped only a few inches above the belt quiver wrapped around her tiny waist. In her left hand, she carried a bow made of yew.

Returning her attention to the blue moss path, Zia continued at a slow but sure pace. She chose her moments of movement, synchronizing her steps with the ambient sounds of the forest. While a dark-plumaged Jackdaw cawed to its mate, Zia picked her way silently through the forest floor.

She narrowed her gaze toward the Maiden Hair fern growing at the path's end. Zia thought she saw movement within its leaves, and proceeded with quiet care as not to alarm whatever creature might be taking refuge there. She placed the heel of her foot down first and rolled it slowly and gently toward her toes, all the while focusing on the fern just a few yards away.

Then suddenly, it appeared! At first Zia could see only its tiny pink head poking out of its hiding place. Its large ebony eyes darted from side to side, checking to make sure its emergence would be into a safe environment.

Amazingly, the enormous coal eyes ensconced inside the diminutive cranium had overlooked Zia's presence. She dared not breathe as the creature slowly emerged from its hiding place.

Upon its fuzzy head grew tufts of soft shimmering antennae. They protruded in all directions, delicate and pencil thin. Zia could count at least eight of the projectiles, all moving and tilting in a manner that suggested the creature was anticipating danger.

Slowly the animal stepped from the cover of the fern, allowing Zia to scrutinize it closer. Fully exposed, it was magnificent to behold. Its six legs moved cautiously, the back two locked in a position indicating it was prepared to flee the instant it sensed peril.

With its entire body now in full view, Zia could see that it was, without question that which she hunted for. She couldn't believe her good fortune. Her heart raced as she drank in the beauty of the elusive, the one, the only – Squeezle!

For an instant, Zia thought she couldn't allow herself to take the life of such a beautiful creature - the last of its kind. But the idea quickly left her mind as she imagined the vast rewards she would soon acquire. The praise of the entire kingdom would be hers when she delivered the creature to King Bourdaine.

She alone would be the archer to bring this most sought after prize before the thrown. Oh, the riches she would receive, the glory she would be lauded with! But most importantly, King Bourdaine would bestow upon her a new adventure - her next quest!

Before the moment of victory was lost, Zia reached into her quiver and removed an arrow. While balancing her weight between the ball and heel of each foot, Zia raised the bow in her left hand and pulled the bowstring back until it rested on her coral lips. Zia's bow arm moved to align the sight pin into the center of her target, but just as her fingers prepared for release a voice pierced the moment.

"Zia, Zia," it shouted from the sky. "Stop Now!" The voice was everywhere. It boomeranged off the trees and rocks. A flooding panic swept over Zia, and she removed her attention from the Squeezle.

"No!" she screamed, but it was too late.

Her green eyes watched in horror as the sun slowly began to melt. The turquoise sky began to break apart into tiny pieces, and with each second, another piece of the vista fell away. It was as if someone had thrown a rock through the plate glass window horizon, and Zia was watching it slowly shatter. The world appeared to be dissolving around her. The landscape was rapidly changing. Trees vanished and sounds of the forest became hushed, replaced with nothing but the sound of Zia's own breathing.

The remaining azure moss on which Zia stood, shimmered for a moment, and was then, extinguished. The world she'd inhabited was gone, and there was nothing around her but darkness. Zia could see nothing through the opacity, which now engulfed her. She screamed and screamed at the top of her lungs! She screamed until her aching throat was raw.

For what seemed an endless period of time, Zia stood motionless in the abyss. Then, slowly, a white light appeared far above her. She watched as it became brighter and brighter, until finally, the light engulfed the entire area. It hurt her eyes, and she blinked to stop the stinging. Using a raised hand to shield her face from the burning glow, Zia turned to inspect her new surroundings. She stood in a small, twelve-by-twelve-foot room. The walls, floor, and ceiling were all bare and as white as the alabaster light shining far above.

Her own appearance had also altered. The bow had disappeared from Zia's hand, and her beautiful gown was gone, replaced with a simple grey tank top and denim shorts. A pair of ordinary white tennis shoes substituted for the golden rings that had only moments before circled her delicate toes. Even Zia's long golden tresses had reverted to a disheveled dirty-blonde ponytail.

A buzzer sound emanated from one of the walls, followed by a loud click. Zia waited. A door opened to reveal Zia's brother, Shane, standing in the hallway of their townhouse.

"I hate you!" Zia shouted to her older brother who was leaning cross-armed against the game room door. "I've been playing this game every day for a week," Zia whirled on Shane, her eyes blazing with anger, "Every single day to get to this level, and now you shut the system off - just when I'm about to win! I can't believe it, I just can't believe it!"

Throwing up her arms, Zia stormed past Shane, extending her middle finger as she passed.

"Listen," her brother's voice rose. "It was Mom who buzzed you over and over to stop and come to dinner, *not* me. I just got picked to come upstairs and get you." A smirk settled on Shane's lips before he continued, "Don't hate me Trinity. I'm just the messenger."

The movie quote wasn't lost on his sister. "This aint *The Matrix*, smart-ass," Zia shot back.

Shane shook his head in exasperation. He closed the game room portal, clicked off the red blinking light on the control panel, and followed his sister down the hall.

The command switch flashed in response, *Game Over*.

CHAPTER 2
BELLABOO, BELLATOO

Zia stomped into the kitchen not sure which person she was angrier with, her mother or her brother. Why there was such a rush to eat some pre-fabricated dinner spit out of a food replicator, she had no idea. Zia would love to have microwaved meals like everyone else, but her mother's ideas about cooking were summed-up by the two magnets on the replicator's door - *Eating Out Is In* and *My Favorite Thing To Make For Dinner Is Reservations*.

Zia's mother and great-grandmother were already sitting at the table when she entered the room.

"Well, sunshine, thanks for deciding to join us." Zia's mother glanced up from her plate.

She tried to give her daughter a smile, but Zia looked the other way and plopped down in her chair. She kept her arms crossed and her jaws locked. She was mad, and she was going to make sure everyone knew it.

Shane strolled in behind his younger sister. "Hey Oma," he patted his great-grandmother on the shoulder as he walked behind her chair.

What an asshat her brother was. Always kissing up, always trying to be the family favorite.

"You make me wanna hurl, churl," Zia spat the words across the table to Shane.

"Be quiet, Zia. You're so deficient." He nonchalantly pulled out his chair, refusing to make eye contact with his sister.

Was she so unimportant, so non-threatening, that he couldn't waste a passing glance on her? Shane really knew how to push her buttons, and he was well aware of how angry it made her when he wrapped himself in that blanket of condescending smugness. Zia was ready to fight back, but because her mom and Oma were watching, she suppressed the words aching to leap from her tongue.

"Please, please don't fight during dinner," their mother begged, trying to diffuse the tense situation.

"Now, Chessie, that's just what brothers and sisters do." Oma's tone was light and pleasant in contrast to her granddaughter's pensive posture. Obviously, a century of listening to sibling bickering had desensitized Oma to the rigid atmosphere hovering over the dinner table.

"Well, Iden and I never fought like these two." Chessie shifted her glance between her two offspring.

Oma smiled. "Well, that's only because he was ten years older. You didn't see each other as rivals."

Zia looked across the table at her brother. Maybe Oma was right about the rival part. Shane was, without question, her adversary, and Zia was positive their mother favored him.

She glared at her brother over the dinner plate and squirmed irately in her chair. He might be two years older, but being a college freshman didn't give him the right to boss her around constantly. She was happy he was away at college; happy that he only made the forty-five mile trek back home when he needed some favor from Mom. Let's see, what was it today? Oh yes, he needed his laundry done.

But the worst thing about her brother was that all her girlfriends thought he was *so* nice – *and* handsome.

Shane stood a little over six feet tall and had the muscular build of the athlete that he was. He had been the captain of both the soccer and hockey teams in high school, and he'd even received a college scholarship to play for UCF's hockey team. His hair was a wavy ash brown, naturally highlighted by the bright Florida sunshine, his ice blue eyes enhanced by his perpetual dark tan.

Zia never tanned. She burned. And she was burning now, fuming as she watched him gab away with their mom and Oma, flashing that perfect white toothy grin of his. Zia wanted to wipe that sugary smile right off his face, but instead, she decided to give her entire family the silent treatment.

Unfortunately, no one noticed, so after a considerable amount of time spent pouting, Zia finally decided the meal didn't look too bad and proceeded to eat something. She nibbled at the food on her plate, silently watching her mother and Oma discuss the day's events.

They looked remarkably alike. Both were tall and slender with chestnut colored hair and fair complexions. In fact, the resemblance between the two was so great one could easily mistake them for sisters rather than a grandmother and granddaughter.

For a woman of one hundred and twenty, Oma looked fantastic! But why shouldn't she? As Oma was so fond of pointing out, there was no reason for a woman to age gracefully anymore. That is, not if she didn't want to.

In the past fifty years, aesthetic surgery had advanced farther and quicker than anyone could ever have imagined, and with all the medical breakthroughs – cures for cancer, heart disease, Alzheimer's, arthritis, the list went on and on – why shouldn't people look beautiful while enjoying their extended life spans? Oma certainly did. In fact, Zia was certain that her great-grandmother had to be New U Medical Resurrection Clinic's best customer!

While Zia analyzed the appearance of the family's female members, Oma's pug, Bellaboo, bounced between the chairs, waiting for a handout.

"Oh Chess, give her just a little bite," Oma begged her granddaughter.

"Nope. Table scraps are bad for dogs." Chessie gave Zia and Shane a *don't-you-do-it-either* look.

Zia smiled at her mother, but quietly slipped Bellaboo a quick bite under the table anyway. When Oma leaned over to baby talk her beloved pet, Zia kicked her brother under the table.

"You know, Shane," she giggled, "Its not healthy for *Bellatoo* if we give her people food."

His eyes bore into Zia, indicating he'd heard her use the name Bellatoo rather than Bellaboo.

Shane glanced quickly at his great-grandmother, but she remained oblivious to the name change and continued with her meal, ignoring her granddaughter's lecture, and feeding the bouncing pup from her plate.

Unbeknown to Oma, Bellaboo had met with a very unfortunate event several years before, and Zia used the tragedy for her continued entertainment whenever she found herself angry with her brother.

The accident had occurred three summers earlier while Oma was in Texas visiting her daughter. Shane had just gotten his driver's license, and in his youthful rush to go cruising around with friends, forgotten to close the back door completely. He never saw the fat little pug follow him into the garage.

As Shane backed the car out, he felt the thud. He cursed to himself, thinking how angry he would be if the snap he'd heard was caused by the breaking of one of his hockey sticks. They usually leaned cautiously against the garage wall, supported by his hockey bag, and he wondered how he could have been so careless!

He jumped out and slammed the car door, walking to the back of the vehicle to look under the rear wheel. What he saw made him wish it had only been a hockey stick he'd heard snap - but it wasn't. Shane could tell from the angle of her body that Bellaboo was dead. In a panic, he ran to the back door, yelling for his sister to come outside.

Zia was watching one of her favorite programs on the den's wall screen, and his urgency annoyed her. She grudgingly lifted her body from the sofa and strolled lethargically to the garage. Shane met her at the back door, holding the lifeless dog in his arms. Now she understood his desperation.

"Oh my god!" Zia couldn't bear to look, and buried her face in her hands. "What happened?"

Shane tried to explain the accident, but Zia was inconsolable, and he instinctively knew that if his sister couldn't be calmed down, his great-grandmother would be hysterical.

"Shit! We have to get her to the vet now!" He motioned for his sister to get in the car.

Zia nodded in agreement but didn't understand what he had planned. The dog was obviously dead, but she slid in on the passenger side anyway. Shane passed her the limp body of Bellaboo, and Zia cradled the pug in her arms, still wondering why her brother was rushing them to the vet's office. Veterinarians couldn't raise animals from the dead, could they?

In uneasy silence, the siblings drove to Water Tower Center where the animal clinic was located. Luckily, the distance to Dr.

Mundy's office was short, and they were able to park near the front door.

Shane grabbed the dog from his sister's arms and rushed into the clinic, Zia trotting behind. The receptionist looked up as they entered the building. Shane didn't have to say a word. The seriousness of the situation was obvious, and she immediately escorted the siblings to a private room.

Dr. Mundy entered soon after, but before she could even examine the pug, Shane began to question her as to where they might get the dog cloned. Zia sat and cried quietly in a corner chair, trying to absorb what was happening around her. She leaned forward to focus on their conversation.

Dr. Mundy was recommending several pet cloning clinics to Shane. "I would suggest either the Second Life Cloning Center or Carbon Copy Pet Cloning," she said.

Zia tried to pay attention, but her thoughts continued to float in and out of the ensuing conversation as she imagined the reaction Oma would have upon returning home and finding her pet deceased - or more precisely - smushed! Engrossed in her own somber contemplation, Zia was startled when Shane suddenly lifted her by the arms and directed her to the exit. He thanked the doctor as he whisked his sister out the door.

"Wha…what did she say?" Zia asked, wiping the tears from her cheeks.

Shane opened Zia's car door and placed Bellaboo on her lap as she slid in. "She gave us two choices," he said. "I'm choosing the second one because it's here in town. You've probably driven past the place. It's Carbon Copy Pet Cloning. The doctor said it'd be less expensive."

"Okay," Zia sighed, and looked out the car window. She didn't really care what Shane's reason was for choosing this particular clinic, she just wanted to get there as quickly as possible.

Shane pulled away from the veterinarian's office and headed toward Celebration Place, where a variety of hospitals and medical clinics were located. Just before reaching the main hospital – the one for humans - the siblings spotted the cloning center and pulled into the parking lot.

Out front marched a small group of protesters carrying signs proclaiming *Pet Cloning Is Not For Pet Lovers*!

"Zealots," Shane muttered under his breath.

He and Zia exited the car, racing past the group and into the center's opulent lobby. Several individuals sat on overstuffed chairs in the waiting area. Some cradled packages or blankets in their arms. Were these also 'recently deceased' pets Zia wondered? There was no odor of decay in the lobby, but the thought made her stomach rise into her mouth.

Zia tugged at her brother's sleeve. "I'm gonna be sick," she said, but Shane was unsympathetic.

"Shut up and sit down," he commanded, walking toward the receptionist's desk.

Zia decided that not looking at the other people in the waiting room might help, so she selected a chair far away from the others and sat down. She closed her eyes, but it was only an instant before Zia had the uncomfortable sensation that she was being watched. She slowly opened one eye. The entire waiting area was staring at her!

She suddenly realized it was because Bellaboo was the only cadaverous pet displayed in plain view. Zia scrambled to remove her sweater, and carefully wrapped the little dog in it.

She shut her eyes again, and pressed Bellaboo against her chest. But as she did, Zia felt a cold caress stroke the back of her neck. Rigor mortis must already be setting in, because the dog was no longer flopping in her arms, but felt rigid and unmovable. The sensation made Zia shudder.

She quickly - but gently - laid the canine on the chair next to her, once more closing her eyes to block out the view of the room. Eventually, Shane rejoined his sister, giving her a sharp poke in the side. Zia opened her eyes with a start.

"Ouch! Watch it!" She glanced around the room. "What did the receptionist say?"

Shane settled into the seat beside Zia, glancing at the canine corpse lying next to her. "She said the cloning process can be performed immediately since the animal just died – or in her words - only just expired."

"How much is it gonna cost?" Zia asked.

"More than you and I have in our savings combined." Shane let out a deep sigh, and looked down at his folded hands.

Poor Oma, Zia thought. She couldn't begin to imagine what this loss would do to her. "Please, call Mom. She'll want to help…for Oma's sake." Zia was adamant. "She won't be mad at you."

Shane didn't look convinced, but he nodded and walked to the far corner of the room. He removed a small black and silver device from his pocket and placed it to his ear. Zia watched from a distance. She could tell by Shane's hand gestures that he was giving their mother the complete story. He paced back and forth as he talked, nervously running his fingers through his hair. Finally, he nodded and returned the palm-sized device to his pocket. He walked back toward Zia, his shoulders drooping, his chin only inches from his upper chest.

"What did mom say?" Zia asked impatiently as he returned. Shane raised his eyes, noticing the anxious expression on his sister's face.

"It's okay. Mom will cover what we can't pay for." He let out a relieved breath, and collapsed in the chair next to his sister. "And I promise I'll pay you back your money."

Funny, he hadn't even asked her if she'd lend him the money from her savings account. But it didn't matter. She would, and he already knew it.

They waited in silence for over an hour, but the receptionist finally called Shane's name. As the two stood up, Zia leaned over to pick up Bellaboo but recoiled at the stiffness of the little dog's body. She stepped back with a shiver. Shane reached around his sister and picked up the body wrapped in her sweater.

They walked toward the heavy wooden doors, which the receptionist had opened for their admittance into the cloning area. They followed her through the massive entrance, and began walking down a seemingly endless hall. The floors gleamed like ice, and floor-to-ceiling stained-glass windows lined the walkway. It reminded Zia of the long hallway Dorothy and her friends were required to march down before their audience with the Wizard of Oz.

The receptionist walked several paces ahead of the siblings, occasionally glancing over her shoulder to make sure they were still following. The place was eerie, and Zia felt as nervous as the Cowardly Lion as they continued down the cavernous hall.

After several turns, they arrived at an ominous looking door marked *Neither Truly Gone Nor Forgotten*. The receptionist stopped and motioned with her well-manicured hand for them to proceed without her.

"Patients with pets enter here," she instructed.

Zia and Shane stepped though the doorway, and were immediately greeted by a doctor and his assistant. Both wore green scrubs and broad smiles. The doctor was short in stature, with dark hair and a grey streaked goatee. He smiled and introduced himself as Dr. Kuitu.

"That's pronounced Kweetoo," he said, repeating the name more slowly. "And this is my assistant, Nurse Frieda." The doctor turned to his assistant.

Nurse Frieda also displayed a broad smile, but little else on her face. She wore no makeup, and her hair was pulled back in an exceedingly severe style. Zia wondered if having her hair drawn back so tightly was what created the nurse's wide grin.

Dr. Kuitu interrupted her thoughts. "I understand your little baby has had a most regrettable accident, and you wish to remedy the situation. Yes?" He smiled, waiting for a response from one of the siblings.

"Uh...yes," Shane found his voice first. "Our great-grandmother's pug was uh...well, run over...and we don't want her to find out. It would kill her."

"Oh, we can't have that happening now, can we?" grinned the doctor. "So, you'll want the little angel cloned immediately. Yes?"

"Yes." Shane's voice was full of nervous uncertainty. "Will that be a problem?"

"Why, no, not at all," beamed Dr. Kuitu. "But the sooner you want to be reunited with your beloved companion, the costlier the procedure." He still had that frozen smile on his face, as did nurse Frieda.

"Ok, ok." Shane appeared slightly agitated. "What's the timeline?"

"Well," began Dr. Kuitu, "the procedure involves taking a canine egg and replacing it with the genetic material of the dog to be cloned. The process can be accelerated by ..."

"We don't care about the procedure," Zia interrupted. "We just want to know *how soon* we can have a full grown dog that looks and acts just like this one." She motioned to the lifeless canine in her brother's arms.

"Well, it can be done of course." The doctor glanced sideways at Nurse Frieda. "However, as I said before, the sooner you desire the return of your companion, the higher the price."

"Just tell me when and how much!" Shane was losing his patience.

The doctor removed Bellaboo from Zia's sweater for closer examination. He looked at Shane and shifted his glance to Zia, finally returning his eyes to Shane.

"I can have your beloved back in your arms within two weeks." He smiled.

"Looking just as she does now? I mean…full grown…not a puppy." Zia wanted to make certain.

"Why, yes, my dear," he replied. "You'll have your same sweet companion, and the time apart will be so brief, you'll think your beloved was only away at the pet motel for a vacation."

Zia and Shane looked at each other, reading the others thoughts. What if this didn't work out the way Dr. Kuitu said it would? They had no real guarantee. What if they lost all their money - and Mom's? Zia looked her brother squarely in the eye, shrugged her shoulders, and moved her head from side to side as if to say, 'What choice do we have?'

She glanced over at Nurse Frieda and Dr. Kuitu, waiting silently with those stupid grins branded on their faces. If they meant for the frozen expression to be comforting, it wasn't working. In fact, it created just the opposite sensation. A feeling of having just woken up in the middle of some creepy B Movie was beginning to crawl through Zia's body.

Her imagination raced, and she envisioned the doctor imprisoning her and Shane in his clinic, running human-animal transplant experiments on them. She was fantasizing about the demonstrators in front of the clinic refusing to come to their rescue, when her brother's sudden movement interrupted her frightening daydreams.

Apparently Shane knew there was no other choice, and quickly handed the animal to the doctor.

"Thank you, then," said Doctor Kuitu. "And please, stop at the receptionist's desk on the way out to complete some minimal paperwork."

His face beamed as he turned on his heel and carried poor, lifeless Bellaboo from the room. Nurse Frieda trotted after him, turning at the door to glance back at the siblings. Was it Zia's imagination, or had the silly smile vanished from the nurse's lips just as she exited the room?

Left alone in the examination area, Zia and Shane looked hesitantly at each other. They retraced their steps down the chambered hallway and returned to the receptionist's desk in the lobby.

After completing what turned out to be a mountain of paperwork, Shane made a down payment and the two left the center. They pushed past the protestors still shuffling about outside the clinic, and walked to the car.

At home, the two rehashed the day's events with their mother, and as Chessie had promised earlier, she agreed to pay any remaining balance needed. Oma would be home in just over two weeks, so they would be cutting the cloning process close.

If Shane had the same concerns as Zia, he never said, but Zia spent many sleepless nights envisioning Dr. Kuitu as a mad scientist, performing unspeakable experiments on animals. One night she even dreamed that he replaced Bellaboo's brain with a chicken brain, and all she could do was cluck and cackle when she returned home.

However, two weeks later when the siblings returned to the cloning center with their final payment, they received - surprisingly to them - what by all outward appearances was Bellaboo – the one and original.

After a quick refresher course of the home's layout, daily activities, and favorite toys, Bellatoo settled right in. She was sleeping peacefully in her usual chair when Oma returned a few days later.

Everyone was relieved that Oma was none the smarter, and although Shane kept his word about paying Zia back, she often found herself feeling increasingly annoyed that her brother had created such a catastrophe. It was this feeling of vexation that snapped Zia's thoughts back into the present.

"Sunshine," Oma smiled at Zia, and slid a small pink device across the table to her. "Your cell phone was ringing while you were in the game room. You might want to check it."

"Thanks, Oma." Zia returned her great-grandmother's smile. "But they aren't called cell phones anymore. It's a tess."

"Well, I'm too old to change." Oma grinned at her great-granddaughter. "I still say cell phone, video game, face book - all those outdated terms. What the heck does tess stand for anyway?"

Zia smiled at Oma. She adored her great-grandmother, even if her vernacular mainframe was obsolete.

"Tess is short for Tessellated Information Transmitter," Zia explained. "And just be glad I don't refer to it as my tit like some of the guys at school." Oma snickered at Zia's comment, but Chessie looked shocked.

Why did her mom have to be so dull? Why couldn't she be more like Oma, Zia wondered. Oma was like…well, like a very wise teenager. Mature when necessary, but full of rowdy fun the rest of the time.

Zia didn't really know why her great-grandmother was that way. Maybe it was because she no longer had to worry about paying a mortgage, or working long hours at a job she didn't enjoy, or wondering how to send two children through college. Retirement had taken care of all that. Those worries were over, and Oma made growing older seem like something which to look forward. Yes, Zia wanted to be just like her when she hit the century mark!

"Despite what you say, a tess is still like a cell." Oma twirled the transmitter in her palm. "It's a phone, a camera, an ipod…sorry…I know that's another obscure term."

"Well, yes," Zia agreed. "A tess is all that, but a lot more." Oma handed the device to Zia, and she began checking it for messages. "Anyway," she glanced up with a smile. "Call it what you want."

Most of the texts were to remind Zia about the shopping trip she had planned for later in the day with her two best friends, Zoolynne and Gentry. Zia glanced at her watch. She had just over an hour before it was time to meet the other girls.

Zia excused herself to get ready, and followed her brother out of the kitchen. Shane could take the stairs to his room on the second floor, but Zia preferred the quicker route to the third level she shared with Oma. She strolled to the elevator located just off the dining area and stepped inside.

"Third floor," she instructed.

The door closed and the conveyer whisked Zia to the top floor of their townhome. She stepped off the elevator and proceeded down the hall, past Oma's room and toward her own bedroom located at the front of the house.

Zia loved her third floor retreat. Even though she had to share the top story with her great-grandmother, Zia felt her room was sequestered from the rest of the family and considered the space her own private penthouse. She especially loved the view from her window. She could easily see all of North Village and beyond - all the way to Old Town. And she had a fantastic view of the nighttime fireworks over EPCOT.

Zia kicked off her shoes as she entered the room. She approached the wall opposite her bed and commanded, "Screen on." The wall flickered, and a blue colored screen emerged.

"Television on," Zia instructed. "No," she said, changing her mind. "Music on. Soft Rock. Random Selection." A tune floated out from the wall, and satisfied with her choice, Zia plopped down in the chair facing the blue screen.

"Computer on," she commanded. Zia leaned back in her seat and rummaged through her purse for a stick of gum. After intense searching, she gave up on finding the packet, and instead pulled out a slip of paper caught in the zipper. It was from a fortune cookie she'd opened at a Chinese restaurant a few days earlier.

Zia turned the slip of paper over in her hand. It said, "The wise thing to do is to prepare for the unexpected."

CHAPTER 3
LIFE IN A BUBBLE

Zia leaned back in her chair and stared at the computer, trying to decide where she'd like it to take her. "Friends Abroad," she commanded.

No, bad choice. She'd been to that site too many times. She needed to try some place new. What was the name of that site a classmate had recommended? Oh, yeah, now she remembered.

"Far Away Friends," she requested. The screen scrambled for an instant and then just faded out. "What? No!" This couldn't be happening. "Refresh," she commanded the computer. Nothing.

She stared at the blank wall, cursing under her breath. Suddenly, the computer screen reemerged with dozens of words and phrases zipping quickly across the bottom - *Abend Search, Bytecode Interpreted, Communication Reset* - they flashed before stopping unexpectedly. Zia had no idea what all the terminology meant and was about to restart the computer, when a startling image suddenly appeared on the wall screen.

It emerged as a blur, but slowly the image came into focus, revealing the face of a young man about Zia's age. As the picture settled into a higher definition, Zia was startled by the young man's appearance.

He was beautiful, but in a completely masculine way. His hair was the color of ebony, but when he tilted his head ever so slightly, it gave off the shimmer of soft plum. The style was straight and heavy, with side swept bangs and jaggedly cut ends, giving his hair a great deal of texture and a rounded shape.

His high cheekbones and strong jaw accentuated his flawless complexion, but as she scanned his features, Zia realized it was something about his eyes that created his incredible allure. He appeared to have an epicanthic fold on his upper eyelids, giving him the almond shaped eyes found in certain East Asians. His lashes were thick and dark, but it was the orbs they framed that created his striking appearance. The iris was a profound, rich purple! The hue complemented the tint that shimmered through his hair whenever he slightly shifted in his seat.

Zia considered for a moment that he might be wearing contacts, or maybe he'd even had optic polychromasia surgery to alter the color, but still...she couldn't recall ever seeing anyone's eyes this particular shade.

She remembered reading somewhere that the color, texture, and pattern of each person's iris were as distinctive as their fingerprints. If that was true, his must be inherently unique.

As Zia gazed at the face before her, she suddenly became self-conscious of her own appearance. Darn it! Why hadn't she taken the time to fix her hair and makeup? She should have been prepared, but she hadn't expected a live person to appear on the screen so suddenly.

Usually, when Zia traversed the various Friends sites, she had time to weed out any uninteresting or unattractive guys before settling on a specific one to chat with face to face. This time she wasn't given that opportunity, and she could only hope her appearance was somewhat presentable.

She smiled at the handsome face, which wore a friendly expression. His lips moved, speaking what was obviously a greeting, but Zia didn't understand the words.

That was strange. Zia had spent days, if not months, on Friends Abroad, and she easily recognized a "hello" in most languages, but his words were unfamiliar. His accent sounded British, but the words were definitely not English.

She checked to see if the language translator was on. It seemed to be scrambled. She tapped the screen's *Refresh Elucidator* button. It was an old Jargon brand – Lingoline edition - and a piece of crap!

How many times had Zia told her mother they needed a more sophisticated elucidator if she was going to chat with friends from other countries? But no, Mom had insisted their translator would be sufficient, and now look where it had gotten her! A gorgeous guy sat waiting to talk – hopefully flirt – with her, and Zia couldn't understand anything he said.

Letters appeared in the translation bar at the bottom of the screen, revising and rearranging. Zia hated having to read subtitles, but she supposed she'd be willing to do it if the translator couldn't get itself to work properly.

She watched as words - and then sentences - zipped across the bottom of the screen, transposing and amending themselves in various ways. This event repeated itself half a dozen times until the jumble of words abruptly disappeared, and the white translation bar suddenly reset itself with four simple words scrolled across the center.

"Hello. How are you?"

Zia returned her gaze to the face before her and smiled. The boy on the screen returned her smile.

"Hello, my name is Zia. Where are you from?" she asked.

"One moment please." His words scrolled across the translation bar. "I am readjusting my language translator."

Zia nodded, and watched as he pushed unseen buttons on the bottom of his screen. He smiled at her again and spoke. Zia glanced down at the elucidator's translation bar, but the words beneath his image had disappeared once more.

Zia's frustration was beginning to get the better of her, but she tried to remain composed – at least outwardly – with a pleasant expression on her face. The young man continued to speak unrecognizable words in his foreign dialect, but slowly a word here and there sounded familiar.

The sentences still made no sense, but his cadence was so mesmerizing - along with those enticing eyes - that Zia was close to not caring if she ever understood a single word he uttered. She was hypnotized by the modulation flowing from his inviting full lips, when suddenly, his voice crackled, and he spoke in English.

"I am attempting to update my language translator for your region. Please bear with me as it may take awhile."

"I understand you!" Zia responded with excitement.

The translator was obviously working at both ends, because the young man smiled at Zia and said simply, "Very good."

"Your accent sounds British, but I'm not sure about your language. Where are you from?" Zia asked.

"I am from Taotrue." He leaned back in his chair, obviously waiting for her response.

"I live in Florida, but where's your city? What country do you live in?" Zia was anxious to know what foreign country produced such gorgeous young men.

"In the capital city of Taotrue. Where is Florida?" he asked.

"Aww, come on!" she laughed. Even people from other countries knew about Florida, Mickey Mouse and all the tacky tourist stuff that went with it. She'd never met anyone on Friends Abroad who didn't know where her state was. "Florida is in the United States," she answered.

"Where is that?" His voice sounded sincere, but Zia didn't believe him. Still, she could play along.

"It's in North America, on... you know...Planet Earth!"

"Earth!" Kiel was suddenly very excited. "You are the first Earther I have ever met!"

"What?" Suddenly, Zia didn't know whether to laugh or lash out.

Someone was playing a trick on her. She hoped it was a friend, and that in a moment, she and the good-looking guy on the screen would be sharing a laugh – and maybe even phone numbers. He was someone she'd definitely be excited to meet in person.

Zia was wondering which friend had put him up to this asinine joke, when the handsome young man spoke again

"The name I am called is Kiel Shovarga." He stated his name in such a way that Zia knew he was waiting to hear her full name.

"My name is Zia Barrett," she answered hesitantly, wondering just how far he was going to take this prank.

He typed something on his screen's keyboard and then pointed to a map that appeared on one side of Zia's computer screen. "My world is here," he indicated.

The galaxy and positions of the planets were unfamiliar to Zia - probably because they were made up, but just to make certain…"Wait a sec," she said, typing in the name he'd given for his planet.

The elucidator swirled and a galaxy map appeared on the screen. It was similar to the one Kiel had shown her, but the names were in English. She looked at the highlighted planet on her map.

"According to my map, you're in a different solar system, but we call your planet Athena Gliese 44b." Zia looked up with a smile.

"Yes, that is correct." Kiel seemed pleased with her interest in his world. "And we call your planet Charvett."

What a pretty name, she thought. It sounded so much nicer than plain, simple Earth. Zia suddenly felt lightheaded. Oh no, she wasn't going to get sucked into his ridiculous story, and yet…if he was telling her the truth, then he really was from another world. And not just another world, one in another galaxy! But how could their home computers have made the connection? Impossible! This type of information exchange belonged exclusively to the governments of the earth, not for teenagers looking for heavenly body hook ups.

"How did you reach me?" Zia leaned forward in her chair and listened as Kiel attempted to explain the intricacies of his computer's intercommunication system.

Zia didn't understand, but she tried to remember certain technical phrases Kiel used so she could check them out later to determine if a link across a universe was even possible through a home computer. And if all else failed, she'd simply ask Uncle Iden. When Kiel – and whoever else was involved – decided to play their little "space alien" prank, they didn't know Zia had an uncle with a high level NASA position.

She wanted to allow the disbelief she felt to seep into her voice, to let Kiel know she was only playing along with him for the fun of it, but there was something so ethereal about his appearance that she found herself slipping under his spell.

He continued to talk about his home planet, and Zia became so engrossed in the conversation that she jumped when tess's alarm went off.

"Does the ringing signify something?" asked Kiel.

"Yes, unfortunately." Zia wished she hadn't promised Zoolynne and Gentry she'd drive them to the mall. "I have to go," said Zia. "But I'll be back in a few hours. Will I be able to reach you again then?"

"I do not understand hours. Is that a measurement of time?" Kiel appeared to be looking at his computer's elucidator, waiting for a translation.

"Why, yes. Will you be on your computer later?" She hoped the anxiousness in her voice wasn't too obvious.

"It is time for evening retirement here," Kiel said. "But I will find you again when you seek me on your computer."

"But what do I do?" Zia scolded herself for feeling and sounding so frantic, but she just couldn't help herself. "Do I enter your name under Far Away Friends? How can I be sure that I'll find you again?"

Zia was seriously considering phoning her friends to tell them the shopping trip was off, but Kiel's response was comforting and reassuring, and most of all - believable.

"Do not be concerned," he spoke with complete certainty. "I will find you here at the same time tomorrow evening."

"Alright," Zia agreed, but she didn't want to log off. Alien or earthling, she was scared she'd never see Kiel again. "Are you sure?" she asked once more.

He nodded. "Yes, do not worry. I will find you." He gave her a tender smile, and it made her heart race.

In case she never saw him again, Zia wanted to memorize every detail of his face, keeping all the sensuous minutia locked in her memory.

Her eyes moved from his forehead to his chin, but she couldn't stare at him forever, so after a few moments, she despondently commanded, "Computer, end session." The screen flickered, and Kiel's image vanished.

Zia felt dizzy and realized she'd been holding her breath. She lifted her body from the chair and released the air from her lungs in one deep exhale.

She supposed she'd need to apply a fresh coat of makeup before picking up her friends, so Zia walked sluggishly to the bathroom to see what needed to be taken care of in the appearance department. She stopped in front of the dressing room mirror and surveyed her reflection.

She was horrified when she looked at herself. "Damn it. I look like dog poop."

How could Kiel have even stood to look at her? He was more beautiful as a male than she was as a female! Well, there was nothing she could do about it now.

Zia went to work, refreshing her makeup and rearranging her hair into a more attractive style, all the while replaying her conversation with Kiel over and over in her head. One moment she was convinced he was nothing more than some local - albeit godlike gorgeous - guy talked into playing an elaborate joke on her, but the next moment she was equally convinced that no one would go to such extremes just to play a silly trick.

Zia knew if she didn't quit volleying both explanations back and forth in her mind, she would eventually work herself up into a self-induced anxiety attack – one of her specialties.

She finished getting ready and rushed down the stairs, giving a hurried goodbye to her mother and Oma. Zia grabbed her purse from the table in the foyer and walked to the Scion tc20 parked in front of the townhouse.

Zia removed the tess from her purse, and signaled the device to unlock her car and start the engine. After tossing her purse in the back seat, Zia made a quick U-turn onto Castle Gap Boulevard. At the end of the street, she turned left and headed down Celebration Avenue toward Zoolynne's house. Midway down the street, Zia could see Zoolynne already waiting on her front lawn.

She shared the same five foot seven frame as Zia, but was roughly thirty pounds heavier despite a continuous regime of diet and exercise. She had enormous hazel eyes and dark auburn hair cut in choppy, razored layers with long fringy bangs.

Zoolynne was Zia's oldest and closest friend in Celebration. In fact, she was the first person Zia had met at school when she transferred from Texas in the third grade. Zoolynne had welcomed her with instant acceptance. They became constant companions, sharing similar interests and having one common bond – both girls were missing one parent.

When she was barely eight, Zia's father had died rather unexpectedly. Maybe *abruptly* was a better choice of words.

He was found floating face down in the family's backyard pool. It was Valentine's Day.

If Chessie had only allowed Zia and Shane to check the backyard when they first heard the neighbor's dog howling, maybe they could have found their father in time. But their mother claimed the dog was nothing more than a noisy nuisance, and shuffled her children off to bed. When Chessie found him four hours later, the dog's calls had been reduced to a whimper, and it was too late for resuscitation.

Chessie had lovingly, but frankly, explained to Zia and Shane that their father had been drinking – not unusual – and simply smashed his head on the pool's ledge when he passed out. It was a painless drowning she consoled her children. After all, he was unconscious when he hit the water.

Zia couldn't remember now if she'd been upset or not about his death. It was hard to miss someone who'd never been a part of your life - even when they were alive.

In fact, the only person at the funeral who Zia recalled looking even remotely sad was a very beautiful, very young woman. Zia remembered asking her mother who the pretty lady was, and Chessie explained that she was her daddy's personal, private secretary. Obviously, the absentee father had been a very doting boss.

After everyone had left the cemetery and her father's coffin was consigned to the ground, Zia stood alone with her mother, staring at the freshly turned dirt. Chessie had held her emotions in check during the ceremony, waiting to release her anguish in private.

Zia stood behind her mother as she cried over her husband's grave, her tears hitting his headstone at a furious speed. They pounded the tombstone like hail, Chessie's pain hurling them toward his final resting place with a spitting force.

How relieved Zia had been to see that her mother's eyes were clear and dry when she turned and walked away.

Immediately after the funeral, Chessie relocated the family to Florida to live with Oma who was also recently widowed – but more grieving. Chessie had told Zia they were moving to the Sunshine State, and for years, Zia thought her mother had given the state its name.

Chessie certainly had a sunnier outlook on life in Florida, her eyes bright and happy. And even though she now had to work long hours to support her family, Chessie's face was no longer shadowed with fatigue. Gone was the bruised swelling that once surrounded her tired eyes.

Zoolynne's situation was a bit different. It was one of the few topics she refused to speak about in any detail, but the rumor was that her mother had run off with her psychiatrist when Zoolynne and her little brother were still in preschool.

The neighbors still gossiped behind closed doors about Zoolynne's mother, and the talk was that she hadn't moved any farther away than Windermere, remarried and living in luxury with her wealthy second husband and new baby.

At one point, Zia had dreamed about her mother and Zoolynne's father getting together, their entire courtship and marriage planned out in her mind. But it never happened.

Zoolynee was wearing her usual broad smile as she approached the Scion. At least growing up without a mother hadn't affected her too much.

After all, she and her brother had a father who absolutely loved and adored them, and whenever Zoolynne left the house, he never failed to pat her cheek or kiss her wrist - right on top of the horizontal scar.

"Guess what?" Zoolynne had an excited giggle in her voice as she hopped in the front seat of Zia's car.

"What?" Zia glanced sideways at her friend.

"I think Xander is gonna ask me to go to the prom!" She let out a delighted squeal as the car buckled her safety belt.

"You mean Alexander Frisby?" Zia asked.

Zoolynne nodded, and Zia hoped her friend didn't notice the startled expression on her face.

"Wow. That'll be schismatic!" Zia forced some enthusiasm into her response.

She was happy for her best friend, but she couldn't help but be a bit envious at the same time. When Zia, Zoolynne, and Gentry had originally planned their shopping trip to pick out prom dresses, none of them had dates, but now it had all changed.

Only the day before, a senior boy named Axel had invited Gentry, and now…well, if Zoolynne ended up going with Xander, Zia would be the only one without a date. Whom would she even ride to the prom with?

Zia knew it wasn't right to feel sorry for herself at Zoolynne's expense, but she couldn't help it. She knew she was at least as attractive – no, more attractive – than Zoo and Gen, so why could they get dates and she couldn't?

Not that she'd want to go with either Xander or Axel. It wasn't that they weren't cute. They both had great bodies and nice features, but they just weren't her type. Now, Kiel…he was *just* her type…just not readily available.

Zia was feeling depressed about the whole stupid shopping extravaganza now. While Zoolynne chatted away about Xander, Zia focused on the street ahead and replayed her conversation with Kiel. In her mind's eye, she could still see the seductive slant of his eyes and the way they narrowed whenever he smiled at her.

She found herself smiling at her own daydreams and not listening to the conversation that Zoolynne, unfortunately, now continued alone.

Zia turned onto the next street and honked as she stopped in front of Gentry's house. While they waited, Zoolynne prattled on about Xander - Zia still not listening.

Eventually, Gentry appeared on the front porch, still struggling to pull on her shoes. She hopped down the four front steps and headed toward the car.

She was only slightly more than five feet tall with flawless, dark copper-colored skin and a short black bob that hung several inches longer in the front than the back. Her delicate face and tiny stature made Gentry appear fragile, but she shared Zoolynne's colossal spirit and radiated the same frenzied enthusiasm.

Zia gave Gentry a smile and leaned forward in the seat to allow her friend to slide into the back. Sometimes having a two-door could be such a pain.

"Good one, Gen." Zoolynne pointed to the diminutive brunette's top.

One of Gentry's signature pieces of clothing was a form fitting V-neck T-shirt with some clever, controversial or smart-ass saying written on the front. Today's shirt read: *I Don't Want To Be A Checkmark On Some Guys 'To Do' List.*

Zia shut the car door, and the trio headed back through the downtown area and toward the town's exit. As Zia turned the corner, she could see the backside of the large billboard that welcomed visitors to Celebration, Florida.

Lauded as the Walt Disney Company's first master planned community, Oma and Opa had been there when the original residents began arriving in June of 1996. They loved the place from the beginning, and Zia could see why. Besides its close proximity to...well, to everything important to an adolescent – theme parks, water parks, beaches, cruise lines – the place had a distinct spirit all its own.

Victorian homes lined its streets, white picket fences circled yards, large porches welcomed neighbors, and village parks invited residents to come outside and play.

Originally built as an attempt to find the future in the best practices of the past, Celebration, almost a century later, still stood as a testimony to the enduring appeal of traditional American towns. That's what the billboard said anyway.

As she neared the exit, Zia switched on the Scion's computer, preparing the car to leave the force field bubble. She was routinely thankful that she lived in a bubbled community. She wouldn't feel secure inside a strictly gated one, and felt sorry for her friends who didn't live inside an energy shield.

Not that living in a bubble stopped anyone, resident or not, from entering or exiting the plasma field on a daily basis, but it did do what it was solely intended to do – it worked as a shield from damage by natural forces or terrorist attacks. And when fully engaged, a residential force field could quarantine an area subjected to harmful biological or chemical agents, as well as function as a temporary barrier against occupation by enemy forces.

Yes, Zia wondered how people not living in a bubble felt safe sleeping at night.

When she passed Water Tower Place, Zia stopped at the red light and watched the cars zipping past them on Highway 192. As each vehicle left Celebration and exited the force field, it momentarily shimmered. Zia had become accustomed to the exit flicker, but today she found herself paying particular attention to the glimmering lights.

"'Ang on luv. 'Bout to leave the Celly bubble," announced her car's decidedly British computer.

All Scions came standard with a female computer, but Zia hated the woman's monotone delivery and immediately reset her sixteenth birthday present with a distinctive male voice that she named Adam – short for Auto Drive Action Mechanism.

She had wanted Adam to sound eloquent, speaking the Queen's English, but what she ended up with was a British computer with split personalities.

Sometimes Adam used proper English, sometimes he spoke with a Cockney dialect, and on certain occasions he slipped into the confusing Cockney rhyming slang that always left Zia baffled and usually very angry.

She understood its ancient origins, a form of coded speech used by London thieves to throw off the Bobbies, but why anyone – especially a computer – used it anymore, was beyond her.

It was, unfortunately, this third personality that seemed to take over whenever Zia asked Adam for directions, often causing her to end up in the wrong location. She would become so frustrated that she'd yell and cuss at the computer, which would generally respond with more rhyming slang.

"Ye 'ave a right foul north and south!" Translation: "You have a right foul mouth!"

This would only upset Zia more, and she'd usually threaten to disable Adam if he didn't friggin' straighten up. Undeterred, he would retaliate with more insulting slang.

"Don't be such a Berkshire Hunt. I told ye to turn on that frog and toad." Translation: "Don't be such a cunt. I told you to turn on that road."

But when Adam really wanted to irritate Zia, he would slip into what she called his Evil Austin Powers' mode, abbreviating the slang and just using the first word of the rhyme. "Don't be such a berk. I told ye to turn on that frog."

It was definitely a love-hate relationship between Zia and Adam. Thankfully, he had recently decided to speak only Estuary English, a mishmash of dialects somewhere between Cockney and the Queen's, and at least Zia could understand that.

It was her turn, and as Zia exited right onto Highway 192, her departure from the bubble caused a momentary sparkle of white. Like with a camera flash, her eyes still saw the glimmer of light for one or two blinks before fading.

Zia moved quickly to the left lane and turned onto International Drive, passing the Gaylord Palms Hotel before exiting right onto I-4. Once she had safely merged with the oncoming traffic, Zia spoke to Adam.

"Set vehicle in auto drive, please."

"Ye needin' a kip, poppet?"

"No, Adam," Zia yawned. "No nap. I'm just a little tired and don't feel like driving."

41

"Awright darlin'. Auto drive engaged." His buttery soft accent made all three passengers smile.

"Oh, good." Zia removed her hands from the steering wheel and foot from the gas pedal. She turned her clasped palms outward and stretched slowly, arching her back away from the car's seat. "That feels better."

"Where ye headin', luv'?" Adam asked in a flirtatious voice.

Zia glanced at her two friends and then answered, "To The Millenia."

Chapter 4
A TRIP TO MILLENIA

"Approachin' Millenia exit," announced the voice from Zia's dashboard. She and her friends had been so busy chatting that she hadn't noticed the passing intersections.

"Disengage auto drive, Adam," she commanded.

"Disengaged, luv."

Zia placed her hands back onto the steering wheel and guided the car toward the Conway Road exit. The flashing green sign ahead announced:

Holy Land Experience…Mall at Millenia…This Exit.

She whipped the Scion in behind a sporty red Mercedes and headed for the mall parking lot.

"Preparin' to enter Millenia bubble, m'dear," alerted Adam.

With a quick white flash of the force field, the girls entered the parking lot and drove toward Macy's. Zia parked as close as possible to the store's entrance and signaled tess to turn off the ignition. She placed the pink transmitting device in her purse's side pocket and smiled to her friends.

"Let's go ladies!"

The three girls walked across the parking lot and stepped inside Macy's front doors, heading immediately to the 'Formal Dress' area where dozens of shiny silver dressing cubicles loomed before them.

A shopping attendant greeted them. "Would you prefer a dressing room large enough to accommodate all three of you?" she asked.

"Yes, that'd be great," Zoolynne responded with a smile, and the attendant ushered them into one of the larger cubicles situated at the far end of the dressing area.

The friends quickly removed their clothing, tossing it on the chair just inside the door. Clad only in their bras and panties, the girls stepped onto the three round cylindrical bases situated in front of the facing mirrors.

"Please remain stationary while your measurements are taken," instructed the computerized female voice emanating from the mirror. The friends giggled, but remained still and waited for further instructions.

"What would you like to try on today?" asked the mirror in a friendly, singsong voice.

"We're interested in prom dresses," answered Zia.

"One moment," the unseen female replied.

The mirror shimmered, and immediately each girl's reflected image transformed.

Zia wore a beautiful jade gown cut high on one side, revealing her calf and lower thigh. Adorning Zoolynne's figure was a light and loose rose-colored gown that draped across her body in a flowing design, and Gentry's image wore a cream-colored beaded halter that appeared soft and rich against her sepia skin.

All three girls oohed and aahed as they admired their own reflections and the reflective dresses worn by their friends.

For the next half hour, the girls commanded the attendant in the mirror to proceed to the 'next image,' and each time it displayed a new dress on one of the young women, the female voice included a comment about the gown.

"Do you want to be the star of the show? Then this sequined covered dress is perfect for that formal occasion you're looking forward to!"

"Do you want to get the party started? Then this dress is sure to help you do it! Its slender, pleated design traces your curves and is both fun and feminine!"

"Do you want to feel like you're walking the red carpet? Then this gown is perfect for a night under the lights – the spotlight that is!"

As the computer's comments became increasingly more ridiculous, the girls began to giggle uncontrollably and started making up their own comments for each new dress that appeared in the glass.

"Do you want to get laid in eleventh grade?" asked Zoolynne. "Then this low cut, see-through number is exactly what you've been looking for!"

Zia and Gentry fell to their knees laughing as Zoolynne's adlibbed dress comments continued.

"Please remain in a standing position," instructed the female voice in the mirror.

The girls eventually regained their composure, and after a short while, Zoolynne and Gentry settled on their dress selections.

Gentry chose a dress made of saffron taffeta that accentuated her coffee colored tresses, while the soft gathers asymmetrically placed at the waist's shirred bodice complimented her petite stature.

Zoolynne's final choice was a strapless black gown with a sweetheart shaped neckline and dropped waist. The full A-line skirt was well suited to her fuller figure and created a lovely silhouette.

While her friends were satisfied that they'd each selected the most beautiful dress Macy's had to offer, Zia was still trying to make a decision. She had found several that were very pretty and quite flattering, but none that had taken her breath away. And that's what she wanted her prom dress to do – take her breath away, and hopefully, her date's breath as well.

"I'll try just one more dress, and then I'll make my decision," Zia said to the other girls. "Next image," she commanded the computerized attendant.

The mirror blinked, and her image changed.

Zia couldn't believe the dazzling gown worn by her looking glass twin. She had never seen anything so exquisite in her life!

"Do you want to wear a gown deserving of a Greek goddess?" asked the mirror. "Then this Athena inspired design is what you've been praying for!"

Did the voice call this design Athena? Kiel's planet was Athena Gliese. Could it be some kind of sign? No, she didn't believe in that sort of nonsense, but still...

She returned her attention to the image in the mirror and the white satin gown, its Grecian styled bodice wrapped in layers of chiffon that extended into the skirt. Embellished with tiny plum-colored Swarovski crystals, the boned torso emphasized Zia's small waist.

As she turned her body from side to side, the crystals sparkled ever so slightly, casting a lavender glow across the gown's midsection. The color was the same shade that shimmered in Kiel's hair whenever he tilted his head! Again, Zia scolded herself for trying to create something out of nothing. The purple hue was nothing more than a coincidence.

She gazed at the mirror, and the corners of her mouth turned up slightly as she looked at the enchanting image. Yes, this was exactly what she had envisioned her prom dress to be. She did feel like a goddess – that was until she remembered she didn't yet have a date for the prom. What was the point of dressing up and looking gorgeous for no one?

Her spirits fell, until her eyes returned to the girl in the mirror. The dress alone was so stunning that Zia immediately felt a lift to her spirits, and the smile returned to her face.

So what if she didn't have a date? Cinderella went alone to the ball, and look what happened to her!

With a unanimous agreement that they'd each made the right decision, the girls used their thumbs to push yes on the *final selection* button located beside their mirrors.

"Thank you for your purchase," said the woman in the looking glass. "You may pick up your items at final checkout."

The three friends redressed, giggling as they each lavished compliments upon the others' gowns. They walked excitedly to the check out area to purchase and pick up their dresses. Rows of registers lined the storefront, and each girl selected the lane she deemed would be fastest.

Zia moved quickly to the front.

"Place your thumb here," instructed the sales clerk. Zia pressed her thumb firmly on the black rectangular pad, and immediately the tablet responded with a dress number and final price. "How do you wish to pay?" asked the woman.

"By credit," Zia replied, removing the transmitter from her purse. With a few clicks, Zia quickly accessed her credit information and approved the purchase, scanning her tess across the check out pad with a smooth glide of her hand.

"Transaction Complete," the words flashed across the tablet.

Within seconds, a nicely wrapped package zipped through the chute next to the cashier's register. "Thank you for shopping Macy's, and have a nice day," she smiled, placing the item inside a Macy's garment bag and handing it to Zia.

Zia walked to the store entrance and waited for her friends to join her. She glanced around at the other shoppers and spotted two classmates heading her way – Twilah Allcox and Chandra Patel.

Although the three had been friends since middle school, Zia didn't generally spend a great deal of time with either girl anymore. It was too bad, because at one time, she and Twilah had been close friends, maybe even best friends.

That was, until eighth grade when Twilah realized guys carried something around in their pockets she liked even better than their thick wallets.

She'd left the nest early, flying a little too fast for Zia to keep up, and by their freshman year, she'd replaced Zia with Chandra. The two had been inseparable ever since, a walking pair of pheromone bookends.

Both Twilah and Chandra were tall and thin with dark shoulder-length brown hair. They were pretty and smart, and Zia didn't doubt they'd probably end up graduating Valedictorian and Salutatorian of her class. But how two people with near perfect SAT scores could have so little common sense, she couldn't understand.

They were constantly involved in things Zia thought were stupid and risky. Namely, they were part of the Lickers. At least that's what the students at Zia's school called them. They were the kids who spent every weekend - and just as many weeknights - getting high by licking stamps laced with various drugs.

Lots of the teenagers at Zia's school used stamps. It was a quicker high for them than drinking. The stamps were easily concealed in purses and pockets, and when it was time to go home to mommy and daddy, all they needed to do was lick a sobering stamp for an immediate return to lucidity.

"Who ya here with?" asked Twilah, as she and Chandra reached Zia.

"Gen and Zoo." Zia nodded in the direction of her two friends, who were now walking toward the girls.

"There's a big group going to Piper's Alley tonight," smiled Chandra. "Wanna come?"

Surely, Zia thought, they wouldn't be getting into too much trouble if they were staying in town - and Zia did love Piper's Alley!

"Twi and Chandy invited us to Piper's tonight. Ya'll wanna go?" Zia asked, as Gentry and Zoolynne joined the trio.

"Oh, definitely!" Gentry smiled, always enthusiastic about any plans thrown her way.

Zoolynne appeared a bit more apprehensive about spending time with Twilah and Chandra. She'd had more than one evening ruined by their crude social graces, and didn't want to be the one responsible for pulling the stop lever when their hormones raced out of control. "I'd like to, but I've got homework I gotta get done before tomorrow. Would we be out very late?"

"That's up to you." Chandra's naughty grin gave both Zia and Zoolynne the feeling that she and Twilah *did* have one of their usual wild nights planned.

"I dunno, maybe." Zoolynne looked at Zia and furrowed her brow. Zia understood. Zoo just didn't have the patience to put up with their slutty behavior.

"Well, I'll be there for sure." Gentry smiled at Zia, raising her eyebrows as if waiting for an answer.

If Gentry was going along then it should be fun, Zia decided. "Okay, count me in," she relented.

"Great!" Twilah flashed a coy smile. "See ya 'bout nine o'clock then."

She and Chandra turned to walk away. With a prissy twiddle of her fingers, Twilah waved goodbye over her shoulder before blending into the crowd shuffling through the department store.

It was already close to eight p.m. when Zia, Gentry, and Zoolynne returned to the parking lot and placed their packages in the back of the car.

Whether they were tired or just in personal thought on the drive home, Zia wasn't sure, but none of the girls seemed to have much interest in engaging in conversation.

After requesting Adam to set the car in auto drive, Zia spent most of the twenty-minute trip home daydreaming about Kiel and wondering if she would be able to talk with him again.

"Approachin' Celly exit, luv," announced Adam.

"Disengage auto drive," Zia instructed, as she took over the handling of the vehicle.

The British voice warned, "An' remember to fill up this yank tank, duckie. Yer almost on empty."

"Adam, I've told you before. This is not an American made car!"

"Awright pet, but yer still low on petrol."

When Zoolynne was dropped off, she still wasn't sure if she'd be joining her friends later, but Gentry instructed Zia to pick her up before heading over to Piper's. Zia assured Gentry that after checking in at home and putting some gas in the car - to make Adam happy - she'd be right back.

Except for a light on the second floor, the house was quiet and dark when Zia pulled up out front. She didn't like being home alone, so she took the stairs to check the second floor.

Shane's light was on, and Zia stopped at his open door. His wall computer was activated, and it appeared he was busy with some type of homework.

"Hey," Zia greeted him from the hallway. She knew that entering her brother's room without permission could lead to a verbal assault.

"Hey," he said, glancing up.

"Are you spending the night here?" she asked.

"No, I'm heading back to the dorm as soon as my clothes finish drying. I've got early classes tomorrow."

"Oh. Where is everyone?" Zia glanced down the hallway toward their mother's bedroom.

"Mom got a call to go into work tonight. Someone didn't show up or something." Shane's attention remained on his computer, but he answered what he knew would be Zia's next question. "And since its Sunday night, you know Oma's at The Town Tavern with all her friends."

"Oh, yeah," said Zia. Of course Oma would be out. She never missed having a glass of wine with her two best friends every Sunday evening.

Zia had once asked her great-grandmother why they didn't do their celebrating on Saturday nights like most people.

Oma had explained, matter of factly, that she couldn't be expected to get up on Sunday morning and attend church with a hangover!

Across the front of the communion table at Oma's church were inscribed the words, '*This Do In Remembrance Of Me*.' Being a religious woman, she had obviously taken the commandment to heart, because when the evening of the Sabbath day rolled around, Oma remembered Jesus – a lot.

Thus, the Sunday night Eucharist with her friends had begun.

"What about Bellaboo?" Zia asked.

Shane didn't answer, but pointed to the wrinkled brown mass wedged in between the pillows on his bed.

"Oh," said Zia.

Shane said nothing more, and Zia took this to mean that it was time for her to move on. She walked down the hall and took the second staircase up to her floor.

As soon as she reached the bedroom, Zia placed her package on a nearby chair and fell face down on her bed. She rolled over and stared at the ceiling. She tried to stop daydreaming about Kiel, but her thoughts continued to drift back to his shore, pounding against the rocks until they splintered in a pile of confusion. Why couldn't she quit thinking about that stupid boy on the computer? This wasn't like her. She didn't generally carry on over a guy. Oh, who did she think she was she kidding? This was exactly like her! Always wanting the guy she didn't have - or couldn't have.

Tess rang in Zia's pocket, the vibrating motion causing her to lurch off the bed. It was Zoo. "I won't be going tonight," Zoolynne sounded disappointed, but decided.

"Okay, I understand." Zia knew there was no use wasting energy trying to change Zoolynne's mind once it was made up. "Then, I'll see you at school tomorrow." Zia tossed her tess on the bed, and walked to the bathroom to freshen up before heading over to Gentry's.

She picked up the bottle of Laila sitting on the bathroom counter. It was the only perfume Zia used, and short of moving to Norway, the only place she knew to buy it in the U.S. was at EPCOT's Norwegian Pavilion. That was where she and Zoolynne had discovered it two summers ago.

They had just finished their freshman year, and like most of the kids from Celebration, spent lazy summer days traveling the world of Disney.

Some days the plan was to visit every Walt Disney World hotel pool using park buses and monorails to accomplish their goal. Sometimes the game involved hide and seek in the Contemporary Hotel elevators. And some days, the fun was just to stroll around annoying tourists with their juvenile antics.

Gentry always made sure to wear her *If It's Tourist Season, Why Can't We Shoot Them?* T-shirt for those special occasions.

But that freshman summer, Zia and Zoolynne had discovered a new Disney game they enjoyed more than all the others – flirting with the foreign college boys hired as seasonal cast members. And the best place for that was obviously EPCOT.

Zia and Zoolynne could easily spend an entire afternoon circling World Showcase, flirting with their favorite crushes.

There had been Miguel in Mexico, Haing in China, Kurt in Germany, Nino in Italy, and they always finished the day with a visit to Alain in France's Boulangerie Patisserie to have coffee and a strawberry tart.

But Lars, who worked in the Norway Pavilion's gift shop, had been their absolute favorite. They'd spent hours that summer talking to and snapping pictures with him. He was tall and blonde, with a handsome face and blue-green eyes that reminded Zia of sea foam.

One day Zia had spent an obviously annoying – at least to Lars' manager – amount of time following Lars around Puffin's Roost, and Zia had in a split second decision chosen to buy a bottle of Laila perfume to avoid being asked to leave the store for an all-flirting, no-shopping infraction.

The price was hefty, but the scent turned out to be worth the dollar amount. It was heavenly, with a distinctive aroma that never failed to garner compliments whenever she wore it.

Summer eventually ended, and Lars returned to Norway, but Zia decided never to smell of anything but Laila for the rest of her life in honor of his memory.

After applying a liberal amount of the perfume, Zia brushed her hair and teeth. A quick touch up of foundation to cover the tiny freckles sprinkled across her nose, and she was ready to head out the door.

When Zia pulled up to Gentry's home on Jasmine Street, she was already waiting on the front steps. She waved excitedly when she saw Zia approaching and rushed to the curb. She had changed from earlier in the day, and Zia gave her new T-shirt a thumbs-up, laughing as she read the words scrawled across Gentry's chest.

The top summed up life for a teenage girl pretty well: *Life's a Bitch, 'Cause if it was a Slut, It'd be Easy*.

CHAPTER 5
PIPER'S ALLEY

The girls drove to Market Street and pulled into the parking lot behind the Seminole Building. Downtown parking was hard to come by, and Zia drove slowly through the lot, surveying the area for an available spot. How lucky! One of The Radio Disney vans was just pulling out. She sped up and grabbed the open space while she could.

After a quick vanity check in the rearview mirror, Zia and Gentry scooted out of the Scion and strolled down Market Street, passing Seito's and D'Antonios along the way. It was a relatively humid free evening, and most of the Celebration in-crowd was taking advantage of the outside dining areas.

As they crossed the street, Zia spotted Oma and her friends, Jaime and Pam, sitting comfortably in the Town Tavern courtyard.

All three women were in their early to mid hundreds, but Zia had to admit they looked pretty hot. Each woman held a wine glass, and Zia could tell by their demeanor that they were reliving adventures and telling stories of events that had happened years, possibly decades earlier.

"Hey, your great-grandmother's friend's T-shirt is even more out there than mine." Gentry pointed at Jaime's pink top. Across the front in big black letters were the words '*Eat Me!*'

"Oh, yeah," Zia laughed. "But that doesn't mean what you think."

"No?" Gentry looked almost disappointed.

"Read what's written underneath it in small letters." Gentry squinted. It was hard to make out the tiny writing at such a distance. "Central Florida CRT Institute," Zia translated the miniscule wording.

"Still don't get it." Gentry shrugged.

"CRT stands for calreticulin, a protein which is found in cancerous cells. It instructs immune cells to devour it, so it became known as the "eat me" protein."

"So that's how cancer is cured." Gentry looked impressed that Zia knew so much on the topic. "I take it Oma's friend has cancer."

"Had." Zia corrected her. "Jaime was diagnosed with breast cancer last month, but she's fine now. Scientists just had to develop a way to eliminate the "don't eat me" signal put out by the CD47 antibody. After that, they were able to develop effective cancer drugs that weren't toxic to normal cells."

Gentry smiled. "Wow, I'm impressed."

"Yeah, the folks at Stanford were pretty smart way back in 2010," Zia agreed.

"No." Gentry shook her head. "I meant with you. I never knew you had such a scientific mind."

"Well, don't be impressed." Zia wasn't taking any undue credit. "I only know about it 'cause I eavesdropped on Jaime and Oma's discussions."

"Oh." Gentry gave an approving nod to Zia's snooping skills.

The girls slowed down their pace to check out the Tavern patrons. There were usually some cute guys from school waiting or bussing tables, but they didn't see any of them tonight.

Several men seated at the outdoor bar glanced at Oma's table with admiring looks. Zia laughed, thinking what a surprise it would be for these gentlemen of forty to find out they were flirting with women old enough to be their grandmothers.

Then a thought hit her. What if they were as youth conscious as Oma and her friends, and were really over a hundred themselves. Each group would think they were victorious in seducing someone of a younger generation, but in truth, none of them would be the victor. The idea struck Zia as being very funny, and she giggled to herself.

Although rejuvenation procedures were a godsend for those desiring them, the clouding of reality they created was sometimes more than Zia could handle. She looked at the women again, and her smile faded.

She strolled by Oma and her friends without a wave or acknowledgement. The amount of wine already consumed guaranteed that Oma wouldn't notice Zia as she passed.

Zia and Gentry crossed over to Bloom Street and headed toward the Celebration Hotel, following the unlit cobblestone path running parallel to the hotel around to the back. The girls crossed over a small wooden bridge hidden behind some trees, and there it stood – Piper's Alley.

For the teenagers of Celebration, it was their own private Xanadu. Adults seldom ventured there, and tourists were generally unaware of its existence.

Piper's Alley wasn't really an alley at all, but a narrow, pedestrian street hidden away behind Celebration's Main Village. Not that it was so well concealed it couldn't be located, or even viewed, from across the lake. Anyone standing in front of the movie theatre could easily see its flickering lights beckoning across the lake. However, most visitors to the town simply didn't take the time to search for the entrance into the sequestered area. This was just fine with most Celebration residents, especially the ones under twenty. Piper's Alley was their own personal retreat.

Teenagers immediately engulfed Zia and Gentry as they entered the alley. Zia knew most of them. They dominated the area, snaking through the slender street and devouring every inch of sidewalk space. Loitering was not only allowed, but encouraged in Piper's.

The alley itself was no longer than half a block with very few shops. There was a small Anime/Manga bookstore, Mama Lomba's Pizza Emporium, Frankie's Tattoo and Piercing Parlor, a T-shirt shop featuring Celebration logos, Cobbledick's Candy Store, and a few other small shops that changed names as quickly as the wind.

But at the end of Piper's Alley, facing the lake, was the magnet that drew the town's youth to the area.

Cheezy Winn's wasn't much to look at from the outside, and not much more on the inside. It was a simple two story, wooden building with screened-in porches, lantern lights, and a heavy smell of grease perceivable from fifty feet away.

The menu wasn't much either. The establishment sold nothing more than burgers, fries and a variety of beverages, but the simplicity was part of the draw. The fact that the place was noisy and cluttered enough to keep most adults away was an added bonus. Rarely was anyone under thirteen or over twenty-one even seen in the place.

After stopping to chat with a few friends, Zia and Gentry headed to the restaurant. The place was packed, but there was one empty table near the back window. Gentry took Zia by the hand, and they pushed through the crowd toward the table, feeling lucky to have found a seat overlooking the lake. The girls plopped down and placed their purses on the two vacant chairs. Zia texted Twilah, letting her know they were in Cheezy's and saving a table in the back.

Twilah responded immediately, "On our way."

While they waited, Zia and Gentry passed the time by reading the names carved into the wooden tabletop. One of the surprisingly simple and fun things to do at Cheezy's was to see what new names and messages had been carved into each table - and maybe even add a few as well.

Most of the carvings said nothing more than so-and-so loves so-and-so, but there were some pretty dirty sayings mixed in as well, and those were the ones Zia and Gentry began searching for. They took turns reading messages, adding their own comments after each one.

Men are like toilets, either occupied or full of shit.

"Sad but true."

Mother Mary, who conceived without sinning, please help me to sin without conceiving!

"Wonder if that prayer worked?"

Please don't throw toothpicks on the floor. The cockroaches can pole vault.

"Do you think Cheezy's really has cockroaches?"

I love defacing private property!

"I think I know the guy who wrote that one."

I'm gonna draw a picture. A picture with a twist. I'll draw it with a razor blade. I'll draw it in my wrist.

"That's sick…no, that's sad."

A kiss is two questions answered at once.

"Oh, how romantic."

I had sex under this table.

"I wonder if that's true?"…"It is. I was there."

Zia and Gentry looked up at the added voice. Twilah laughed as she and Chandra settled in at the table. Immediately Zia could tell they'd been with the Lickers before coming in.

"How many stamps ya gone through tonight, Twi?" Zia asked Twilah under her breath.

"Look, you're not my goddam mother," she snorted, tossing her thick brown hair over one shoulder.

Zia crossed her arms and slumped back in her chair. "Ok, Twi," she said, glancing at her friend with disgust.

Twilah and Chandra had no idea how sleazy their stoned-out antics appeared to others - especially guys. Not that it mattered. Most of the teenage boys Zia knew were more than happy to watch Twi and Chandy's intoxicated escapades – and wait. Zia knew that from experience. She was always the one stuck holding back their hair while they puked in public toilets, a line of guys waiting outside the restroom door for them to sober up.

After placing their order, the girls passed the time texting friends and chatting about unimportant things. There was a steady stream of students coming and going through Cheezy's, and Zia was enjoying people-watching until Twilah poked her in the side and motioned to the young man entering the door with several friends.

"Hey, isn't that the type you always go for? You had a crush on him all last year, didn't you?"

Zia looked over and watched as Kim and two of his friends entered the café. He was Korean and had the Asian features and thick straight hair Zia found so irresistibly appealing. One of the other guys, Jinho, was also Korean and shared Kim's full lips and sultry eyes. The third friend, Danny, was a British boy Zia had actually dated her sophomore year. She'd thought the relationship was going along pretty well, but over the summer months, things between them just slowly fizzled out. He told Zia he'd simply grown tired of her. He didn't even take the time to lie.

"Ooh, yeah," Chandra chimed in. "There's everything our little girl finds attractive in a man. Hard Korean abs and a sexy British accent."

As the words left Chandra's lips, Zia began to feel sick to her stomach. Suddenly, everything was clear. Chandra and Twilah were behind her earlier conversation with Kiel. Why had she ever confided to them that she had a secret crush on Kim? They knew exactly what she found sexy in a guy, and they'd used it against her!

That's why they'd invited her to join them in Piper's Alley - so they could all have a good laugh at her expense. Zia felt sure Twilah had also invited Kim, Danny, and Jinho. Just one big party to witness the freakin' hilarity that would ensue when she and Chandra revealed to Zia that Kiel was a personality they'd created! The guys might even be in on the joke. Kiel could easily be one of their friends. Maybe he'd even recorded their earlier conversation so he could play it back later, and they could all have a good laugh over Zia's naïveté.

Just then, Jot, the co-owner of Cheezy's, walked over with the girls' order. "Here ya go," she said, with her usual cheerful disposition.

She appeared to be about thirty years old - but honestly, who really knew these days - and seemed unfazed by the noisy immaturity displayed by the patron's of her restaurant. Zia assumed

Jot had either a high tolerance for teenagers or a great love for the money her establishment brought in. Whatever the reason for her unrelenting good humor, Zia liked Jot and smiled at her as she sat down the tray of burgers and fries.

Jot handed Twilah a large ceramic mug and gave Zia a wink as she headed back to the front counter. Zia was surprised to see that coffee was all Twilah had ordered. She usually had several orders of fries and a large coke when it was her bulimic week, so…since she was only drinking black coffee tonight, it must be her anorexic week.

"Ugghh, this coffee tastes jotty!" Twilah closed her eyes tightly and stuck out her tongue. Jot was famous for her bitter tasting coffee, and whenever a customer got a bad cup, they said it tasted jotty. Cheezy Winn's patrons repeated the expression so often, that the local kids eventually started using 'jotty' to refer to anything that was bad.

Zia watched Kim, Jinho, and Danny as they walked to a table on the other side of the crowded restaurant. They were talking with some friends from the varsity soccer team. Zia imagined they were giving their teammates the heads up on when to come over to her table and join in as Twilah and Chandra unveiled their cruel trick.

While Gentry, Chandra, and Twilah gossiped and laughed together, Zia nibbled at her food and gazed out the rear window at the reflections on the lake. The lights from the restaurant's lanterns danced on the water like brightly colored fireflies. Back in Texas, the people called them lightening bugs.

65

Any other time, the image bouncing across the lake would make Zia smile, but not tonight. She had already wasted most of her afternoon, worrying she might never speak to Kiel again because he was an alien from another planet. And now, she was wasting her entire evening, upset she'd never speak to him again because he was an asshole from her own planet.

An hour passed. Chandra and Twilah excused themselves numerous times to go to the restroom, always returning a bit more loopy and incoherent. Eventually, only Gentry still pretended to listen to their rambling, disjointed discussions. Zia ignored the idle chatter swirling around her, and instead, snuck intermittent glances at Kim.

But even through her foggy vision, Chandra noticed, and leaned over to Zia. "He's way too high voltage for you," she said.

"Huh?" Zia looked at Chandra.

"He'd want to add a little alcohol to your Virgin Daiquiri."

"What are you talking about?" Zia glared at Chandra. She had such a big mouth, and now Gentry and Twilah were listening as well.

"I'm just saying that Kim's the kinda guy who goes to the bar for a cocktail, not a cocktease."

Chandra was really starting to piss her off. "You mean I'm not easy," Zia snapped. She wanted to add "Like you and Twilah," but Zia knew Chandra would take the tacked-on come back as a compliment.

"No." Twilah couldn't resist jumping in. "Chandy just means you're cold, you know, frigid." She pretended to shiver violently, pulling her sweater tightly across her breasts in a display of faux safeguarding.

"You're both disgusting!" Zia folded her arms and leaned back in her chair, glancing over at Gentry who mouthed the word, "sluts."

Despite what they'd said, Zia clandestinely continued to watch Kim and his friends. Chandra and Twilah were such whores. She hated them right now - and they were wrong about her! Just because she wasn't like them, it didn't make her frigid. She looked back at Kim. If she were cold, she wouldn't mind having a guy like him help thaw her out.

After 11:00 p.m., some of the crowd began to disperse, and Gentry suggested the four girls head up to the second floor. The screened-in balcony would be a nice change of scenery she told Twi and Chandy before whispering to Zia, "And the fresh air might help sober them up."

By this time, Twilah and Chandra could barely take more than a few steps without weaving in one direction or the other. Even so, they led the way, and Zia and Gentry followed their stumbling, giggling girlfriends to the staircase. Halfway up, Twilah dropped her purse. As she leaned over to retrieve it, the guy walking down the stairs paused, his crotch eye level to Twilah's face.

"Last night was titanic." He tousled the back of her hair with his fingers before continuing down the steps. Zia knew exactly what that meant – Twilah had gone down like the Titanic. Typical!

"Who was that guy?" Zia asked.

"I don't remember," Twilah said, picking up her purse.

When they reached the upper balcony, Zia's eyes darted around the room, settling on Kim. He was sitting with at least a dozen of his friends and several senior girls. The group turned to look at the four friends as they stepped onto the balcony, but quickly returned their attention to conversations already in progress. Kim laughed lightly, leaning casually back in his chair with his hands clasped behind his head.

In Zia's mind, she was sure they were deciding which among them would be the one to tell her of their elaborate trick - before the entire group joined in with a big ass laugh.

Zia clenched her teeth. She wondered what she'd done to these people to make them want to play such a heartless prank on her. It didn't matter. She knew it was coming and took a deep breath.

She walked over to an empty barstool and sat down. The other girls fanned out across the second floor, heading toward friends in various directions. Zia moved restlessly on the seat, preparing her body to take flight from the situation the instant they decided to reveal their trick. Maybe it would be better *not* to see it coming.

She turned her back to everyone and waited.

And waited.

And waited.

Nothing happened - not for a good fifteen or twenty minutes. What the…. Zia swirled around on the barstool. The place was practically deserted! A few freshman boys were still playing pool at one of the tables on the far side of the room, but on her side, only Gentry, Kim, and Danny remained.

Gentry was laughing and talking with the guys, and Zia felt awkward and embarrassed as she approached them. "Where is everyone?" she whispered in Gentry's ear.

"Left," answered Gentry. "Didn't you hear the announcement over the speaker?" Zia shook her head. "Its closing time," Gentry said.

Zia looked around. "Twi and Chandy left too?"

"Umm hmm. They got a better offer, if you know what I mean." Gentry's smile morphed into a smirk.

"Okay, let's get outa here too." Zia's voice was full of urgency.

Gentry was surprised that Zia would want to rush out without talking to Kim or Danny, but she picked up her purse and said goodnight to the young men still standing near the railing. Zia grabbed Gentry by the arm and glanced over at the guys, giving them a half hearted smile as she nudged her friend down the stairs in front of her.

"What's going on with you?" Gentry looked confused.

"Nothing." Zia continued toward the exit.

"Then why are you in such a hurry to leave? I thought you'd be thrilled to talk to Kim."

"I just need to get home. I didn't know it was so late." Zia pushed open the screen door and hustled Gentry outside. She moved to follow her friend but then stopped. She was aware that someone was watching her, and glanced over her shoulder.

Kim had descended to the bottom of the stairs and was leaning on the banister, his thumbs hooked casually through his jeans' belt loops. He grinned at Zia, and as he did, the corners of his eyes curved up. The thick lashes outlining their angles were so dark that Zia could almost assume he was wearing eyeliner if she didn't know better. She returned his grin with a faint smile, but quickly stepped out the door and into the night air.

If she gazed too long into those deep brown eyes, she felt she might fall in.

CHAPTER 6
THE PARALLAX ROOM

The next morning Zia woke up before her alarm even went off. She rolled over and glanced at the time. It was only five a.m. Why had she woken up so early?

She stretched and turned over. It was always easy for Zia to slip back into sleep, but suddenly, she remembered...remembered Kiel. She began thinking about everything that had happened the day before, and a mountain of questions crashed down on her in an avalanche of uncertainty. Her mind raced through different scenarios, none of which would allow her to relax and go back to sleep.

If Chandy and Twi hadn't been playing a trick on her yesterday, then it meant Kiel was a real person. Well, of course he was real.

He wasn't computer generated, but was Kiel really who he said he was? Maybe he was the one - the only one - playing the joke on her, but what would be the reason? She didn't know him.

Two hours later Zia was still lying in bed asking herself questions, when the intercom buzzed.

"You'll be late for school if you don't hurry. We've already finished breakfast." Her mother's voice was pleasant but insistent, and Zia panicked when she saw what time it was.

"Coming down now," she yelled back at the intercom. Zia threw off her covers and rushed to the dressing room, tripping over her robe and house shoes on the way. She rushed back and forth across the floor. Makeup...check, hair...check, clothes...check, personal hygiene...check. Now...go!

Monday classes proved to be both uneventful and uninteresting. The only class Zia was even remotely looking forward to attending was sixth period Musical Theatre. Their teacher, Mr. Cicero Petty, always made the class a special event, if for no other reason, simply to watch his dramatic contortions whenever a student didn't live up to his expectations.

He would throw his hands in the air, look to the heavens, and declare, "I'm done here. I'm just done." Of course, he never was, and his students actually looked forward to these flamboyant explosions.

Behind his back, some of the guys in class referred to him as Mr. *Pretty* because of his effeminate mannerisms, but none of the students were really sure about his true sexual orientation - and honestly, they didn't really care. All that mattered was that he was fun and entertaining, and everyone looked forward to his class.

As soon as Zia turned the corner, she could tell Mr. Petty had something special planned for this humdrum Monday afternoon. He was waiting in the classroom's doorway, hugging himself and bouncing up and down like a kettle on a hot fire. Whatever the surprise, he could barely hold it in, his obvious excitement literally bubbling up and boiling over.

The instant all his students had taken their seats, Mr. Petty made an announcement. "Today class, I have a special treat for you." He paced back and forth in front of his desk, one hand on each hip and a mysterious smile on his lips. Everyone leaned forward waiting for what he would say next.

After a dramatic pause, he continued. "As you know, our final production of the year is *Le Miserables*, so… I have decided to take you all to Paris!"

Excited chatter filled the room. "Now calm down," Mr. Petty said, making a circular wave with his hand. "We are using the Parallax Room for our trip."

"What's that?" asked Annie. She was a pretty, petite, blonde who had just transferred to Celebration from Kissimmee and was usually very quiet.

"Even if your old school didn't have a Parallax Room, you *must* have seen one somewhere!" Spotswood swirled around in his chair, staring at poor Annie.

Although he often ran around with Zia's group, Spotswood was one person, who for the most part, she couldn't stand. Even though he was actually an extremely good-looking guy, he was so arrogant and condescending, that most days Zia couldn't even tolerate the sound of his voice.

"I don't think so," Annie's voice became small.

Spotswood squinted at the timid girl and pursed his lips. It looked as if he was studying her to determine her intelligence. "You have used a game room, right?"

"Yes," she nodded.

"It's the same thing, but you're really in the place you travel to. Or at least your image is." Spotswood tried to make himself more clear. "You can actually see and feel things inside the portal."

Annie still wasn't sure what the difference was. "But you can see and feel things in a game room too."

Spotswood cleared his throat before continuing his lecture. "Yes, but it's all just a holographic image in there. Unless you're playing with a partner, there's no one real, nothing real in the room with you. But when you use a Parallax Portal, the place you travel to *is* real. The people can see you, talk to you, touch you. They don't realize you're not a Breather because you're existing in real time."

"Oh." Annie still looked a bit confused. "A Breather?"

"Figure it out." Spotswood rolled his eyes, but continued his explanation. "The only things you can't do in a portal are eat, drink, and use the bathroom. So go pee now if you need to."

"I don't need to," Annie dropped her voice. "But what would happen if I did....uh...use the bathroom while in the portal?"

"Are you deficient? You'd wake up with wet pants!"

Annie looked embarrassed. "Oh, I see."

"And one other thing," Spotswood added. "If you're a guy - which you aren't - you shouldn't have sex in a portal. My cousin did once and when he woke up his pants were all...."

"Enough jibber-jabber!" Mr. Petty clapped his hands, looking appalled. "I only have permission to use the room for one hour, and our tour guide on the other end is waiting for us."

"I thought you said the people in Paris wouldn't know we were only virtual images?" Annie asked Spotswood in a hushed voice.

"The people we pass on the streets won't know, but we still have to have permission to enter through a portal. Someone on the other end has to know we're coming and be waiting for us," Spotswood whispered back, looking down his nose.

"Silence," Mr. Petty instructed. "Now, follow me." He exited the classroom with an exaggerated stride, the students quietly following him down the hall to a small silver door adjacent to the Band Room.

Zia felt as excited as poor, shy Annie. She had only experienced a Parallax Room twice before, both for school trips, but never to any place this exciting.

In fifth grade, her science class had used the room to pop over to Alligator Alley near Naples. Their class project was to appraise the alligators inhabiting the waterways along the Everglades Parkway and write a report about their observations. Going to Gatorland just down the street had been more fun.

The other time was on a freshman choir trip to Radio City Music Hall to watch the Rockettes perform. It was exciting, but Zia had physically been to New York many times and was a little disappointed that the excursion hadn't involved some place more distant and exotic.

Mr. Petty swung open the shiny gray door, and the students entered the room. He instructed them to line up two by two, and Zia immediately grabbed her friend Breckin's hand, pulling him over to her. She knew he'd be looking around for a cute boy to line up with, but he was her only close friend in Musical Theatre, and she didn't want to be stuck with someone she didn't like.

"Oh my goddess!" Breckin looked at Zia. "Quit pulling my arm. I'll go with you."

"Thanks, Breck." Zia slid her arm through his. He patted her hand and gave her a smile, but she could still see him eyeing one of the boys ahead of them.

Breckin was about Zia's height, maybe a bit shorter, with a slight build. He had glacial blue eyes and unusual blonde highlights in his straight brown hair. Zia never asked how Breckin accomplished the look, but it appeared he pulled his hair into a quarter-size ponytail on top of his head and dyed only that part blonde. With the highlights in place and the ponytail removed, the cascading blonde accents created a flattering butterscotch tuft.

The silver door opened again, and an ungracefully, lanky women joined the group. Laverne Lavendusky was in charge of the Parallax Portal, and despite her awkward appearance, she was a favorite with the students. If Ms. Lavendusky had ever experienced a bad day in her life, no one was around to witness it. She had flaming red hair and a big toothy smile that never left her face.

"Now," she began. "For those of you who don't know, before you may actually enter the Parallax Room you must first have what we call your Simulacrum scanned onto a disc."

Annie raised her hand.

"Yes, dear," said Ms. Lavendusky.

"What is a Simul... what you just said?"

"Roughly translated, it means a reasonable image of reality which attempts to copy precisely the original." Annie seemed satisfied with the somewhat rambling answer, so Ms. Lavendusky continued, "Now, everyone grab their partner, and get in line."

The students proceeded in pairs toward what appeared to be nothing more than the full-body scanners used in every airport in the world. Once they entered the apparatus, the students were asked to stand very still while the mechanism burned their whole image onto a disc.

When it was Zia and Breckin's turn, they stepped forward and stopped. A soft buzzer sounded, and a swirling, intricate pattern surrounded them. The sensation lasted only a few seconds before Ms. Lavendusky instructed them to move into the next room, handing Zia and Breckin each a small disc as they exited.

They joined the others and found that Spotswood was continuing to lecture an unresponsive Annie on intensity fringes and something about sequences of holograms being strung together to replicate movement. Zia and Breckin instinctively moved to the area farthest away from him.

Approximately thirty pearl colored chairs filled the stark white room, each adjusted to a reclining position. With all the students' images successfully burned onto a disc, Ms. Lavendusky entered the room and asked that each student select a seat.

"Your Simulacrum disc will be inserted here." Ms. Lavendusky pointed to a slot on one of the vacant chairs."

"Ms. Lavendusky?" Annie raised her hand again. "Why do we have to sit in these chairs?"

Ms. Lavendusky's large toothy smile spread across her face. "So your body doesn't fall down when your Simulacrum is transported to its destination, my dear."

Everyone laughed, including Annie.

"Now, remember. Please close your eyes to avoid becoming dizzy. When the faint buzzing sound stops, open your eyes, remember that you will be standing upright and walking at that point, and enjoy your trip to Paris!"

Breckin and Zia inserted their discs into the appropriate slot, and then squinted tightly.

There was a brief drone suddenly replaced by the sound of several French voices welcoming the students to Paris.

"Quickly, quickly," Mr. Petty summoned the students out of the Parallax Portal. The students laughed quietly and elbowed each other in the ribs as they walked past their teacher and noticed the silly looking azure blue beret he'd donned before passing through the portal.

"Please follow Mademoiselle Aumont. She will be your tour guide on our brief visit," Mr. Petty instructed, using a highly elaborate and showy French accent

Everyone sniggered at Mr. Petty under their breath, except for Spotswood who pulled poor Annie with him to the front of the line. Mademoiselle Aumont swung open the doors facing her, and on the other side stood the Champs Elysee - the most famous avenue in Paris. The students spilled out onto the avenue and turned their eyes toward the west end where Paris' most recognized symbol of pomp - the Arc de Triomphe - greeted them.

After a very quick discourse with Mademoiselle Aumont, it was on to the Eiffel Tower followed by a swift survey of the Seine River. The brief tour was over before it began, but everyone was abuzz with excitement while walking back to the Parallax Portal - everyone except Spotswood, who was busy expressing his sorrow that the class hadn't been able to tour the Louvre Museum or take in an exotic show at the Moulin Rouge as he'd done on his last family vacation.

When the class stepped back into the hallway of Celebration High School, the dismissal bell was just ringing.

"You may all thank me later," Mr. Petty said, with a flourish. "Now, go forth mon petits!"

"I'm not sure how what we toured today translates to the Paris underworld of the 1800's," laughed Breckin, as he and Zia headed back to Mr. Petty's classroom. "But it was fun."

Zia nodded in agreement and gave Breckin a hasty hug. She had to hurry if she was going to catch up with Zoo and Gen before they left school. "Thanks again for being my sight seeing buddy." Zia smiled at her friend before rushing off.

She ran ahead and quickly retrieved her holdall from the classroom, meeting Breckin again as she headed back down the hallway. Zia made a beeline for the parking lot, hoping she hadn't missed her friends. She couldn't wait to tell them about the unexpected European vacation she'd taken during sixth period, but by the time she reached the lot, both of their cars were gone.

Out of breath from her unnecessary dash across the school campus, Zia walked listlessly to her car, dragging her satchel. When she reached the Scion, Zia placed her items on the hood and began rummaging through the holdall to find her tess. After several minutes of useless searching, Zia got so frustrated that she dumped everything on the ground in front of her car, cursing loudly as she did. She leaned over to look through the discarded items. As she did, she could feel the transmitting device in her pocket. She cursed again - this time even louder.

In a fit, she threw everything back into the tote, glancing cautiously around to see if anyone was watching. She hoped no one had witnessed the monumental tantrum she'd just thrown. Her eyes carefully scanned the area for onlookers, and then she spotted Kim, standing near the gym doors.

He was dressed in his soccer uniform and talking to some buxom redhead. While Zia watched, several more girls swarmed over to him. He never had any trouble attracting females – he didn't have to put forth the slightest effort. They buzzed around him as if he was some sort of giant honeycomb.

It was a silly thought, but she'd love to squash a few of those oversexed bumblebees and keep his saccharine sweet secretions all for herself!

Chapter 7
Air Castles and Sand Castles

Back at 321 Castle Gap Boulevard, Zia let herself in and flung the holdall on the entry table. Bellaboo ran to greet her, and she patted the dog on the head. "At least you're always glad to see me," she smiled at the wrinkled face.

Zia headed to the kitchen to grab a drink from the fridge. As she turned the corner, she noticed her mom was standing by the back door holding her purse, as if about to leave.

"What's up?" Zia asked.

"I just have to update some data on my work computer, and then I'm coming right back. Wanna join me?" she asked, smiling.

Why not? The short trip would give Zia time to fill her mom in on the school trip before she forgot any of the details.

She followed Chessie to the garage and slid into her white BMW. It was almost a year old but still had that new car scent Zia loved. Her great-grandmother's purple PT Cruiser sat next to it. The thing had to be over fifty years old, but Oma refused to get rid of it. Across the back window was a graphic cling that said *Foolish Mortal,* a nod to her former position in Disney's Liberty Square.

While they visited, Chessie guided the car out of Celebration and onto Osceola Parkway. As they drove, Zia recounted all the fantastic sights of Paris. Chessie had never been to France but was excited to hear her daughter's description of its beautiful attractions.

After awhile, Zia leaned her head on the passenger window and watched the white clouds floating overhead. She'd never seen such a blue sky, the clouds scattered across it as if milk poured from a pitcher.

"Are you making air castles?" Chessie asked with a smile.

"What's that?" Zia liked the way it sounded, whatever it was.

"Oh, just something my mother used to say. That's what she calls it when you stare at the sky and daydream."

Chessie was right. Zia had been making air castles. She'd been daydreaming about Kiel, remembering his magenta eyes and full lips. He looked delectable. Did he taste the same, she wondered.

Zia looked over at her mother. She felt guilty about having such devilish thoughts with her parent sitting so close, and forced herself to return her attention to their conversation.

Chessie was assistant manager at the Sand Castle Hotel, one of the area's most popular lodges, and easily Zia's favorite. It was located in the middle of dozens of vacation attractions dotting the Lake Buena Vista landscape, and before reaching their destination, the car whizzed past one tourist trap after another.

There was a giant orange shaped building selling – what else – Florida oranges, a medieval castle boasting authentic jousting tournaments, a tiki-themed miniature golf course, and a futuristic house touted as the "Home of the Future," but unfortunately outdated before its official opening.

For someone who didn't live in the area, the surrounding sights were almost too much to take in. Tourists became hypnotized by the imposing attractions that closed in around them. Those in cars looked every which way but at the people in the crosswalks, and those crossing the street looked anywhere but at the cars heading toward them. No wonder Central Florida led the nation in pedestrian deaths.

But Zia had seen it all, so she once again leaned her head against the car window and continued to look up rather than out.

They soon reached The Sand Castle hotel. It was located on a small, fabricated island just minutes from Walt Disney World, its construction designed to recreate a particular undersea castle featured in a certain mermaid movie.

"Here we go," Chessie smiled at Zia and switched on her headlights, guiding the BMW into the tunnel that began under the man-made lake and ended on the island at the rear entrance to the hotel.

After Chessie parked her car, the mother and daughter walked through the employee parking lot and up through the rear doors to the lobby. No matter how many times she saw it, the sight always astounded Zia.

Resplendent Chihuly sculptures hung from the ceiling, enhancing the hotel's ambient feeling of submersion. Aquatic motifs and open-air aquariums substituted as backdrops for the hotel's thalassic lobby. A nautical staircase led to the restaurants, gift shops, and nightclubs located on the upper levels, while a row of seashell elevators waited to submerge guests in their underwater accommodations.

"Be right back." Chessie walked toward the front desk. "Almost time for the show anyway."

Zia loved everything about the resort, but her favorite part was the twice-daily underwater pageant. It was an elaborate production recreating scenes from Hans Christian Anderson's *The Little Mermaid*, more a rip-off of the famous Weeki Wachee mermaid show than the Disney movie.

Hotel guests always had a front row seat because the window of each suite looked out into the mermaid's own private world. Constructed cleverly in a circle, the design of the hotel created a privacy that guaranteed guests could not see into the rooms of those around them.

Of course, that didn't mean the subaquatic performers couldn't see into the rooms during show time. The swimmers were equipped with special contacts, which worked like goggles to remove any water blur that might interfere with their choreographed underwater ballet. The actors could clearly see hotel guests if they swam close to the windows during one of their performances.

Zia had asked her mother one time what the actors did if they saw someone behaving inappropriately in one of the rooms. Chessie had laughed and told her that all employees were required to notify hotel management of the room number where anything considered *improper* might be ensuing.

Guests couldn't see that above each room's window were four-foot letters indicating the suite number – placed there specifically for the performers to use whenever something censurable did occur. And according to Chessie - it occurred daily!

Sometimes, witnessing a licentious act was merely by accident. Most guests left the curtains open during their entire vacation to enjoy the beautiful ocean scene, but more often than not, when a tasteless exhibition did occur, it was intentional.

There was always some guest who thought their high jinks were funny and that they wouldn't - or couldn't - be identified. However, they were wrong. With the goggled contacts, it was impossible for performers to mistake what they witnessed through a guest room window.

Large coral displays worked as shields to hide the actors' air tubes, so if a performer did witness something tawdry during a performance, he or she would swim behind one of the barriers, return to the surface, and hit the corresponding room number on a large sensor board located just above the lagoon. This action would immediately darken the window, disallowing the guests to see out or the performers to see inside.

Although the rules of conduct were clearly stated to resort patrons before and during check in, there were always those who didn't follow the expected decorum. These guests were ultimately mortified when they realized that the only way to have the window re-lightened was to appear at the front desk - in person. Phone calls concerning the offense were not accepted, and usually, one embarrassing trip to the lobby to speak with a manager was all it took.

The offending guest did not repeat their mistake, but for those still protesting their innocence, there was a bonus vacation video – the last thirty seconds of their lewd conduct before the window darkened.

Travelers not staying in the hotel could still view one of the two daily performances by entering the underwater viewing theatre, and one of the presentations was beginning in a few minutes. Zia followed a large group of tourists down the slanted walkway leading to The Little Mermaid Theatre.

Even though she'd seen the show a million times, the intricate ballet the performers were required to maintain, while dressed in mermaid fins and other seagoing costumes, still kept Zia mesmerized. The underwater animatronics were magnificent in their design and sophistication as well, and even in its twentieth year, the show never failed to please. As the audience broke into a round of loud cheers and applause, Zia quickly made her way to the exit and rejoined her mother who was waiting in the lobby under a giant statue of Poseidon.

"Good?" Chessie asked, smiling.

"Always," Zia answered.

At home, Zia grabbed a quick sandwich in the kitchen before heading upstairs. She explained to her mother that she had enormous amounts of homework, but secretly, she was in a hurry to search for Kiel again.

Zia rushed to the bathroom, expertly reapplying her makeup and styling her hair before sitting down in front of the wall screen. Since she'd been unprepared the previous day, she wanted to make darn sure she looked her very best tonight.

Zia glanced at her watch. The time was fairly close to when she'd spoken to Kiel the day before. He promised he'd find her again, so maybe he was online searching for her now. She kept her fingers crossed that they'd be able to reconnect.

"Computer on," Zia commanded. She wasn't taking any chances with her requests. "Random Search...Kiel Shovarga...Far Away Friends...Planet Athena Gliese 44b," Zia continued, but the computer screen remained blank. No response whatsoever. She slumped forward in her seat.

"Damn it!" Zia kicked the wall so hard it made her chair spin around.

She was just about to ask the computer to connect her with Zoolynne, when it began a repeat of the previous day's events. Words scrambled and reset, the screen turned off and on, and then suddenly – he was there.

He appeared on the wall screen, just as beautiful as he had the day before, and once again, Zia found her chest hurting as she tried to move air into her lungs.

"Hello, Zia." He smiled. "I told you I would find you again."

With most guys, Zia could at least make a tiny effort to play it cool and aloof, but with Kiel, it wasn't so easy.

"I was afraid I wouldn't see you again," she blurted out, immediately feeling embarrassed by her lack of restraint. He spoke so eloquently. Why couldn't she talk like that? She wanted to rip her tongue out and start over.

Kiel gave Zia a bright smile. "Let me assure you. I will always be able to find you." At least he looked happy to see her again.

Zia didn't really know what to do or say next, but after a long pause, she asked, "How old are you?"

Kiel tilted his head to one side, the wine colored highlights shimmering through his hair. He responded with a faint grin, "I am - the elucidator scrambled to translate the number he spoke with a comparable earth age – eighteen. And you, my shooting star?" Why did he call her that she wondered?

"I'll be seventeen this weekend." He smiled at her answer. "But why did you call me your shooting star?" Zia's voice sounded so anemic she was afraid he might not have heard the question.

"Because you flew across the universe and burst into my life like a shooting star." Kiel laughed when he said it, but his expression remained sincere. That was either the weakest line she'd ever

heard…or…maybe it was the most romantic. She didn't want to fall
for such a lame come-on, but she was sure she felt her heart flutter.

"Did you think of me after we spoke yesterday?" she asked.

"Yes. I hope you thought of me as well." He answered with such
apparent honesty that Zia wasn't sure how to continue with the
conversation. She certainly wasn't used to any earth guy being
completely honest and straightforward with her. It must be a quality
only the teenagers of Taotrue possessed - if there really were
teenagers in a place called Taotrue.

A humming sound came from the screen. "Excuse me one
moment," Kiel said. He rose from his chair and walked to an area
out of the screen's view.

As he stood, Zia was taken aback by his physique. He wore what
appeared to be a black jersey top, the low cut neckline extending
past each side of his collarbone and resting loosely on his shoulders.
Although the neckline draped freely, the body of the garment fit his
torso snuggly, emphasizing his broad chest. Even beneath the
clothes, his abdominal and pectoral muscles appeared so well
defined, that had he been shirtless, Zia would have assumed body
make up had been added to the crevices to add definition. On his
lower torso, he wore a pair of what appeared to be loosely fitting silk
pants tied at his narrow waist.

Zia had learned in art class that this physical form and shape -
the one Kiel possessed - was trapezoid, the perfect male body.

He reemerged and returned to his chair, placing his closed fist to
his chin and leaning on one arm. As he did, his bicep noticeably

expanded, and Zia found herself staring until he summoned her eyes back to his.

"Zia?" he asked.

"Oh, yes," she fumbled, trying to recover. "Sorry, I was just daydreaming while you checked on that humming sound." She hoped he believed her.

"It was my parent summoning me," he explained.

"Oh, do you need to go?" Zia wanted to sound polite.

"No, I was able to answer his question," Kiel replied, with a smile. He used the word *his*, so now Zia at least knew with *which* parent he'd been speaking.

For an hour, they continued to make small talk, asking each other any question they could think of about the other person's home planet. Zia learned that Kiel lived in a galaxy only discovered by the people of earth in 2006. They named it the Olympian Galaxy. He explained to Zia that his was the twelfth dwarf galaxy associated with Andromeda - the Earth's nearest galactic neighbor - and that his galaxy was 115 kiloparsecs from the center of Andromeda. Zia had been musing about how they'd meet someday, but when she cross-referenced the distance on her computer and discovered that 115 kiloparsecs translated to 375,000 light-years, she knew it would never happen.

"You must be very smart to know so much about astronomy." Zia tried to keep her voice light, but she felt depressed by the continued planetary discussions. It only added to her realization that they were really, truly living in two different worlds.

"Yes," said Kiel. "It is because of my father that I have learned so much."

"Is he an astronomer?" Zia asked.

"Yes, as well as a physicist and….." Kiel paused. He glanced toward the unseen door before continuing. "He is also Primus Superior of Taotrue."

The elucidator bar appeared on Zia's screen. Translation: Prime Minister.

Could his father really be the leader, the president of an entire planet? At first Zia didn't believe it, but then, why would it be so impossible? If someone had told her a week ago she'd be talking to some guy from another planet, she wouldn't have believed that either.

Suddenly, certain things began to make more sense. If his father was, not only a theoretical genius, but also the Prime Minister of their planet, then he must also have the knowledge and means to communicate with inhabitants from other worlds. Was that how Kiel had stumbled upon her, by plugging in some classified planetary coordinates he'd purloined from his father's computer?

A million assumptions dashed across Zia's mind, crashing against the sides of her skull and falling into the middle of her nervous contemplation.

If Kiel had used some searching device his father was unaware he'd taken, then maybe that was why he continued to contact her and not some other earth girl. That was the reason he was so interested in her. Not because he found her attractive, but because he'd already made the connection with her computer and couldn't risk searching again for fear of being found out. He was simply interested in her because she was an alien being! Zia felt like an organism under a microscope.

"Why do you suddenly look so sad?" Kiel asked. "Are you upset by my father's position?"

"Oh no, that's not it." Zia tried to regain a pleasant expression on her face, while she considered Kiel's motives. That was why he'd called her his shooting star. When he wasn't examining her under a microscope, he was looking at her through a telescope!

"Zia?" he spoke again.

"Yes?"

"I must say goodnight now, but will you look for me again during this same time frame?"

Zia tried to smile. "Yes, I will."

"May I ask you one more question?" Kiel leaned forward and tilted his head to one side. When he came close to the screen, his lavender eyes were so penetrating that they caused Zia to blink.

"You may," she answered.

"Are all the girls on Earth as beautiful as you are?"

CHAPTER 8
ZIA

The remainder of the week passed quickly. Zia no longer had to create air castles because she was floating inside one. She and Kiel continued to talk every evening after supper. Their conversations were sometimes brief and sometimes lasted for hours, but each time, Zia felt more and more certain that her feelings for Kiel were reciprocated.

Friday evening rolled around, and Zia was especially anxious to talk with Kiel, because the following day was her seventeenth birthday. She was finally old enough to get into a nightclub, and her friends had plans to take her to Church Street Station - Orlando's main nightlife scene. Even Chandra, Twilah, and Spotswood were coming along.

And as usual, her mother was worried about *something*. This time, it was the sketchy area of town and the possibility of the kids venturing into an unprotected area that had Chessie concerned. Just a few blocks in either direction, and the friends would be out of the Church Street bubble.

Sometimes her mom could be such a pain. None of the other kids' parents worried about anything – ever! Why couldn't she be more like Twilah and Chandra's folks? If they ever paid the slightest bit of attention to what those two did, they'd need an industrial strength defibrillator to revive them!

Immediately after dinner, Zia hurried to her room and settled down in front of the wall screen, anticipating another evening spent visiting with Kiel. But after waiting half an hour for him to *find* her, Zia decided to click on the special message link - Kiel called it a dispatch folio - he'd established for them to use when face-to-face visits weren't possible.

Although his posts were always brief, they were usually reassuring. Sometimes he said things like, "I am thinking of you," or "How is my shooting star?" but tonight, the text said only, "I am occupied this evening with a personal affair and will not be able to visit with you."

"Noooo!" Zia whined.

If her heart was a red balloon, the little kid in Kiel's message had just popped it with a sharp, shiny pin!

His words sounded so impersonal - and what was this stupid, important affair he was involved with anyway? She'd never asked him how Taotrue's weeks were structured. Was this a weekend for him as well? Did he have a date? She supposed he could. He owed her nothing. They could never be anything more than celestial pen pals anyway.

"Computer off," Zia instructed. She leaned forward, placing her chin in her hands and strumming her cheeks with her fingers.

What to do, what to do? Well, she darn sure wasn't going to sit in front of the computer and feel sorry for herself! She'd stroll down to her great-grandmother's room and see what she was up to. Oma was the one person who could cheer Zia up – always.

If Oma was only a hundred years younger - and not related to her - Zia felt sure they'd be best friends. She often imagined Oma as a teenager, going places with her friends – probably cussing, definitely drinking, and maybe messing around with boys - but always having fun. The *messing around* part Zia didn't like to dwell on for too long. Oma was her great-grandmother after all, and it was a little creepy. But if she imagined Oma as a young girl, it was pretty easy to see that she would've been entertaining to be around – she still was!

As she neared Oma's bedroom, Zia could hear the sound of singing. Oma must be watching an old musical. She loved those, and so did Zia. Oma was the one who had actually introduced Zia to classic movies, way back when they first moved in with her. In those days, she and Zia would spend almost every Friday night watching time-worn musicals.

Zia stopped at Oma's door. She could hear Gene Kelly's voice and recognized the movie – *Singing In The Rain*, one of Oma's favorites.

"Can I join you?" Zia asked from the doorway.

"Of course!" Oma placed the movie on pause and waved Zia into the room. "Get in here."

"What's this?" Zia picked up a box from Oma's bed and turned it over. Across the front, in 3-D lettering were the words *Silver Screen Squeeze-Ins*.

"Oh, Oma! Have you tried it yet?" Zia was excited.

"Just did. Wanna see how it turned out?"

Zia pulled up a chair. "Definitely!"

Silver Screen Squeeze-Ins was a new computer program that promised to let fans seamlessly insert themselves into their favorite movies, and Zia was anxious to see how well it worked.

"So, what character are you in the movie?" Zia asked her great-grandmother. "Lina Lamont?"

"No way," smiled Oma. "No one but Jean Hagen could ever play Lina. I know her character steals the show, but I inserted myself as Kathy Seldin, so I can sing and dance with...and kiss...Gene Kelly." Oma giggled like a teenage girl, and it made Zia laugh.

"So, tell me how this works." Zia turned the box over, reading the back. "I've never actually seen the finished results."

"It's so easy, even I can do it!" Oma winked at Zia. "All you do is upload a digital recording of yourself, and the program simply copies your image. You just have to make sure it's a full body recording. You know...walking and talking...so it can accurately duplicate your voice and movements."

"Oh, I don't like my speaking voice," said Zia. Although it wasn't true, Zia often worried that she still had a hint of Texas twang when she spoke.

"Well, you can always let the program dub over your voice with the original actor's voice," Oma suggested.

"Did you insert your own singing voice, Oma?" Zia hoped her great-grandmother had, because she was a wonderful singer.

"Yep. I sure did," Oma replied, looking rather pleased with herself.

Zia pulled a small wireless mic from the box. "Did you record all the songs just now?"

"Oh, no. I just uploaded some of my old…very old…recordings and let the computer replicate my singing voice from those." Oma paused to lift Bellaboo onto her lap. "Anyway, I wanted my movie image to be when I was young…still in my twenties."

Zia couldn't wait to see the finished product. "Let's watch some of it right now," she eagerly suggested. If the results were as seemless as the manufacturer promised, she might want her own *Silver Screen Squeeze-Ins* for Christmas.

"Okay." Oma turned her attention to the wall screen. "Run *Singing In The Rain Squeeze-In*."

The screen flickered – *Silver Screen Squeeze-Ins* Presents a *C. U. N. The MooVz* Production of *Singing In The Rain*.

The opening sequence began. And Oma appeared - young and beautiful.

There she was. Recast in the Debbie Reynold's role, singing and dancing while sandwiched in between Gene Kelly and Donald O'Conner.

Zia couldn't believe how well the software worked. "That's freakin' majestic!" she exclaimed, her eyes focused on her great-grandmother as she hoofed across the screen.

"Cool, huh?" Oma gave Zia a sly grin. "Now watch this! Sequence, please fast forward to final scene."

Oma appeared on the screen, barely older than Zia, held in Gene Kelly's arms while he kissed her passionately. Both great-grandmother and great-granddaughter screamed with delight.

"Oma?" Zia was curious. "How did you develop such a crush on Gene Kelly? He must've died before you were born."

"No. I was a teenager when he passed away, but I discovered his movies by watching them with *my* grandmother. Some of my favorite memories are of watching musicals with her." Oma smiled, and looked into the distance, obviously remembering.

"So tell me," Zia wanted to know more. "Out of all the old musical actors, how'd you pick Gene Kelly to crush on?"

Oma wiggled around in her computer chair. "Well," she began, and Zia could see from the glimmer in her great-grandmother's eyes that this was going to be a good story. "Fred Astaire was a great dancer, but not attractive. And Frank Sinatra was a great singer, but too skinny. And then...there was Gene Kelly. Gene was sex on the dance floor." A sly grin crept across her face. "Wanna see?"

Was she kidding? Zia couldn't wait. "Of course I do!"

"Now, this wasn't his greatest movie, but it does have some good parts." Oma's grin continued to spread. "Computer, play *The Pirate*, 1948, starring Gene Kelly."

The main title appeared on Oma's computer screen. "Jump sequence to Pirate Ballet," she commanded.

Gene appeared, dressed as a pirate and cavorting in calf high black boots and tight – very tight – black shorts. His bare legs were lithe and powerful as he bounded across the screen. He made ballet masculine...athletic...sexy.

Gene lept over a parapet and took a Tarzan-like vine ride up a ship's rigging, landing smoothly in the crow's nest. He descended with a javelin spear, slinging it with unbelievable speed and vitality around his neck and waist, the dance propelling him into a furious spiral. Gene held the spear upright, one leg wrapped seductively around the pole's shaft, its sharpened head gleaming as the dance climaxed in a smoldering spin.

"That's hot!" Zia was almost embarrassed to look Oma in the eye, knowing now what her great-grandmother considered the *good parts* of the movie.

"Yes, but that's not *the scene*," Oma quotationed the words with her fingers.

"No?" Zia wondered what could have been sexier in 1948 than watching Gene Kelly curl his muscled legs around a phallic symbol.

"Skip sequence to *Nina* number," Oma requested. "Just watch. You'll know when you see it." She had that wicked grin again.

Zia watched as Gene danced through the mythical streets of San Sebastian, again in skin-tight pants, courting every maiden with his acrobatic ballet. He moved from girl to girl, seducing each one with his panther-like grace.

Okay, he was looking good, Zia thought. But what erotic dance move was it going to be that hooked Oma all those decades ago? And then, Zia saw it. She knew this was *the scene*…but it didn't involve dancing at all!

Gene took one of the beautiful senoritas in his arms, throwing her provocatively across his lap and removing the cigarette from her lips. He placed the tobacco roll between his teeth, and using his tongue, suggestively flipped the lit cigarette backward into his mouth. He then leaned into the girl and kissed her - long and hard - before using his tongue's curve to flip the cigarette out of his mouth and back into his lips, seductively blowing smoke in the maiden's face.

"Dang! That *is* sexy!" Zia found it titillating to say the least, and Oma nodded her head in agreement. "Well, I guess I know *what* I'll dream about tonight," Zia said jokingly.

With that, she decided it was probably time to leave Oma and Gene alone, so Zia gave her great-grandmother a goodnight kiss on the cheek and headed to her bedroom, tap dancing along the carpeted hallway as she went.

The next morning Zia was awakened by a hard thump to her upper body. "What?" she awoke with a start. It was only Bellaboo, who had jumped onto her chest.

Singing drifted in from the hallway, and Zia sat up, trying to focus through bleary eyes. In walked Mom, Shane, and Oma holding a candle-lit birthday cake and harmonizing to the tune of *Happy Birthday*.

Generally, Zia was a pretty grumpy person in the morning - okay, she was an out and out bitch - but the site of her family standing in the doorway created a warm spot in her anti-aurora heart.

"Yay!" She jumped out of bed and skipped toward the door, holding Bellaboo in her arms. "I'm seventeen today!"

"Make a wish," Chessie instructed. Zia looked at her mom and smiled a wide happy smile before blowing out the candles.

"What did you wish for?" asked Shane.

"I'm not telling – especially not you – or it won't come true! And why did you wake me up so early?"

"You really are deficient." Shane reached over and gave Zia's forehead a knock, knock tap. "It's not early. It's already noon, so get your lazy ass moving!"

Those were fighting words, but the grin on Shane's face told Zia he was kidding.

"Let's get going," said their mother. "We need to open presents and eat some cake before I have to go to work." Chessie ushered everyone from the bedroom and into the elevator, descending the family to the kitchen.

Zia didn't really like sweets, and the idea of piling nothing but sugar on her stomach first thing in the morning - okay, afternoon - made her feel a bit nauseous. While she scraped the icing off her piece of cake, Zia excitedly read the birthday greetings her friends and family members had sent.

On the table sat three beautifully wrapped packages.

"May I open them?" Zia looked up at her mother.

"Of course," she replied. "But Oma wants you to open hers last."

The first package was from Grandma back in Texas. It was the newest, most advanced peripheral game on the market, and Zia had been dying to experience it.

"Don't interrupt me when I play this." Zia smiled at Shane.

"I won't," he promised. "But open this one next. It's from me and mom."

Zia tore into the box but found nothing but paper. She looked at Shane with a puzzled expression. "Look harder," he advised.

Zia shuffled through the paper again. It appeared to be only an empty box, but there, hidden at the bottom, was an excessively generous gift card to her favorite boutique. Zia turned it over and looked at the dollar amount.

"Oh, shit...I mean...Oh, wow!" She couldn't believe the dollar amount printed on the card. What an extravagant shopping spree she was gonna have! "Thank you, thank you, thank you!" Zia gave her mother and Shane each a big hug around the neck.

"And this is from me." Oma pushed a small box over to Zia.

Shiny red paper and an equally flashy gold ribbon decorated the package. Zia tore away the paper and found what appeared to be a ring box. She gently lifted the lid. Inside rested a delicate ring made of gold.

The center stone was turquoise, inset with a sparkling diamond. From the ring's center circle extended four aurous beams, stretching in four separate directions. Each beam was comprised of four smaller rays, giving it the appearance of a sun.

Zia looked at Oma, "It's beautiful."

"I'm glad you like it, sunshine, because this is where your name comes from."

"It is?" Zia looked at her mother, who nodded.

"It originated with the Indians of the Zia Pueblo in New Mexico…where I was born."

"You were born in a pueblo, Oma?" Shane looked surprised.

"No, silly. In New Mexico - The Land of Enchantment." She let out a mammoth laugh, but Zia rolled her eyes. She wasn't sure if her brother was kidding or clueless.

"The Zia design represents the sun, and is the official state symbol of New Mexico," Oma tried to clarify her earlier comment.

"Oh, Oma." Zia removed the ring to examine it more closely. "It's the most wonderful, beautiful thing I've ever seen."

Her great-grandmother looked gratified as she continued her explanation of the symbol's significance. "Four is the sacred number of the Zia. The four sun rays at the top represent the winds." Oma pointed to the top four rays. "They are the North, South, East and

West winds. The east rays are for life phases: Childhood, Youth, Womanhood, and Old Age; and the west rays are for the times of day: Morning, Noon, Evening, and Night." She gestured to the lower rays. "On the bottom are the seasons: Winter, Spring, Summer, and Autumn. And the circle shape stands for everything bound together, the circle of life and love, without beginning or end." She finished with a smile.

"I will *never* take this ring off, Oma," Zia said, sliding it onto the ring finger of her left hand.

Oma leaned over and gave Zia a kiss on her forehead. "I love you, sunshine."

"I love you too, Oma."

Zia glanced around the kitchen table. The three most important people in her life sat across and to each side of her. They cussed and fussed, fought and made up, disagreed and agreed to disagree, but in the end, this was her family and she loved them - and they loved her.

Oma was right. The number four *was* special and sacred.

CHAPTER 9
CHURCH STREET STATION

Zia had just finished dressing when her friends arrived. She'd been so busy primping for her special night on the town that she'd forgotten to watch the time. But the extra preparations had paid off, and she was unusually pleased with her appearance. She turned to admire her aquamarine mini dress in the mirror. It flowed like water over the delicate curves of her body.

Zia had taken a tiny gold ribbon and loosely tied back her long, blond hair. She hoped it created the appearance that the she had more important things to do than worry about her casually coifed tresses, but in fact, she'd spent just under the better part of an hour getting her hair to look so carefree and noncommittal.

She was wanting to visit with Kiel, but with everyone waiting downstairs, all she had time to do was leave him a note in their special dispatch folio.

"Today is my birthday," she told him. "I'm out celebrating with friends tonight." Maybe now he'd know how she felt when all she got was an impersonal message. Maybe.

Zia glanced at herself in the mirror one final time before heading downstairs. She held her hand in a nonchalant way, deciding how to best show off her new ring. Hand on the shoulder...no. Hand under the chin...no. Hand on the hip...yes. That was it. Perfect!

"Happy Birthday!" her friends cheered, as Zia exited the elevator and joined everyone in the living room.

Zoolynne was the first to notice Zia's jewelry. "Is that a new ring?" She rushed to Zia's side and took her hand. "I love it, but what's that design? Is it supposed to mean something?"

"It's a Zia," Zia replied.

"Funny, it doesn't look like you," Zoolynne made a silly sounding guffaw.

"Very funny, sassy-ass! That's what it's called. It's a Native American symbol for the sun." Zia held up her namesake for everyone to see.

"Ooooh!" Her friends crowded around for a closer look.

Zia couldn't have been more pleased with the gushing admiration and was showing off the ring to Chandra, when Spotswood pushed forward.

"Let me see that!" he said, grabbing Zia's hand. "What size diamond is that?"

Zia wasn't really sure. "A half carat, I think."

"The cut is nice, and the color appears adequate, but I'll need my magnifying glass to really check its clarity." Spotswood continued with his pretentious examination until Chandra grabbed him by the arm.

"Give it a freakin' rest, will ya?" Chandra dragged him to the front door, and the others followed. "What an asshat," Chandra mumbled under her breath.

Usually, even one haughty comment from Spotswood's ego-inflated lips could destroy Zia's good mood, but not tonight. No, not even his bloated bravado could ruin this special evening. It was *her* birthday, and Spotswood could go to hot-air hell for all she cared. And apparently the others agreed, because the atmosphere was full of high-spirited revelry as the group walked to the waiting cars.

Zia rode with Zoolynne, Gentry, and Breckin in his slightly dinged and dented Volvo, while Twilah, Chandra, and Spotswood followed behind in his father's Lamborghini Estoque.

Luckily, the traffic was light and they arrived at their destination in a comparatively short time. Zia could see the bright lights of Church Street Station beckoning to would be party goes even before the cars exited I-4.

The name Church Street was a bit deceiving, and the antagonistic avenue suffered from dual personalities. While the east end was dotted with one house of worship after another, Church Street Station on the west end was dotted with one nightclub after another. "Drive east to get saved. Drive west to get smashed," Oma always said.

The place was more congested than the friends had anticipated, and after circling around the club area several times, the group realized they'd have to park their cars in a non-bubbled area. Zia's mom had warned her about doing just such a thing because there would be no security officers in an off site area, but none of the others seemed overly concerned - not even Spotswood in his posh automobile - so Zia said nothing.

They found a parking area several blocks away. It was unlit, but filled with relatively nice cars and seemed safe. Breckin pulled in first, and Spotswood pulled into the spot just beside him.

After exiting their vehicles, the schoolmates linked arms, laughing and talking as they walked to the entertainment district. Even before they entered Church Street Station, the atmosphere was electric. Each time one of the clubs' doors opened, sounds of music poured out. The vibrations flowed through the ground and into Zia's body, heightening her anticipation about finally stepping inside an adult nightclub. The excitement created a thrilling, stinging sensation in her limbs.

Once they were ushered through the Church Street bubble, the group stopped to survey the area, deciding which club to go in first. Zia was still trying to absorb all the new sights and sounds, when Breckin squealed, "Oh my goddess! Look who's appearing at Riff Raff's."

A neon sign above the club announced *Commotio Cordis* and *Krackin Skulls* as the evening's entertainment.

"They're fuckin' subfusc!" Spotswood seemed even more excited than Breckin, and the others were just as enthusiastic. Zia was apparently the only one with no idea who the bands were, but if Spotswood's outburst was any clue, their music style was metalcore dark.

Everyone agreed on going to Riff Raff's, but while Breckin, Zia, Zoo and Gen queued up, the other three excused themselves and disappeared around a corner. Zia knew it was to give them an opportunity to lick a few stamps before entering the venue, but tonight she couldn't care less. This was *her* night, and their junked-up antics weren't going to ruin her good time.

The line moved quickly, and the friends were at the door before the others had returned. Zia presented her I.D., and with barely a second glance from the attendant, motioned through. Once inside the club, the four friends found an open area near the stage and claimed the space before anyone else could crowd in around them.

The first band was just about to go on when Twilah, Chandra, and Spotswood made their appearance and pushed in next to their companions. All three were excited, jumping up and down and raising their arms as *Krackin Skulls* took the stage.

"I think they must've done some Zoom, or maybe Shuggercaine," Breckin whispered in Zia's ear. She glanced at the trio but quickly returned her attention to the stage. He was probably right. That's what it looked like, but so what? She didn't have to ride home with them.

After the first band exited the stage, Gentry and Zoolynne decided it was time for a bathroom break; Twilah, Chandra, and Spotswood decided it was time for a stamp break; and Breckin decided he just needed to get a drink from the bar. He was no more drinking age than Zia, but he was friends with several of the gay bartenders who were more than happy to serve their cute little crush.

He leaned over to Zia, "Will you be ok here alone?"

Zia nodded, and Breck gave her a quick hug before vanishing into the throng of bodies pushing toward the bar. After he disappeared, Zia glanced around at the horde of patrons, regretting her decision to wait alone while Zoo and Gen when to the toilet.

Across the floor, she saw an old acquaintance named Riley Danker. Maybe acquaintance wasn't the right word. Nemesis, perhaps? Tormentor?

Riley never lived in Celebration, but she attended the dance academy there and was in the same jazz class as Zia all through middle school. She never knew the reason, but Riley had taken an instant dislike to her, christening Zia as her official punching bag – figuratively, if not literally. She never let an opportunity pass where she could make Zia cry. Riley was, in fact, the reason Zia had dropped out of dance class after junior high. It simply wasn't worth the constant harassment.

Looking at her now, Zia remembered Riley easily being the best dancer she'd ever seen. Even at a young age, she had the powerful legs of a professional dancer. There was no movement, no step, she couldn't accomplish with minimal practice.

Some time after Zia left the dance studio, she asked several friends if Riley had found someone new to pick on, but all they could tell her was that Riley had simply disappeared after freshman year. With her natural talent, everyone assumed she'd moved on to one of the more professional dance studios in Orlando, but no one really knew. Riley didn't leave behind any friends eager to maintain contact.

Through her skin-tight pants, Zia could see that Riley still had the muscled legs of a dancer, and from the size of her calves, Zia felt her friends were correct in assuming she'd continued to pursue her dancing elsewhere. Although her legs appeared graceful and sculpted when performing on stage, up close they took on a masculine appearance. Her face was manlike as well, and when she applied heavy makeup, as she had tonight, she resembled an extremely macho drag queen. She was standing with two seriously rough looking guys, the kind she'd always gone for - even in middle school.

Before Riley could spot her, Zia turned her back and began watching the line entering and exiting the girls' restroom. She didn't like standing alone in the club and hoped Zoo and Gen would hurry back. While she continued to concentrate on the stream of young women exiting the toilet area, Zia felt a hand on her shoulder and jumped. Please don't let it be Riley, she thought.

"I didn't mean to scare you." It was a male voice.

Zia turned around and was shocked to see Kim. An extreme side part caused his sienna bangs to fall across one eye. The club's red lighting intensified the hue of his burnished hair, making him look mysterious, sensual. Why did he always have to look so freakin' hot, she wondered.

"Oh, that's okay." Zia tried to remove the surprised expression from her face. "You just startled me because I was watching for my friends and didn't see you walk up."

"I didn't know you were old enough to get into a club," Kim commented, casually placing his hands inside the long ivory jacket he wore.

"Today's my birthday." Zia grinned sheepishly, and shrugged her shoulders.

Kim leaned over and whispered in her ear, "Well, happy birthday."

As he moved his head away, he paused for an instant, making Zia think he was about to kiss her. Her instincts were wrong, however, and she watched him through side glanced eyes as he resumed his upward stance.

"Shall we drink a toast to your day then?" He smiled down at her.

"I'm not old enough for a bartender to serve me."

"You think I am? Come on." Kim took Zia by the arm and guided her toward the bar.

"Hey Chad," Kim called to one of the bartenders he obviously knew. "It's my friend's birthday." He motioned toward Zia. "How about two cherry bombs for us to celebrate with?"

Chad smiled and filled two shot glasses with a red liquid. Zia couldn't believe he didn't ask *which* birthday she was celebrating. She certainly didn't look drinking age.

"Cheers!" Kim raised his shot glass, waiting for Zia to do the same.

"Cheers!" she replied, repeating his movement.

Kim tilted his head back, quickly emptying the glass. Zia mimicked his hurried gesture, but the liquid didn't flow quite as easily down her throat. She was able to empty the glass, but the taste reminded her of some awful cough medicine she'd been forced to take when she was a little girl. Still, she smiled at Kim and tried not to make a face.

He took the shot glass from Zia's hand and sat it on the bar next to his. "You missed some," he said, cocking his head to one side.

"Huh?" she asked.

"Just here." Kim took Zia's chin in his fingers and leaned into her. He extended his tongue and slid it softly and slowly across her upper lip, removing the crimson liquid that remained.

Zia's eyes closed with pleasure. His breath smelled delicious. She'd love to sample his entire mouth. Actually, she wanted to devour it, but after his one unexpected advance, Kim stepped back. Couldn't he see that she wanted more? He'd made his move, and she hadn't protested, so why had he stopped? His actions – or lack of – left her completely baffled.

Zia was trying desperately to think of some clever banter when Kim's usual group of friends surrounded them. They didn't seem to notice Zia as they ushered Kim away from her and toward a group of girls Zia recognized as CHS cheerleaders. He left with no protest. Zia was dumbfounded. He was so easily whisked away – not even a second glance over his shoulder.

She was still standing at the bar, watching Kim, and wondering why he'd even approached her, when Zoolynne and Gentry returned.

"Dear lord!" exclaimed Zoolynne. "What was Kim Song doing talking to you? He is scrumptious!"

Zia looked blankly at her friend. "I really have no idea."

"Did he just kiss you?" Gentry was equally interested in what she'd just witnessed.

Zia didn't know how to respond. It wasn't really a kiss was it? "I'm not sure about that either," she murmured.

Zia honestly wasn't certain what had just happened between her and Kim, but before she could worry about it further, Breckin rejoined them with Spotswood in tow. Spotswood was as overbearing as ever, rambling on about one of the Church Street nightclubs his father owned.

According to Spotswood, it was far superior to Riff Raff's, and he promised to take the group in for a free drink after the next band played. While he continued bragging to an obviously unimpressed

Breckin, Zoolynne turned to Zia, crossed her eyes, and stuck out her tongue.

"Yuckity-fuckity," she said in a funny voice, and both girls giggled.

Just as the announcer welcomed *Commotio Cortis* to the stage, Twilah and Chandra returned. They were even more animated than before, but their artificially induced enthusiasm didn't bother Zia this time. Even though Kim's actions had left her feeling off balance, they had also, in some strange way, elevated Zia's spirits to such a point that Twi and Chandy's mania simply added to her exhilaration. Zoolynne and Gentry seemed to be floating on a natural high as well, and soon all five girls were bouncing in rhythm with the band.

The time passed much too quickly, and when the performers exited the stage, the club began to empty out. Zia kept a close watch for Kim, but apparently, he'd already left the venue with his friends. Zia's group followed the other patrons through the exit and into the night air. It felt good to be back outside, much easier to breathe.

"Most of the other clubs stay open 'til four a.m.," said Chandra. "Why don't we go to Scruples or Kickin' Kitties?"

"Oooh yeah." Twilah liked the idea. "There are always hot guys there, and I'm feeling like letting some lucky guy snatch a little slice tonight."

"I wouldn't mind nabbing some shaft myself," Chandra gave Twilah a high five.

Their choice of words made Zia want to gag, and now she was stuck with the disgusting image of their planned activities seared into her brain. How could her friends be such total gutter-dregs!

"You girls wanna join us?" teased Twilah.

Zia frowned at the suggestion. "I don't think I'm ready for that."

"You don't have to be ready, just willing, and able." Chandra gave Twilah another high five.

Zia wanted to change the subject. "Maybe we should just leave now since there'll be more people walking to the parking areas outside the energy field."

Twilah moaned and rolled her eyes. "What do you think is gonna happen?" she complained. "Think somebody's gonna...getcha?" Twilah jumped forward and grabbed Zia around the waist.

Zia didn't like anyone treating her like a baby. "No, I don't Twi." She pushed Twilah's hands away.

"Zia's right." Breckin came to her rescue. "I'd feel better if I got my car out of that jotty side-lot now."

"You guys are such..."

Zoolynne jumped in before Twilah could say anything more. "I don't really wanna wait two more hours either."

Twilah crossed her arms and looked up at the sky. "I give up," she said in a disgusted voice.

Zia hated that her birthday night was going to end like this, but she'd made up her mind. It had been fun, but it was time to go.

The four friends said goodnight to Twilah and Chandra, and waved a goodbye to Spotswood, who was still complaining about their lack of appreciation. He just couldn't believe they'd pass up a free drink at his father's club.

"You don't know what you're missing," he called after them.

The classmates passed through the bubble, the exit flicker sparkling around them, and joined the already thinning line of pedestrians. Zia and Breckin walked in front with Gentry and Zoolynne in the rear. Just before they reached the parking lot, Zoolynne called for Zia and Breckin to stop.

"Hey, wait up," she yelled. "I left my tess in Chandy's purse."

"Do you have to get it tonight?" Breckin didn't want to walk all the way back to Church Street Station and get into it again with Twilah.

But Zoolynne was insistent. "If I don't get it, I can't get into my house without waking my dad. It has all my key codes on it."

"Here, use mine to call her." Gentry pulled a neon-green tess from her purse and handed it to Zoolynne.

"Oh, thank goodness." Zoolynne looked relieved when she finished her call. "Chandra said she'll meet me at the entrance." She handed Gentry the transmitter. "Gen, please walk back with me. I'm afraid to go alone." Gentry agreed, and the girls turned to begin the long walk back to Church Street.

"We'll drive down and get you," Breckin yelled after them. "Let's go." He turned and took Zia's arm, continuing toward his car, now less than a dozen yards away.

They were the only two people left on the dark side street, and Zia picked up the pace, forcing Breckin to hurry along with her. She'd feel safer as soon as they were inside the car with the doors locked. Zia waited beside the passenger door while Breckin walked around to the driver's side. She reached for the handle, but just as her fingers touched the cold metal, she heard a familiar voice.

"Well, look at the Celebrats!" It was Riley and the two boys Zia had seen her with in the club. One had a short red Mohawk and the other had his head completely shaved except for a long black ponytail hanging halfway down his back.

Zia motioned with her eyes for Breckin to get in the car without responding to Riley's taunts, but as he clicked unlock, the two guys with Riley grabbed him by each arm.

"What do we have here?" Riley walked closer to survey Breckin. "Why, we have a Celebrat *and* a Faglodite!" She tossed back her head, and let out a long, low chuckle. "Look here, Johnny," she said, turning to the guy with the long black ponytail. "I do believe this little one is totally cruising down Boy-Boy Avenue."

Johnny, as Riley had called him, turned his body toward Breckin, and pressed his mouth against his ear. "I guess that means you know how to drive a stick shift."

Zia watched helplessly as Breckin's eyes widened and a look of absolute terror spread across his face.

Zia winced. She had always been scared of Riley and she still was. In fact, she was terrified, especially with the two sidekicks Riley had along tonight. But Zia was also feeling something else while listening to Riley mock one of her best friends. She was frightened and enraged at the same time, and the combination wasn't a good mix. A rampant feeling took control, and Zia reacted in a way that surprised even her.

"You bitch!" Zia screamed, grabbing Riley by the hair. "Let him go!" she demanded.

Riley's cheeks pulsated and then settled into a bright blood red. She yanked Zia's hand from her hair, and turned toward Breckin. "Yeah, let him go," she snarled to her two thugs.

As soon as they released their grip, Zia yelled, "Run Breck," and the two bolted toward the street lamp just beyond the darkened parking lot.

Breckin took off first and Zia followed, her heart pounding furiously. She ran wildly, the trio at her heels. Just a few more feet and she would be out of the parking lot and back under the street light. Just a few more feet. But as she reached the curb, she felt a hand grab her roughly around the waist and another hand slap across her mouth. She couldn't move. It felt as if Johnny was going to crush her ribs.

Riley sauntered casually toward Zia, followed closely by the boy with the red Mohawk. As she walked, Riley pressed her palms to her hips. There was a choreographed sway to her step, and under other circumstances, Zia could have easily imagined Riley choosing a partner and breaking into a Tango.

"What did you call me?" Riley thundered, as she descended on Zia.

Johnny uncovered her mouth. "An ugly bitch," Zia spat back at her.

Riley's eyes flashed, and her nostrils distended contemptuously. "Wrong answer!" she screeched. Riley gestured for Johnny to return his hand to Zia's mouth, but Zia clawed fiercely at his fingers with her hands.

Riley tapped her foot while watching the struggle, and then suddenly, something caught her eye. "Well now, what do we have here?" Riley asked, glancing at the diamond in Zia's ring.

The nearby street light was causing it to sparkle brightly in the otherwise dusky parking lot. Zia tried to shake her head, but it was no use. She was held too tightly to move or call for help.

Riley grabbed Zia's hand and began to pull at the ring. But with the Florida humidity and the blood pumping furiously through her veins, Zia's fingers had swollen, and Riley was unable to remove the piece of jewelry.

"Get it!" She nodded to the boy with the red Mohawk.

As Zia watched, the second boy removed a switchblade from his pocket. She screamed into the hand covering her mouth. The knife snapped open, and the blade gleamed. He reached for Zia's hand, but she fought against him as he tugged at her finger.

Then she felt a searing, wrenching jerk! The pain was blazing, and the parking lot began to spin. Zia's consciousness was crumbling, and she needed air, but she could only breathe in catches.

She was aware that Riley had moved in close beside her. Her face was so near that Zia could smell Riley's putrid breath. It polluted Zia's nostrils with a contaminating waft.

She turned her head and looked into Riley's eyes. They had no pupil, no life. But Zia couldn't look away. Her gaze was fixed, her subconscious aware that something outside her periphery vision was coming closer. She watched as the darkness around the soulless face began to close in. The well of ink flowed to the center of Zia's sight, until it erased Riley's presence…and everything was black.

CHAPTER 10
THE SALAMANDER SHOT

Zia struggled to open her eyes. Why was the light so blinding? Breck must have come back with help, and they'd carried her under the direct glare of the street lamp.

Her eyes watered as she fought to open them, confused as to where she was. Whatever she was lying on was soft, so she wasn't outside. She must've been taken inside one of the clubs, but why were the lights so damned bright? After several attempts, Zia finally succeeded in opening both eyes, and the face above her slowly came into focus.

"Shane, what're you doin' here?" Zia's voice was frail and tottering.

"Hey kiddo," her brother smiled.

"We're all here, sunshine," said another voice.

Zia turned her head and saw that her mother and Oma were both in the room as well. But where was this room? Something was terribly wrong! Zia struggled to sit up, but as she did, she felt a strong tug at the bend in her arm and looked down. Why was there an I.V. inserted into the vein in her arm?

Oh dear god, she was in a hospital room! A wave of panic crashed over Zia.

She remembered what had happened! She remembered Riley, and the knife, and the pain, and…. Zia stared straight ahead. She couldn't bear to look down at the hand, which she now sensed was numb. Her heart raced, and she could feel the blood pounding in her temples.

Suddenly, an unfamiliar face appeared above her bed. She had been completely unaware there was even someone else in the room.

"Hello," said the man in the white coat. "I am Dr. Markison." He placed both hands on Zia's shoulders. "I want you to calm down, and just focus on what I'm about to tell you, ok?" He used a commanding but caring tone as he spoke.

Zia couldn't respond. She felt as if there was a jellyfish bobbing up and down in her esophagus, stinging her stomach as it rose and fell. She grabbed at her throat with her right hand, but nodded that she understood.

"Your left ring finger was amputated just above the knuckle," explained the doctor. Zia felt the acid in her stomach rise, and she moved her hand to cover her mouth. "Now, listen to me," Doctor Markison instructed, noticing the horrified expression that had appeared on her face. "This is as easily repaired as a broken finger."

Unblinking, Zia stared at the doctor. She was finding it difficult to arrange her thoughts, and she struggled to understand his words.

He continued in a compassionate tone, "As you may know, in its natural state the human body will form a scar at an amputation site. However, in recent years scientists have discovered a way to recreate the salamander's ability to reactivate an embryonic development program to build a new limb." Zia blinked. "Technology now allows us to control the human wound environment, so you have been given a hypospray injection that will enhance your fibroblast growth factors."

"Wha...?" Zia tried to focus, but the room bounced in sync with the jellyfish lodged in her throat.

"The injection will accelerate the fibrocytes in your body that work in several stages of tissue repair, including wound contraction. In other words, salamander-like regeneration of large body parts." Dr. Markison smiled at Zia, pausing to insure that she understood his diagnosis of her injury. She looked at her mother, and then to her brother.

"Kid, he means you'll have a new finger in less than a month!" Shane smiled. "And just be glad you weren't wearing a necklace that chick wanted." He slid his forefinger across his throat in a cutting motion, and rocked his head from side to side. Shane winked at his sister, and Zia started to relax a bit.

With her heart slowing down, the hysteria began to subside.

Dr. Markison continued, "We've placed your injured digit in what we refer to as a limb guard or bud guard. It will protect your finger as it re-grows, and the gel inside the guard will aid in the healing process."

For the first time, Zia found the courage to look down at her mutilated finger. She was gratefully surprised that it didn't frighten her as much as she would have expected. A single fingered glove-type sling encased her injured ring finger. The glove extended up the back and palm of her hand, fastening around the wrist.

"Now, what appears to be a flaccid finger within that pouch is actually the antiseptic gel to aid in your healing. As the finger re-grows, it will displace the gel in the pouch. And until then, it will give you the appearance of still having a ring finger." He concluded with a smile and a pat on her shoulder. "Any questions?"

"No….I don't think so." Zia turned her hand over and examined the bud guard from every angle. At least it was a flesh tone, which shouldn't appear too noticeable.

"Very well, then. I will see you in four weeks." Dr. Markison walked to the door. "But now, I think you have a few visitors."

Zia's family excused themselves to allow for more room in the cramped quarters, each giving her a kiss on the cheek as they exited.

As the doctor left the room, he held the door open, and Zoolynne, Gentry, Spotswood, Twilah, and Chandra entered. Breckin stood back in the doorway. Zia could tell he'd been crying and motioned for him to come in and join the others.

Everyone hugged Zia, all noticeably avoiding looking at the bud guard on her left hand. They each told her how sorry they were, making polite small talk to fill in the awkward pauses. Even Twilah and Chandra seemed sincere, and Zia found tears forming in the corners of her eyes. When he saw this, Breckin ran forward and flung himself across the hospital bed, almost dislodging the I.V.

"I'm so sorry," he cried. "I ran and didn't help you. Please forgive me."

"Breck," Zia stroked his hair as he lay across her lap. "I told you to run. You did the right thing."

Breckin wiped his wet face with the back of his hands and repositioned himself on the bed. He gently placed his head on Zia's shoulder and circled her waist with his free arm.

"I guess I passed out." Zia smiled down at Breckin. "But what happened? How'd I get here?"

"When I finally got back with help, Riley and those two mizzis were gone, but I was too late. You were already being taken care of."

"By the paramedics?" Zia questioned. "Who called them?"

"No," Breckin shook his head. "Someone else...and he wants to see you too, if you don't mind."

"I don't," Zia assured him, and with that, Breckin rose from the hospital bed and looked at the others.

"We'll leave so you can talk in private, ok?"

"Sure." Zia was more than a little surprised that everyone was shuffling out so quickly.

Zia did her best to prop up on the pillows and smooth back her tangled hair. She didn't want to look too disheveled when the police officer or security guard enterd her room. A minute passed, and finally the door slowly began to open. A hand circled the doorframe, and Zia watched with anticipation for her rescuer to enter.

The door swung back in a prolonged unsealing, and there stood the last person Zia expected to see - Kim.

A faint smile appeared at the corners of his lips as he walked toward her. Zia was aware that there was a massive amount of dried blood smeared across the front of his shirt and jacket. His beautiful ivory suit was ruined, her blood preserved in a repugnant henna stain.

Zia opened her mouth to speak, but no words came out. Nothing. Not a sound. She fought to stay calm, but her body involuntarily convulsed and then saline poured from her eyes. It tumbled down her cheeks and pooled at her chin, finally sliding down her neck. The tears obscured Kim's handsome features, and his face became nothing more than an indistinct outline.

While Zia struggled to regain her vision and her voice, Kim moved closer and sat on the edge of her bed. Without a word, he gently placed one thumb on each side of her nose's bridge, and gently wiped the falling tears to the outer corners of each eye. She found the caress of Kim's hands to be both soothing and salacious, and she remained motionless, paralyzed by his touch.

"Such a pretty girl shouldn't cry," he said, continuing to hold her head in his hands. Kim leaned over Zia and she closed her eyes, feeling the strength of his body upon her chest and the softness of his lips upon her forehead.

Her savior.

CHAPTER 11
TAOTRUE

When Zia arrived back home later that afternoon she went straight to her room and crawled into bed. The whole ordeal had taken more out of her than she'd realized. Even getting from the garage to the townhouse elevator had been draining.

She pushed her head deep into the pillow and pulled the covers up underneath her chin. She tried to sleep, but the day's events kept playing over and over in her mind.

The police officer who came to take her statement said no one had witnessed the previous evening's events. When Breckin returned with security from the Church Street Bubble, Kim was already sitting on the sidewalk, cradling Zia in his arms. He'd heard the commotion coming from the lot, but the trio saw him approaching and took off, and it was too dark for Kim to identify whom they were.

Although Breckin and Zia were able to give the officer Riley's name, they didn't know the guys with her. The police were questioning everyone who was at Church Street Saturday night, but as it stood, they hadn't located the thugs – or Riley. As with dance class, when she left a place, she seemed to vanish.

Zia's core burned at the thought of Riley, but now that she knew her finger would re-grow, the worst part was accepting the fact that her birthday ring was gone.

She pulled the covers over her head, but sleep was impossible. For hours, she tossed and turned, finally settling into a fitful slumber. When Zia awoke, she was in a tangle of sheets and blankets, her injured hand asleep from hanging over the side of the bed.

She gave her hand a few brisk shakes and the feeling began to return, but she wondered why her throat was so sore. Was she getting a cold? No, that wasn't it. Oh, yes, now she remembered. She'd done a lot of screaming at the football game the night before. Hadn't she? No, it wasn't a football game. It was a concert. She recalled the band. But it wasn't a concert, it was a performance at a nightclub, and she hadn't been screaming then. It was after that…but where was she? Somewhere dark. She was screaming, but she couldn't hear the sound of her voice because something was stopping it. Something kept the sound from exiting her throat. Something…and then her memories came into focus.

Zia shivered and reached for the glass of water on her nightstand. It fell to the floor with a sloshing thud. Apparently, operating with the limb guard was going to take some getting used to.

She flopped over and peered at the clock. It was within the time frame she usually found Kiel online. Zia still felt shaky, but she needed to get up if she was going to talk to him. Zia stepped over the spilled drink and slowly maneuvered toward the bathroom to examine her image in the mirror.

Just then, her mother entered the room. "Good morning, sunshine. I was going to let you sleep in today, after all you've been through."

"What?" Zia was confused. She looked back at the clock and then toward her bedroom window. The sun was trying to peek in through the shutters. The time on the clock wasn't p.m., it was a.m., and it wasn't Sunday evening it was Monday morning!

She felt panicky. Had Kiel tried to reach her last night? Zia rushed to the computer and connected to Kiel's dispatch folio. Nothing. The last posted message was the one she'd left for him on the night of her birthday. Was he no longer interested? Did he think she was no longer interested?

"Are you looking for a message from one of your friends, honey?" Chessie watched as Zia frantically rushed around.

"Oh, no. It's nothing." Zia climbed back under the covers, but she wasn't alone. Anxiety was a wonderful companion. "I just wanna stay in bed today."

"I think you should." Her mother leaned over and kissed her forehead. "I'll see you when I get home from work." Chessie softly closed the door, and Zia tumbled onto her right side, trying not to hyperventilate.

A distraction - that's what she needed. She reached for the nightstand and picked up her tess. She had over forty text messages

and voice mails! Obviously, everyone at school had heard about the
events that had taken place at Riff Raffs. Zia spent the better part of
the next hour reading, listening, and responding to her classmates'
questions and comments. She was surprised and flattered at the
number of people who'd contacted her to lend their support. Lots of
them were kids she'd never even spoken to before.

There was a soft tap at the door, and then Oma popped her head
in. "Mind if I join you?" she smiled.

"No. Come in." Zia placed her tess back on the table.

Oma crossed to Zia's bed and sat down. Bellaboo followed her in
and collapsed with a grunt at her mistress's feet. "You doin' ok
today, sweetie?" Oma patted Zia on the leg.

"Yes, but I'm so sorry about the ring and...." Zia was angry at
the tears that threatened to leak from her eyes.

Oma wagged her finger at Zia. "Shush. Let's talk about
something else. What's been on your mind lately?"

How did she know? Oma could read Zia better than anyone –
even her own mom. Zia was at a loss to understand how she did it.
Decades and decades of being a mother, grandmother and great-
grandmother she supposed.

"Oma, I do have one question." Zia looked at her great
grandmother.

"Yes?"

"Do you believe there are people on other planets?" She knew it
was a redundant question. NASA had virtually admitted decades ago

that they were in contact with other planets, and yet, they never actually came out and confirmed it.

Oma smiled at Zia. "Yes, sunshine, I do."

"Then, why don't our world's leaders – people like Uncle Iden – be honest about what they know?"

Oma bit her bottom lip, trying to decide where to begin. "Perhaps they think if people were actually faced with the reality of alien beings, there would be complete pandemonium across the world."

"But why would people be so scared?" Zia pressed her. "Would they be afraid of being invaded?"

"No," Oma shook her head. "I believe the panic would be created in the core of people's religious beliefs, whatever those might be. Their religion wouldn't allow them to accept such an idea. They'd have to reconsider everything they'd believed in for thousands and thousands of years."

"You mean, you think they'd stop believing in God if they knew there were people on other planets?"

"Some might, yes."

"But you *already* know the answer about the existence of extra terrestrials, don't you?" Zia looked intently at Oma, wondering what information her grandson might have divulged over the years. "And you still believe in God."

"Yes, I believe."

"So your beliefs weren't affected, right?"

Oma raised and lowered her shoulders. "I know what I know, and I believe what I believe. But the two are not the same."

Zia sat in silence, trying to digest what her grandmother had just confided to her. After awhile she asked another question, "Wouldn't people just believe that God created many different worlds with people like us? Couldn't we all have been created in His image... you know...just placed on different planets, at different times, and for different reasons?"

"Well, that's where the problem rests, sweetheart." Oma patted Zia's leg again. "You see...they aren't all in *His* image."

Zia felt an icy panic slither up her spine. Now she understood why Oma said there'd be complete chaos in the world if people knew the facts about extra terrestrials.

"What do you mean, Oma?" Zia pressed her. "What do you know, what has Uncle Iden told you?"

"Nothing you need to worry your sweet self with." She reached forward and stroked Zia's injured hand, but Zia was unrelenting.

"Oma, please tell me. Some aliens do look like us though, right?" Her great-grandmother nodded, but didn't say a word. "If I asked Uncle Iden a direct question, do you think he'd answer me? I mean, do you think he *could* answer me? You know, without violating any rules or getting himself in trouble?"

"Why don't you just ask him?" Oma stood up and gave Zia a reassuring smile before leaving the room, Bellaboo trotting at her heels.

Zia vacillated all afternoon regarding her feelings about Kiel. She believed what he told her, yet she couldn't believe him. But then...Oma had confirmed that she knew humans, or humanoid life forms, or whatever they were called, existed on planets other than Earth. And if she knew it, then she'd heard it from only one person, her grandson – Zia's uncle!

She paced back and forth across the bedroom floor, chewing on her nails. Finally, Zia decided she would risk asking her uncle the question she wanted – no, needed – an answer to. All he could do was say no.

"Computer on," Zia commanded. "Connect me with Iden Tracy, Human Space Flight Division, NASA."

Within minutes, Uncle Iden's face appeared on the screen. He looked well groomed in his compulsory NASA attire, his long gray hair pulled back in a fastidious ponytail.

"Well, hello Zia." He looked startled, but pleased to see her. "I was surprised when the computer said I was receiving a call from my favorite niece. How was your birthday? Did you get my card?" He smiled.

"Yes, I did, and thank you. It was a very eventful birthday." Zia tried to return his smile. If Chessie hadn't already told her brother about what happened, Zia certainly wasn't going to go into at this point. Besides, that wasn't why she'd contacted him.

"Uh, Uncle Iden, are you allowed to talk about certain things on your work computer?"

"Well, what things do you mean?" He looked confused.

"Well, personal things."

Now he really looked puzzled. "Zia, are you asking if, for security reasons, I'm allowed to talk about any and everything on this computer?"

"Uh, yeah, that's kinda it." She wasn't really sure how to answer the question.

"Listen, honey. I don't know if you're having some sort of personal problem, but I'm just heading home to Cocoa. If you want me to, I'll call you when I get there."

"That would be great," she said.

"Do you prefer tess or computer?"

"Computer, please." Zia wanted to be able to really see the expression in his eyes when he answered - or didn't answer - her question. The picture screen on a palm-sized transmitter was too small for that.

"Ok, I'll call you in about half an hour." He logged off with a curious smile.

Zia returned to her bed. She stretched out on her back, staring at the ceiling. How would she ask him what she wanted to know? How would she know if he was being honest? Or what if he really didn't know the answer?

She was still contemplating her questions when the computer announced an incoming message.

"Accept," Zia commanded. It was Uncle Iden. She returned to the computer chair, wanting to be as close to the screen as possible.

"Uncle Iden," Zia began. "I know there are people - or beings - on other planets, but is NASA in touch with any planets in the Olympian Galaxy?"

"How would you know about that galaxy?" He wasn't giving anything away. "Are you studying about it in school?"

"No. I've never heard it mentioned at school, or on television, or on the worldnet, or in a book." Zia hoped her answer indicated to her uncle that she knew more than he might assume.

"Well, it was discovered by a team working at California Institute of Technology using a MegaCam instrument. It's the faintest dwarf galaxy ever discovered...."

"Yes, I know," Zia cut him off. "A friend told me about it."

"Oh. A friend from school?" Uncle Iden smiled.

"No. A friend who lives in that galaxy." Zia watched for his reaction. He didn't smile and he didn't laugh. He didn't ask if she was joking around. He simply didn't say anything. "I'm sure you know his planet. It's Athena Gliese 44b."

"Yes, I'm familiar with all the planets in that galaxy." He didn't admonish her for being silly, and he didn't emphatically deny the existence of beings on Athena Gliese, or any other planet for that matter. What he didn't say spoke volumes.

"Of course," Zia tried to keep her voice calm. "That's what we call his planet. The people who live there call it Taotrue." The moment she said the word, Zia saw in her uncle's eyes the look she'd been watching for. It was a momentary startle, but she saw it nonetheless.

"Well, do they now?" he said, clearing his throat.

"Yes...but you already knew that," Zia replied.

Again, no denial came. Just a smile, and then finally her uncle spoke, "Zia what is it you're asking me? What is it you really want to know?"

"Nothing." Zia was satisfied. "You've answered my question, so thank you." She wasn't sure if her uncle was going to say anything more, but before he had the opportunity to respond, Zia commanded, "Computer off."

She waited for Uncle Iden to call back with some logical explanation, or some parental lecturing on her rampant imagination, but he didn't. The computer was silent.

Zia suddenly felt rejuvenated. It was strangely emancipating to feel this way, but she did. Kiel wasn't someone set up to play a trick on her. He was real! He was an extra terrestrial, and he was *real*!

Zia was in place a full hour before the usual time she and Kiel connected on the computer. It had been too long since she'd been able to speak with him - or look at him.

She traipsed back and forth in front of the wall computer, watching its chronograph. The second she realized it was within the time frame Kiel would be able to find her, Zia instructed, "Computer on," and rushed to her chair.

She busied herself, arranging her clothes and hair, and then returned her focus to the computer screen. Nothing was happening.

"Far Away Friends...Kiel Shovarga." Nothing.

"Planet Athena Gliese 44b." Still nothing.

"Taotrue...please." Her words were more pleading than commanding, but the screen remained dark.

Zia dropped her head, but as she did, the cold, insentient computer flickered. It must have her heard her humble request and taken pity on her, because the screen suddenly jumped - Zia jumping along with it.

There was a loud buzz, and then - Kiel's face appeared.

Each time she saw him it was as the first, startled anew by his physical perfection. She honestly didn't think she'd ever truly become accustomed to it.

He was wearing a royal blue Mandarin collared tunic that accentuated the rich color of his eyes. The side cut jacket was a variation of the traditional center-opening Thai styles with which Zia was familiar. This one folded over at the breast and secured close to the shoulder, emphasizing Kiel's broad chest.

"Zia!" He smiled widely. "I have missed speaking with you. I am sorry I have been away for so many days."

That must mean Kiel hadn't tried to contact her since his last message in the dispatch folio! Suddenly, Zia was glad she'd slept through Sunday night and not been awake, trying to contact him. She would have just cried herself to sleep when he didn't appear.

Kiel leaned forward in his chair as if to look at Zia more closely. "How have you been, my little star?"

She found his voice annoyingly cheerful. "Just fine," Zia replied, trying to appear detached. She hoped Kiel would notice that she hadn't missed talking to him.

"Was your birthday pleasant?" He smiled broadly, apparently oblivious to her dispassionate verbal cues.

"Oh, yes. It was very nice," she lied, tucking the damaged finger beneath her skirt to avoid any questions.

"I bought you something for your birthday." Kiel held up a small black box.

Zia wanted to remain apathetic, but the onyx colored package aborted her mock disinterest.

"What is it?" She couldn't believe he bought her a gift, much less, even remembered it was her birthday.

"I cannot show it to you until I can give it to you in person," he teased.

"Oh, please," Zia begged.

"No, not until I can place the gift in your hand." He smiled again. "Now, tell me what Earthers do to celebrate birthdays." Zia loved it when he used that word – Earthers. It was cute and silly, and she told him so.

Kiel laughingly responded, "I like the way you speak as well. You have a funny way of shortening your words."

"Huh?" Zia thought for a second. "Oh, you mean contractions?" Now she realized why Kiel's speech was so articulate. He never contracted his words.

"So, please tell me about your birthday," Kiel returned to his earlier question.

Zia described her cake and the gifts she'd received, and then she recounted the trip to Riff Raff's - carefully omitting her encounter with Kim and the evening's conclusion of events.

Kiel seemed very interested in the interactions and rituals of the young people on Earth, asking Zia dozens of questions. He wanted to know what else, besides dancing and shopping, she enjoyed doing.

"I love watching movies and swimming at the beach," she answered.

Zia was just about to ask Kiel what teenagers on his planet enjoyed doing, when he suddenly asked, "Zia, will you go on a date with me?"

"Huh?" Zia was confused. "How would that be possible?"

"We could have dinner together...tomorrow night." He looked pleased with his idea.

"But where?" Zia asked.

"Here. In our rooms."

As crazy as the idea sounded, Zia was giddy at the prospect of spending an entire evening with Kiel, doing something more than just staring at each other.

They'd dress up, he explained, just as if they were really going out to dinner – apparently, there were restaurants on Taotrue. Zia could prepare whatever she wanted to eat, and he'd do the same. They would be able to converse across a dinner table. But the best part was that they could interact like any real couple on a date - albeit through a computer screen.

They were putting the final touches on their plans, when Kiel's face suddenly took on a frightened expression.

"What is it?" Zia felt alarmed.

"Stay still," he commanded. "Something has infiltrated your space. It is in the room with you, and I am afraid it could be harmful."

Chilling apparitions congealed in Zia's imagination. What if some alien virus had entered her computer through his and was now seeping out into her room? She was sure she'd be dead within minutes.

"Do not move," he instructed. "I can see your door. If you can exit through it quickly enough, you may escape unharmed. But please, be quick. It is right behind you." He sounded anxious.

Zia's heart was pounding so fast she thought it might burst through her chest.

"On the count of three, I want you to run," he ordered. Zia slowly rose from her seat and waited for Kiel's command. "One...two...run!"

She jumped from the chair, her chest heaving. Zia turned to race for her life, but as she did, she looked down. The *thing* that had entered her bedroom was nothing more than Bellaboo! The poor little pug sat with her head tilted to one side, looking as if the top part of her body was being held up by all the wrinkles around her neck.

Zia fell to her bed, laughing hysterically. Kiel thought she had been attacked by the animal, and pressed himself against the computer screen.

"Zia, are you alright?" he screamed. "Please, tell me you are alright."

She slowly rolled over and sat on the edge of her bed, wiping away the tears of laughter.

"Kiel," Zia finally composed herself. "This is our dog." She leaned over to pick up Bellaboo.

"Watch out." He still wasn't sure about the creature's safety.

Zia moved to her computer chair and placed Bellaboo on her lap, carefully sliding the limb guard under the pug's ample behind. Kiel seemed to have regained his composure, but had a strange look of revulsion as he glanced at the dog.

"This is our pet," Zia motioned toward Bellaboo. "Don't you have pets on Taotrue?"

"Yes, we do," Kiel relaxed, looking amused at his mistake. "But we do not bring them into our homes - and they do not look like that!" He pointed at the dog and let out an unfettered laugh. Its blissful sound bounced through Zia's room, and she found herself laughing as well.

Some time later, Zia fell into bed feeling happier and healthier than she had in days. She hugged the pillow to her chest and imagined it was Kiel, their bodies wrapped together in a maze of winding passion, searching for the exit to their desire.

Then, she surrendered to sleep, yielding to her dreams of Kiel and tomorrow – their first date.

CHAPTER 12
WAY BACK'S

Chessie was surprised to see her daughter emerge from the elevator looking so happy the next morning. She had expected Zia's usual morning sluggishness, but today she was fully animated.

"Well, what has you so happy this morning?" Chessie asked.

Zia smiled. "Oh, just life," she answered, grabbing her purse and holdall before heading to the door.

"No breakfast?" Chessie called after her.

"Not hungry." Zia waved over her shoulder as she bounded down the front steps and headed to the car.

At school, Zia's cheerful mood only increased. Friends and classmates, who gathered around to examine her limb guard and ask her to recount the events of Friday evening, treated her like a celebrity.

Everyone was amazed that Riley still hadn't been located and arrested.

"She must not be registered in school anymore, or they'd have gotten her by now," Zoolynne told the crowd of students surrounding Zia.

"What about checking local dance schools?" Gentry smiled at her idea. "The police should try those."

Zia appreciated her best friends' concerns, but today she didn't really want to think about Riley, so she excused herself and began walking to her first class a bit earlier than usual. As she navigated through the students in the outside courtyard, Zia spotted Kim across the way.

He was talking with some other seniors, leaning with his left side against the wall, his back to Zia. Just seeing him from a distance made her heart race the way it had in the club, and then again in the hospital.

She turned and strolled toward the upper classmen. She wanted to thank Kim again, especially now that her appearance was vastly improved. She could only imagine how she'd looked in the emergency room that day. As she neared the group, Kim moved away from the wall, giving Zia a clear view of Becky Stone. She was leaning against the shared area, her shoulders pressed to the brick.

Becky was a *very* well endowed senior cheerleader, whose boobs appeared to have doubled in volume over the summer. Zia figured Becky's brains must've fallen into her chest cavity and puffed up her bustline, because they certainly weren't in her head anymore. Zia had known Becky since middle school and still wasn't sure just how real anything was about her. The only thing she knew for certain was that Becky had two faces and two ta-tas as fake as her personality - and her Prada purse. Zia called it her Frauda.

The bell rang and Kim leaned over, giving Becky a kiss on the cheek. Zia watched the pair say goodbye, and then Kim walked away in the opposite direction.

Zia was relieved he hadn't seen her approaching with the big stupid smile on her face. She would've been humiliated if she'd reached him, and then realized he was standing cozily with another girl. Especially Becky - whom she hated!

Perhaps hate was a strong word. Maybe she should say disliked - a lot. No, now that Zia had seen her with Kim, she was pretty sure she definitely *hated* Becky.

Zia turned and walked to her homeroom, not feeling quite as happy as she had when she'd arrived at school. When she entered class, all the students were talking excitedly and passing around a memo. Zia took her seat next to Twilah.

"What is it?" she asked.

"Prom details." Twilah handed her one of the slips.

"I love it, I love it, I love it!" Breckin said, poring over the memo.

Zia began reading. Ok, an Arabian Nights theme wasn't all that exciting. Proms always had romantically silly themes. Her eyes jumped to the next paragraph. Suddenly she understood everyone's enthusiasm. It was the venue that was exciting. The Celebration Junior-Senior Prom was going to be held at Way Back's, a nightclub inside the Hyperion Wharf's adult entertainment district.

It was just one of the many clubs inside Disney's newly re-opened Pleasure Island, but it was by far the most popular. Absolutely anyone might be performing there - live and in person! Well, anyone who was dead!

The club's theme centered on entertainers from the past, and because the venue was also a Parallax Room, the performers could be viewed in real time thanks to a technology not too dissimilar from the Simulacrum used by the living. Guests were able to watch long gone entertainers – and experience their shows just as the audiences of their own time.

"I'd rather watch some Breathers perform," Twilah said, glancing through the list.

A roomful of negative responses followed her comment. Everyone else was excited, reading frantically through the list and discussing the names of the entertainers who would be appearing. There were literally dozens!

On the two occasions Zia had been to Way Back's, there were only one or two performers.

She went once with Oma to see some group called The Monkees and a guy named David Cassidy. She enjoyed the show and could understand why Oma thought they were so cute. She asked her great-grandmother if they were popular when she was young, but Oma just laughed at the question and shook her head. No, it was *her* mother who'd loved them as a teenager, and that's why Oma wanted to see them.

Zia's other trip to Way Back's was with her mom to see an actress and singer named Judy Garland. Zia was much younger then, maybe eight, or nine and didn't appreciate the show perhaps as much as she should have. At the time, she was bothered by all the gentlemen in the audience warbling along with Miss Garland. She found it hard to hear the singer, but thought she must have been a wonderful lady for all these men to still love her so much.

She remembered asking her mother, "Do all these men wish they could marry that lady?" Chessie had replied, "No dear, they all wish they could *be* that lady."

At the time, Zia didn't understand what her mother meant, but in middle school, a friend educated her on why they were friends of Dorothy.

"Oh, Michael Buble!" Gentry squealed at reading the name.

All the girls sitting behind her launched into an enthusiastic conversation about which one of his songs was the most romantic. The guys listening around them finally had enough of their gushing.

"Shut it!" shouted Spotswood. "He's not that damn handsome, and he's not that great a singer."

"Hey look," Xander handed Spotswood the prom memo and pointed to a name.

"Oh god! Katy Perry! I dream about her at night." Spotswood held the sheet to his chest and let it drop onto his crotch. "And when I wake up, she carries my morning wood!"

Xander leaned over laughing, "Yeah, she's helped me pitch a tent a few times too."

"Oh, shut up!" the girls yelled back.

Zia scoured the memo and was excited to see some of the old bands she liked were included as well. McFly, Asking Alexandria, Super Junior, MBLAQ, and Forever The Sickest Kids were all on the list.

"You know what the best part is?" asked Breckin.

"What?" Zia looked at her friend.

"Since it's a Parallax Room, it means it has a Parallax Portal."

Zia cocked her head to one side. "So?"

"It means, if we have dates that don't live here, they can still come to the prom by Simulacrum." He grinned from ear to ear, obviously planning to invite a beau from outside Central Florida.

Zia stared at Breckin, realizing what his words meant. Zia could ask Kiel to come as her date! He could be her escort to the prom! She suddenly felt so ecstatic she could scarcely contain her giddiness.

Gentry noticed the silly grin on Zia's face and leaned over. "What gives?

"I'll tell you and Zoo later," Zia whispered.

She wanted to keep Kiel her very own secret for just a while longer, her unseen paramour locked tightly inside the chambers of her lovesick heart.

CHAPTER 13
HELLO AND GOODBYE

Six o'clock found Zia bustling about preparing for her date with Kiel, and as fate would have it, both Mom and Oma would be out of the house for the entire evening. Zia couldn't remember if they were going to a bridal or baby shower, but it really didn't matter. The important thing was they *weren't* going to be around.

Zia had already decided what she'd prepare for dinner – spaghetti, partly because it was simple to make but mostly because she thought it might be something Kiel had never seen before.

Deciding what to wear had been much more difficult, but Zia settled on a short, lacy pink evening dress. It had a flattering cinched waist and rhinestone straps that criss-crossed the open back. She pulled her long hair to one side, allowing the dress's low cut back to be seen – and hopefully admired.

Zoolynne had come to Zia's rescue and lent her a pair of lacy, short gloves. They were sheer, but covering enough that Zia felt comfortable Kiel wouldn't notice the flesh colored bud guard on her left hand.

A folding table was set up in front of the computer screen, decorated with a lovely, shimmering gold tablecloth and Oma's finest Noritake china. In the center, Zia arranged a vase of pink roses cut from the bushes in their courtyard, and on each side, she added a crystal candleholder.

Zia returned from the kitchen and placed the pasta, salad, and breadsticks on the table. She poured herself a glass of Chardonnay, using one of her mother's mouth-blown Schott Zwiesel wine glasses. Zia downed it and poured another, anything to calm her evolving nerves. Funny that she'd feel so jittery about a make believe date.

Before turning on the computer, Zia walked to the dressing room to re-examine her image. She twirled in front of the mirror, feeling rather smug. That wasn't an emotion she often felt - the alcohol must have kicked in.

At the designated time, Zia switched on the computer screen and waited for Kiel to appear. She had finally realized that none of the search commands she'd been giving to her computer had anything to do with Kiel's connecting to her. She could request different search sites all day long, and it wouldn't make a bit of difference. He'd been in complete control all along.

Within minutes, the screen went through its usual turning off and on before resetting and allowing Kiel's image to appear. Instead of sitting at the dinner table, Zia remained standing and was happy to see that Kiel had done the same.

She was; however, unprepared for his other surprise.

He had set the computer screen to a full wall, 3-D image, allowing Zia to see his entire body, as well as the depth and breadth of the room behind him. The results caused Zia to gasp unexpectedly, a rush of air filling her lungs. It appeared as if Kiel was really, truly standing just across the room from her, his bedroom nothing but a continuation of hers. She wanted to reach out and touch him, to assure herself that he wasn't really standing in her bedroom.

"Good evening," he smiled.

As always, his appearance was intoxicating, and with the expanded wall image, Zia could see that Kiel was much taller than she'd expected - at least 6'4", maybe even more.

His mode of dress wasn't too dissimilar from what the guys on Earth wore – only he wore it better. His look was fresh and clean with a crisp white shirt contrasted by a gray vest and a pair of tightly cut dark blue pants.

"Good evening," Zia replied. She found it hard to look directly at Kiel now that they were engaging in a 3-D conversation. She felt awkward. It really was like a first date.

"Would you care to join me for dinner? Kiel asked.

"I would love to." Zia smiled timidly, and they both sat down - facing each other.

His dining table was more lavishly decorated than Zia's, and although roughly the same size, it was not simply a card table covered with a gold cloth. It appeared to be made of rich mahogany with gilded designs covering its marble pillared legs. His china was ornate, its lustrous hue dancing in the flicker of the candles resting on his table.

"It looks like we had the same idea," Zia said, pointing to her candles.

"Yes, it does." He nodded in agreement before asking a question. "May I propose a toast?"

He stood with a golden goblet in his hand, and poured what Zia assumed to be something like wine from a beautifully shaped Viking horn decanter, its contents rapturously sloshing around the sleek interior.

Zia was surprised that his people engaged in the same toasting ritual as the people on Earth, but she stood and raised her glass.

"To my beautiful star on our first date." He held his glass to the screen, and Zia did the same, touching her glass to the wall. They both took a sip, smiling at each other across the chalices' rims as they drank.

As they returned their wine glasses to the table, Kiel asked, "May I play some music?"

Zia smiled at his romantic gesture. "Yes, that would be very nice."

"Music on, subdue lighting," Kiel commanded. A lovely tune flowed from the wall, and the lighting in his room turned to a honey colored glow, illuminated only by the candles.

"Lower lighting, please." At Zia's request, the lights in her room dimmed as well, adding to the warm radiance of their shared dinner table.

After she became accustomed to the new 3-D setting, Zia found Kiel unbelievably easy to talk to, their conversation effortless. She explained to him what foods she'd chosen for dinner, and he listened with interest.

As it turned out, his people ate a type of pasta not too dissimilar from spaghetti, only not quite as slender or extended. Kiel had originally shuddered when she'd shown him her plate, thinking she was eating some type of legless, soft-bodied invertebrate.

He was more interested in her salad. Not the leafy lettuce, but the red tomato. He found its pigment fascinating.

As for what was on Kiel's plate, Zia still wasn't completely sure, even after a lengthy explanation. It appeared to be beef from some unknown animal, garnished with blue and black vegetables, which she found as interesting as he did her tomato.

As soon as they began eating, Zia realized her mistake in choosing spaghetti. What had she been thinking? Could there be anything more unflattering for a young lady to eat than spaghetti? As it turned out, it really didn't matter. Zia felt so uneasy eating in front of Kiel, that after her salad, she could scarcely take another bite. She pushed the pasta around on her plate, finally placing it to one side.

In the flickering candle light, Kiel took on an ethereal quality. His every movement was impeccable. From the way he tipped the wine glass to his lips, to the way he held a utensil in his hand. Every gesture was without fault. Kiel must have sensed he was being watched, because he suddenly sat down his goblet.

"Why do you look at me in such a way?" he asked.

Startled, Zia looked down and cleared her throat. What should she say? How could she tell Kiel that he was the most beautiful creature she'd ever seen? She decided to be only as honest as needed.

"It's because I find your looks...uh...your appearance...uh...," she kept stuttering. "Well, I've never seen someone with purple eyes before!"

Kiel laughed, and leaned forward, resting his elbows on the table. "Well, I have never seen someone with green eyes."

"Really?" Zia suddenly felt pleased with her appearance.

"Really." He shifted positions in his chair before continuing. "Zia, what else do you do with your friends? Something we could do?"

Zia began racking her brains, trying to think of something clever and interesting. "Well, we go out to movies...but I guess you and I couldn't do that."

"Do you and your friends watch movies at home as well?" he asked.

"Yes," said Zia. "But never in my bedroom - unless we're having a slumber party."

"What is that?" Kiel was suddenly very interested.

"You know, a sleepover…when your friends stay over at your house all night."

"No," he shook his head. "I have never done that."

"Well, I guess its something girls enjoy more than boys, but the guys here do have sleepovers sometimes."

"Do you ever have boys come to a sleepover?"

Zia knew friends who had unisex sleepovers, but her mother never allowed her to attend. "Well, I guess some people do…but…well…I've never had a guy sleep over. I mean, I've never had a sleepover with a guy."

"What else do you do at one of these?" Zia had obviously piqued his curiosity.

"Well, besides movies, we enjoy listening to music." Zia was beginning to wonder what he found so fascinating about a slumber party. She knew he'd never seen one of her planet's ridiculous pillow-fighting pornos featuring topless Earther bimbos.

"We also talk about all different things," she added.

"What things?" Kiel pressed her.

"Mostly boys, which I guess is why they're never at our slumber parties. If they were, we couldn't talk about them."

Kiel laughed at her reasoning. "I see," he smiled. "So do you retire early?"

"Retire? Oh, you mean go to sleep early? Oh no, that's part of the fun of it. You try to stay awake as long as you can."

Kiel suddenly looked confused. "Then why is it called a slumber party?"

"Hmm...I don't guess I ever thought about it like that," Zia laughed.

"Could you and I have one?"

His request was straightforward and to the point. And it made Zia's heart race - for several reasons. One - Because the idea terrified her. Two - Because the idea didn't terrify her.

In fact, after the initial shock of his question wore off, the idea of a sleepover with Kiel was the most intoxicating, exhilarating circumstance she could imagine! Kiel was like an aphrodisiac, a drink she craved but couldn't consume. If she agreed to the sleepover, it wasn't as if he could really do anything with her, to her. Not through a computer screen. They wouldn't be existing in the same time and space - but the absinthe would be close enough!

"I think that's a great idea," Zia smiled. "When do you want to sleep over?"

Kiel seemed surprised, but pleased, by her enthusiasm, and for once, he was the one stammering, "Well...uh...I do not know. When do you usually have these sleepovers?"

"On weekends, when there's no school the next day," she replied, her excitement building.

"When is your next weekend?"

"On Friday...in three days. Is it a date?" Zia was anxious for his reply, and crossed her fingers under the table.

"Yes!" Kiel responded with a roguish laugh.

He didn't know it yet, but on Friday night, she would ask him to be her date to the prom.

Wednesday found Zia feeling even happier than she had on Tuesday. She had daydreamed through all of her school classes, reliving her dinner date with Kiel. It had been so romantic, and it was her *own* sweet secret. She still wasn't ready to share Kiel's existence with Zoolynne and Gentry. She would wait until after Friday. By then she'd know if he was going to accept her invitation to the prom, and then she would tell Zoo and Gen everything. Almost everything.

"Hey, Oma," Zia called as she passed her great-grandmother's room upon returning home from school.

"Hi, sunshine," Oma called back.

Zia stopped and thought for a moment. She turned around and walked back to the room. Oma was in her dressing area, obviously preparing to go out.

"You got plans tonight?" Zia asked.

"Oh yes, the girls and I are going to The Tavern. One of Pam's friends is singing in the courtyard tonight, and we don't want to miss him."

"Is he cute?" Zia teased her great-grandmother.

"Cute enough that I'm stopping by New U on the way, just to get a little pick me up," she answered, placing her fingers in front of each ear and pulling up what little loose skin there was.

"Seriously, how many face-lifts can one person get?" Zia laughed, and Oma responded with a sly wink.

Zia wasn't sure of the number or types of aesthetic operations her great-grandmother had undergone, but at the speed she was moving, she'd soon look younger than her own great-granddaughter. But more troubling to Zia than the outward plastic surgery was the inward rejuvenation treatment.

No one ever discussed it, but Zia often wondered what type of procedure Oma had to endure in order to remain physically young. Was it painful? What was involved in the monthly rejuvenation process she underwent at the Resurrection Clinic? Just the name of the place sent shivers down Zia's spine, and visions of decaying corpses rising from morgue tables crept through her imagination.

The only thing Zia knew for sure was that it was expensive, because even though everyone was living longer, they weren't all living as long as Oma and her friends, and they sure weren't looking as good while doing it.

"Oma?" Zia started again. "Can I visit with you while you're getting ready to go out?"

"Sure," Oma smiled over at Zia from her dressing table.

"Do you remember the other day when I asked you about people from other planets?" Zia sat down on the edge of Oma's bed. "Well, there was a reason for that."

"I assumed there was," Oma grinned. "So you want to tell me now?"

"Yes," Zia started talking and before she knew it, she'd told Oma everything about Kiel. She did conveniently forget their *date night,* and the proposed *sleepover*, but she included her conversation with Uncle Iden.

"Wow," Oma said, once Zia finished. "That's some story."

"You don't believe me?" Zia couldn't believe she'd confided everything to Oma, and now she wasn't going to believe her.

"Oh, no. I believe you. I just said that was some story." Zia let out a sigh of relief, and Oma walked over to sit beside her on the bed. "So, you want to ask this boy if it's possible for him to come to a prom on Earth."

"I want to, but I don't know if it's possible for his Simulacrum to travel that far." Zia looked down at her hands, picking restlessly at her cuticles. "And...well, I don't want my friends to make fun of me if I don't have a Breather as a date."

"Honey, I hear you and your friends use that expression, Breather, all the time, but I have no idea what the hell you're talking about!"

Zia laughed at her great-grandmother. For some reason it was always funny to hear someone Oma's age curse – even if she didn't look her age.

"A Breather is a real person," Zia explained. "But I just don't know what to do. If Kiel *could* come by Simulacrum, we'd at least get to share the same experience, and a regular person like me doesn't get to use a Parallax Portal all that often." She nervously chewed on a fingernail before continuing. "If I don't take this opportunity, I don't know when I'll have another chance to see him as a whole image."

Oma smiled, "Is that what you're really worried about? Or are you afraid of falling in love with Kiel once you've actually experienced being with him?" She looked carefully at Zia's face before continuing. "And having to accept the reality that you can't be with him again until you have access to another portal?"

Zia nodded, "Or worse. That even having him as a Simulacrum wouldn't be enough. That I would die because I couldn't really be with him in the same physical world."

"You feel that strongly about him?" Oma put her arm around Zia's shoulder. "First loves are never easy." She gave her great-grandchild an understanding squeeze, and Zia leaned her head onto Oma's shoulder. "Zia, I think the question you're asking me is if it will be worth spending one wonderfully romantic evening with this boy, knowing that it will most likely be the only one you two will ever share. Is that it?"

"I guess so." Zia hadn't even realized it herself until Oma put it into words.

"One moment." Oma walked to her dressing table and picked up a small music box. She placed it on Zia's lap and instructed her to open it. Zia had heard its nice little tune many times before, but she did as her great-grandmother instructed. "There are words that go along with that melody. Did you know that?"

"There are?" Zia had never thought about lyrics accompanying the sweet sounding music.

"Yes, they were written by a man named Elmer Bernstein over a hundred years ago. The song was even used in a movie once."

"It was?" Zia's eyes widened.

"Would you like for me to sing it to you?" Oma asked.

Now that Zia was older, Oma rarely sang to her anymore. "Oh yes, please do," she said.

"Then, listen carefully." Oma wound the music box and reopened the lid. As the tune began to play, Oma sang.

Some have a lifetime, some just a day
Love isn't something you measure that way
Nothing's ever forever, forever's a lie
All we have is between hello and goodbye.

It's not how long the spring, it's not how wide the sky
It's just how sweet the time between hello and goodbye.

The music has ended, I still hear the song
Our moment was brief, but our kisses were long
Though the loving is over, the love of you stays
And the memory will warm me the rest of my days.

It's not how long the spring, it's not how wide the sky
It's just how sweet the time between hello and goodbye.

Oma tenderly closed the lid and glanced over at her great-granddaughter. "Thank you," Zia said, wiping away the tears. "I know what to do now."

She stood and walked down the hall to her room. She wasn't certain if she was more happy or sad. It was a combination of feelings hard to interpret, but at least now, she knew inviting Kiel was the right thing to do - no matter *how* things turned out.

She had just sat down at her computer, ready to begin homework when she heard the ding of the elevator and her mother's voice as she entered Oma's bedroom. The two women were speaking in subdued tones that sounded very somber. Zia strained to hear what they were saying. What were they talking so seriously about? Was it her?

Several minutes passed, and Zia heard someone approaching her room. Chessie walked in with a concerned and scared expression on her face.

"What's wrong mom?" Zia felt alarmed.

"It's your grandma. She isn't well, so Oma and I are flying back to Texas this evening."

Zia always forgot that Grandma was Oma's daughter because, unlike Oma, Grandma used neither internal nor external rejuvenation procedures. She looked and felt her age.

"Mom," Zia watched Chessie as she paced back and forth. "How come Grandma never used anything to stay young like Oma?"

"I guess it's just something Mom never believed in." Chessie continued pacing, wringing her hands. "I don't know why."

"It's bad though, huh, Mom?" From her mother's facial expression, Zia already knew the answer.

"Yeah, it is. Very bad." Chessie walked over and sat next to Zia. "I don't know when we'll be back. Do you want me to ask Shane to drive over from UCF to stay with you?"

"No, mom. I'm not a baby!"

Chessie looked at her daughter sideways, and Zia knew what she was thinking. Zia was terrified - absolutely petrified - of being home alone at night. But the thought of having the house all to herself while Kiel *slept over* was thrilling enough to alleviate her usual fears.

Before Chessie could become suspicious about her teenage daughter's sudden bravery, Zia gave a quick explanation, "I'll have Zoo or Gen stay over. That way I can be here to take care of Bellaboo."

"If you're sure then." Chessie was still looking suspiciously at Zia.

"I promise. I'll be fine." She smiled reassuringly at her mother. "I just don't want ya'll to worry about me while you're in Texas."

Convinced her youngest child would be fine alone, Chessie headed downstairs to begin packing. Half an hour later, she and Oma were gone, and Zia was all alone on the third floor. The sun had now set, and Zia was already starting to feel apprehensive, until she glanced at the time. Kiel would be looking for her online!

She rushed to the bathroom to perform her usual refreshing ritual. Satisfied with the overhaul, she activated the computer's wall screen and dropped into her chair.

Whenever she had to wait for Kiel, she always felt the butterflies begin to swirl around in her abdomen, and nothing could make their wings quit beating. Not until she saw the screen flicker did her nerves subside, and the insect in her stomach flit away. Finally, almost half an hour later he appeared.

"I am sorry for the long delay this evening." Kiel grinned, but didn't offer any other explanation.

"That's ok," Zia lied.

"You look very pretty this evening." Kiel smiled at her. "Which is why I am sorry I can not talk to you longer."

"You have to go…right now?" Zia was unable to hide her disappointment.

"Yes, my little star. I am afraid I must leave again on another short trip with my father."

Zia wanted to ask Kiel what *his* role was when traveling with the Primus Superior of Taotrue. Was it just to accompany him as his son? Was the travel for official business or pleasure? She wanted to ask him all these things, but instead she asked him another question.

"Will you be back by Friday?"

Kiel understood the meaning of her inquiry. "Yes, I will be back for our sleepover. I am looking forward to it." He flashed a bright smile. They chatted for a few more minutes, and then Kiel bid her a hasty goodnight.

With the computer off, the house was suddenly a big, frightening structure. Zia immediately called Zoolynne. She was well acquainted with her friend's phobia, and invited Zia over without hesitation.

Zia grabbed Bellaboo and her pajamas, commanding the home's computer to turn on every light as she walked through the townhouse. On the front porch, she pulled out her tess. She quickly locked the door, switched on the security alarm, and ran to her car.

The lights behind the second floor's half-drawn shades created the appearance of eyes, and Zia was sure they were watching her. But it wasn't only the house her terror-stricken imagination brought to life – it was the entire property! While she fumbled with her transmitter's vehicle command buttons, the limbs from the yard's oak trees reached out to grab the car. The ignition finally started and Zia accelerated from the curb, looking back at the three-story structure as she sped away.

She was positive the house was breathing.

CHAPTER 14
SEOUL KISS

Zia woke up early the next morning and headed back to the townhouse. It stood just as she had left it, but somehow it didn't look quite as foreboding as it had the night before. She unlocked the door and let herself in. No ghosts… no vandals…just a big, empty - but brightly lit - house.

She hurriedly walked and fed Bellaboo, and then grabbed a quick bite for herself. Her mom probably wouldn't consider a soda and a bag of chips a balanced breakfast, but it worked for Zia. She glanced at the time. Classes started in a half hour, and she still needed to get ready.

Zia rushed to the elevator, Bellaboo at her heels. She was just about to step inside, when a horrible thought occurred to her. What if the elevator stopped? What if she was trapped and no one knew, no one came to her rescue? What if her tess had no reception and she couldn't call for help? She could just see the headlines now:

Teenage Girl Found Dead in Elevator. Eaten Alive By Ravenous Pug!

Zia glanced down at Bellaboo. "You wouldn't do that, would you?" The pudgy little canine just stared at her, wagging its tail. "Better take the stairs," decided Zia, smiling at her four-legged friend. "Besides, you need the exercise."

When Zia arrived at school, she spotted Gentry heading to their homeroom class and rushed to join her. Gentry's mood usually determined which T-shirt she wore. Today's top read: *Friends Are God's Way of Apologizing For Family*.

"Fighting with your mom again?" Zia asked as she caught up to her friend.

"You got it," she laughed, but from the wide grin on Gentry's face, the family argument couldn't be too serious.

Once inside the building, Zia made a quick stop at her locker to retrieve a few items. She was fumbling with the combination pad - tess never could scan the code in correctly - when she felt a tap on her shoulder. It was Kim. This was the first time he'd approached her since his visit to the hospital.

"Hi," he said, giving Zia a flirtatious smile. "How's the hand?"

"It's doing much better. The finger has re-grown a lot, but it itches most of the time." Zia laughed, and held out her hand for him to see.

As she did, Kim took her hand and turned it palm side up, placing a white envelope on top of the limb guard. Zia looked at him with a puzzled expression.

"It's an invitation to my graduation party tonight," Kim explained.

"But graduation isn't for another three weeks." Zia glanced at the envelope. "And tonight's a school night."

Kim leaned casually against Zia's locker, his eyes locked on her profile. "Yeah, but my parents are gonna be gone, so it's the *perfect* night." He traced the length of her arm with his finger, and Zia turned her face to his, able to see her startled reflection in his cinnamon-colored eyes.

Before she had a chance to reply, the bell rang, and Kim sauntered away with a devilish grin. After a few steps, he stopped and turned around, pointing a finger at Zia.

"Be there!" he commanded.

She turned the envelope over in her hand. Written across the front in very neat, masculine cursive was *Zia Barrett*. She didn't think Kim even knew her last name. Zia carefully opened the invitation. It was to be a pool party at Kim's house in Artisan Park. That was on the opposite side of Celebration from her home in North Village.

She watched as he continued down the hallway, handing invitations to several other students standing by their lockers. The second bell rang, and Zia rushed to her homeroom, still holding the invitation in her hand.

She quietly began asking friends if they'd received invitations to Kim's party. None of them had. That seemed odd.

"It's because he's still interested in you," whispered Gentry.

Zia shook her head. "I wish he was, but he's not."

"Yes, he is!" Gentry was insistent. "Ever since Church Street."

"It's hard to resist that Asian Persuasion!" Twilah leaned over to join in on the discussion. "So, do you think you two are gonna finally lock bits?"

"Is that all you think about?" Zia glared at Twilah.

"Pretty much," she flashed a wicked smile, turning forward in her seat as the teacher entered the room.

Zia ran her fingers across the invitation on her desk, and a naughty grin spread across her lips as well.

During morning classes, Zia's search to find a friend - any friend - invited to Kim's party continued, but she always got the same answer – no. Some of the girls she asked were obviously jealous, and Zia hated to admit it, but she was beginning to feel somewhat special.

Why would one of the most popular senior boys ask her to attend his party? Why was he suddenly so interested in her? Not that she was complaining, but Kim was a dream she'd woken up from a long time ago.

By the time afternoon classes rolled around, Zia had quit asking her classmates about Kim's party. She was obviously one of the chosen few.

Zia set her elbows on the desk and let her chin slump down in her hands while she stared out the math room window. Even on the best days, Zia found it hard to concentrate in algebra class, but today it was downright impossible. She felt as if she'd been given a shot of novocaine directly between the eyes. She aimlessly clicked through the pages on her desk computer, allowing her daydreams to turn into psychedelic chimera involving Kim, air castles more rousing than royal.

Finally, the school day ended, and Zia rushed home. She walked and fed Bellaboo, and then fixed herself a quick snack before calling her mother to see how things were in Texas.

Chessie answered on the first ring and tried to sound strong, but her tone gave away her true feelings. Her voice broke abruptly whenever she tried to discuss her mother's condition. The conversation was depressing, but thankfully, brief. Zia wasn't uncaring, but she just didn't feel like dealing with any bad news. At least, not on a night when she'd been invited to a party with Kim – okay, a party *at* Kim's.

Suddenly, a thought occurred. What was she going to wear to the party? She hadn't even considered it. This was a serious decision too. Did she even own a swimsuit that could grab Kim's attention?

Zia took the stairs two at a time and dashed to her bedroom. If he'd only given her the invitation earlier, she could've gone shopping and bought a slinky new bikini. But as it was, she'd just have to settle for what was already in her wardrobe.

She rummaged nervously through her drawer, a growing pile of swimwear resting at her feet. Finally, she found something halfway acceptable. It was from last summer, but Zia considered it her most flattering bikini. The top fastened in front with a spinning gold anchor that, when twisted, added the illusion of a non-existent cup size to Zia's slim figure.

She slipped into the bikini, parted her hair down the middle, and braided both sides. She surveyed her appearance in the three-way mirror. Not bad. The long blonde plaits, paired with the sailor style swimsuit, created a coy - but sexy - schoolgirl kind of look. A sheer white cover-up and a pair of navy flip-flops completed the ensemble.

Now for the finishing touches. Zia applied a small amount of mascara and blush, but as she reached for the lip gloss, she stopped. Instead, she picked up her toothbrush and gave her teeth a second disinfecting to rival even her dental hygienist's cleanings. After her teeth, Zia brushed her tongue, flossed her gums, and topped it all off with a strong mouthwash. If her oral cavity wasn't an antiseptic marvel now, it never would be!

Better safe than sorry she told herself. And besides, who knew *what* might happen. Pleased with her grooming, Zia added one final thing before exiting the bathroom - a touch of light pink lip stain.

Zia had decided, after a great deal of soul searching and nail biting, to be brave and come back to her *own* house after the party. Still, she wasn't taking any chances of returning home to *House on Haunted Hill*.

Just as she had the night before, Zia turned on every light in the house prior to leaving. Only Oma's bedroom, where Bellaboo was sleeping, remained dark.

As she stepped outside, Zia clicked on the front porch light and walked eyes-forward to her car. It was better if she didn't look back to see if the house was looking back. Instead, she glanced at the invitation again, memorizing Kim's street number before heading to Artisan Park.

As she drove, Zia began to feel apprehensive. She didn't like the fact that none of her close friends would be at the party, and she hated arriving alone. Showing up anywhere solo made her uncomfortable.

When Zia arrived at Kim's house, she was stunned by its size and beauty – and perfection. She had no idea Kim came from such a wealthy family.

A meticulously landscaped yard enhanced the home's timeless Feng Shui architecture, while an elaborate stone driveway invited guests inside. Zia took a deep breath, and buzzed the entry gate for admittance into the Song Family Estate.

The interior courtyard was uncluttered, save for the large number of high-end vehicles already parked in the long driveway. Zia pulled in beside a glistening Bugatti hybrid and slid out of her Scion. Maybe she'd spot a familiar car on her way to the front door. Zia glanced from side to side as she walked.

No luck.

Well, hopefully, she'd know someone already inside. Her finger trembled slightly as she rang the doorbell.

A remarkably beautiful woman answered. She opened the soaring door with a sparkling smile and introduced herself as Mrs. Song. But didn't Kim say his parents would be gone? Then Zia noticed what his mother was wearing - an elegant black cocktail dress - obviously ready for an evening out.

"It's so nice to meet you." Zia bowed and stepped inside the foyer. She placed her flip-flops in one of the long rows lined up by the front door. There appeared to be dozens of shoes already abandoned by their owners, and Zia wondered how many people Kim had invited.

"Everyone's outside by the pool, so let me show you the way." Mrs. Song led Zia through the living room.

She'd never seen a home so lavishly decorated. Elegant lacquered furniture graced the living area, separated from the dining room by Shoji screens. On the far wall, a step Tansu held a collection of exquisite Celadon temple jars, and above them, hung a painting by an artist Zia learned about in art class. Her name was Shin Sa-im-dang. Surely, Kim's family couldn't afford a painting by the most renowned female painter of the Chosun Dynasty! Were they that wealthy? No, Zia decided it had to be a print.

Just as they approached the kitchen area, an attractive gentleman appeared. At first, Zia thought he was a young man - maybe just out of graduate school - but as he walked closer, she could see faint lines around the eyes and a touch of gray in the sides of his hair. Even so, he was - to say strikingly handsome for a man his age was an understatement - no, he was come-hither hot!

Now Zia understood why Kim was so painfully, good looking. His parents - especially his father - were gorgeous!

"I'm Kim's father," he introduced himself with a smile. "And this is Kim's older sister Jandi. She's home for a visit." Zia smiled at the young woman who had entered the room behind her father.

Zia bowed to both and then turned to Jandi. She was as stunning as the rest of the family, with a flawless complexion and waist length black hair.

"My name's Zia. I didn't know Kim had a sister."

"I'm a junior at Baylor," smiled Jandi. "So I'm seldom here."

"Oh, Baylor University in Texas?" Zia was excited, thankful she had something in common to talk about with Kim's sister. "I was born in Texas!"

"Really?" Jandi's smile widened. "I love going to college there. Texans are really nice." She took Zia by the arm, tossing her long black hair over one shoulder. "Come on, let me take you outside."

Zia excused herself, bowing again to Kim's parents, who smiled approvingly as she left the kitchen and followed Jandi into the garden room.

Jandi swung open the French doors leading to the pool area, and the girls stepped outside. Immediately, Zia felt intimidated and out of her league. All the girls were beautiful – and exotic. Every disgustingly attractive girl from school was there - all tanned, well-endowed, dark haired beauties! Suddenly, Zia felt very self-conscious. She seemed to be the only pale, skinny blonde girl at the party.

At least, she could be grateful that Jandi had walked her outside. Maybe the other girls would see them talking and think they were friends.

"What are you majoring in?" Zia asked, hoping it was something requiring a great deal of description.

"Dentistry," Jandi replied. A one-word answer. Well, that conversation starter didn't work out as planned. "Hey, Kim!" she called to her brother.

He was playing water volleyball with some guys Zia recognized from the high school's soccer team.

"Coming!" He waved back.

He handed the ball off to one of his teammates and swam to the pool's edge. With a toss of his head, he flung his thick hair to one side and placed both hands on the pool's side, lifting his body out.

Zia had the sensation of watching an erotic movie in slow motion. As he emerged from the pool, she could clearly see that his body was as magnificent in person as she could only imagine Kiel's to be through a computer screen. He grabbed a towel hanging on a nearby lawn chair and walked over to where Zia and Jandi were standing.

"I just wanted to let you know your friend…Zia, right…was here." Jandi motioned toward Zia and turned to go back inside.

"Thank you," Zia said, bowing again.

"You don't have to do that with me," Jandi laughed. "It's great for Mom and Dad, but I'm all American."

"Oh, sorry." Zia felt doubly embarrassed because Kim had also witnessed her mistake. She dropped her eyes as he greeted her, partly because of the blunder with his sister, but mostly because she wasn't sure where to look.

He lifted the towel to his head and rubbed it briskly across his hair, causing it to fall perfectly back into place. The wet hair only made him more sensual. Wet hair made Zia look like a drowned rat.

"Sorry. I'm a little out of air from the game," Kim apologized, taking several deep breaths. Zia watched the contours of his chest rise and fall, and struggled to find something to say.

"Oh, that's understandable." Zia hoped she sounded unaffected by the close proximity of his mostly naked body.

"I'm glad you came." He smiled at her. "Do you know everyone here?"

"Well, I know *who* everyone is, but I'm not sure I know them all personally," she lied, glancing around. In truth, her eyes were searching frantically for anyone with whom she was even remotely friends.

The crowd consisted mostly of seniors, but Zia did see several juniors, and even a few sophomores. Finally, her eyes focused on a girl she considered a friend. What a relief to see a familiar face! They didn't hang out often, but Zia enjoyed her company when they did get together.

Enrica was an Italian beauty who'd begun a modeling career their freshman year, and Zia often wondered why, with such an exciting and lucrative future already mapped out, she even bothered to continue attending school.

Zia smiled and waved at Enrica in an exaggerated manner, hoping to indicate to anyone watching that the two were closer friends than they actually were. Zia held her breath for a moment, but Enrica waved back, and with a pleasant look on her face, began walking around the pool toward Zia.

While she waited for Enrica to cross the lawn, Zia looked at Kim. "I like your family. They're very nice, and your mother is beautiful."

"I'm glad you think so. I'm named after my mother."

"Your mother's name is Kim too?"

"No," he laughed. "In Korea, Kim is never a first name. Kim was my mother's maiden name."

"So, in America you have a first name, but in Korea you have a last name?"

Zia's reasoning must have sounded funny because Kim chuckled again before responding. "Yeah, something like that," he said, flirtatiously popping Zia on the hip with his wet towel.

His relaxed gesture indicated a playful intimacy between the two, something that really didn't exist – yet. Zia liked it. She hoped someone noticed. Anyone would do.

Their conversation was going so well, that Zia half-expected Kim to whisk her off to a darkened corner of the backyard to get to know her better, but when Enrica reached the pair, Kim seemed satisfied that Zia had found someone to pass her time with and returned to his volleyball game.

Despite Kim's sudden departure, Zia couldn't have been more pleased with the reception she received from Enrica. She gave Zia a friendly hug and a kiss on each cheek. So continental, Zia thought.

Hopefully, everyone noticed the greeting and realized that *she* belonged at Kim's party as much as anyone else. Zia glanced around, but no one seemed to be paying any attention.

"Zia!" At least Enrica was pleased to see her. "I heard about the incident with you and Riley. I always hated that bitch! She was so mean to me in ballet class."

What great news! Not that Riley had made someone else's life a living hell, but that Riley's hatred for Zia wasn't something personal. She felt an instant bond with Enrica.

"I thought I was the only one she ever picked on."

"Are you kidding? She was mean to almost every girl at the dance studio." Enrica took Zia's arm. "So, how's your finger? I'm sorry about what happened."

"Its okay, almost completely healed now." Zia smiled, but kept her left hand tucked inside the cover-up pocket.

"Can you get it wet?" Enrica wanted to know. "Come sit with me in the hot tub."

"I can't get the bud guard wet." Zia glanced down at the hand in her pocket. "But I can sit on the side maybe."

"Okay." Enrica seemed satisfied and walked arm in arm with Zia toward the whirlpool.

Three senior girls were already enjoying the tub's bubbling water, and Zia knew one of them - Becky Stone - the girl she'd seen Kim with at school.

Becky was leaning back on her elbows in an exaggerated manner, allowing only her lower body to settle into the churning pool. It was obvious to Zia that Becky was satisfied to float around like a life preserver if it meant flashing her fake boobs.

And it was probably a good idea that she didn't try to submerge the girls. Zia was positive if Becky tried to lower her upper body into the water, her two artificially inflated breasts would work as buoys, keeping her bobbing up and down on the surface.

Equally endowed, the other two females sat fully, if not modestly, submerged in the hot tub, obviously gossiping about someone. One of the girls turned to give Zia and Enrica a quick smile, but the other kept talking with her hand placed in front of her mouth.

Even though she'd never cared for Becky, Zia felt she should at least acknowledge her presence.

"Hi, Becky." Zia tried to sound friendly as she sat down. "This is my friend Enrica."

Becky grunted an inaudible reply and leaned her head back. She obviously didn't find it necessary to reciprocate the personal presentations and introduce her hot tub buddies. Oh well, easily solved. Zia would just refer to Becky's playmates as Dee and Double Dee.

Zia looked around at all the dazzling figures clad in skimpy bikinis. This place had to be a visual orgy for the horny eyes of its male guests. She glanced down at her own physical attributes. Zia wasn't sure if she even wanted to remove her cover-up, but she'd probably draw more attention if she didn't.

Mission one – get the cover-up off while no one was watching. Zia quickly loosened its sash and let the garment fall behind her where she sat.

Mission two – hide and protect the bud guard. Zia immediately leaned back on her palms and slid her injured finger between the cover-up's folds.

Mission accomplished!

"Oh, isn't your swimsuit cute." Mission *almost* accomplished. Zia's movements had obviously awakened Becky from her self-induced coma. "I can't wear anything off the rack myself. Voluptuous bodies require designer styles, ya know." She grinned at Zia, and wrinkled her nose.

Zia gritted her teeth at Becky's thinly disguised insult. She was seriously considering sliding into the hot tub to hide her off-the-rack bikini, but Enrica came to her rescue.

"Oh, too bad, because that's the exact suit I wore on the cover of Seventeen Magazine's September issue."

Zia knew Enrica was lying. Seventeen would never feature a model wearing a year old navy blue bikini from Target. Zia smiled at her in a way she hoped Enrica could read as a thank you. Becky rolled her eyes and looked the other way.

Just then, Kim's parents and sister walked out to the patio. "We're all very glad you were able to come to Kim's party," said his father. Zia smiled at Mr. Song, imagining what Kim would look like in thirty years. He'd still be hittable.

"We have our own party to attend this evening, but we trust you'll all enjoy yourselves," he paused, and then added. "But please, remember, you are still young ladies and gentlemen whether we are here or not."

"Yeah, right," Becky mumbled under her breath, and for once, she was correct.

Within moments of his parents' departure, the mood changed. Suddenly, it was party time. The guys who'd been happy to play water volleyball only moments earlier abruptly scrambled out of the pool.

Kim pushed open the sliding doors of the outside bar, and motioned for his sister to take over bartending duties. Jandi complied with a surprisingly agreeable attitude, and guests began lining up to place drink orders.

"Let the Carnal Carnival begin," Becky said, with a sly grin. Zia glanced over at Enrica, who returned her look with a shrug of the shoulders. "What I mean, sweet cheeks, is you better get out now while you still have your virtue in tact." Becky stared straight at Zia.

Wasn't it bad enough that she had to endure Twilah and Chandra's lectures, without having to listen to Becky's crap too? "Why are you telling *me* this?" Zia asked.

"Because I saw you eye humping Kim earlier!" Becky narrowed her eyes.

"I was not!" Zia's words came rushing out, and she felt her face go warm.

"Well, this place is about to turn into Copulation Station, and I'm sure you're too straight edge to ride it out."

Zia's eyes widened, and she looked again at Enrica. "Don't pay any attention to her," Enrica said, in a hushed voice. "Kim's parties never get outa control like that. I think she's just trying to scare you into leaving."

Zia was confused. She couldn't imagine *why* Becky would want to do that? Surely, she didn't see Zia as competition. Why on earth would she? But...she obviously did! Without realizing it, the snotty bitch had actually flattered her. Well, she wasn't about to let someone as vile - and apparently insecure - as Becky bother her now. No, Zia wasn't going to budge if she had to sit alone on the hot tub's edge all night.

As it turned out, she didn't have to. Kim, Danny, and Jinho appeared with a bottle of champagne.

"Ladies?" Kim asked. "Would you join us in a toast?"

Becky's two friends were obviously thrilled with the invitation, hoisting their shapely bodies out of the steaming water, and situating themselves beside Enrica and Zia. Danny sat down beside Dee, and Jinho settled in between Enrica and Double Dee.

After a great deal of pretentious maneuvering, Becky finally emerged and sat cross-legged on the tub's edge. She smiled seductively at Kim, and tossed her wet hair over one shoulder in an exaggerated manner. Becky pressed her lips together in what Zia considered a ridiculous looking pout, and patted the ground next to her, calling Kim over like he was a puppy dog.

Zia looked up at Kim, expecting to see him bounce over to Becky with his tongue hanging out. But he wasn't even looking at Becky. He was looking directly at her!

Could Enrica have been right? Was this why Becky had tried so hard to get her to leave the party? No, Zia didn't believe it. But Kim sat down next to her, allowing his leg to brush against hers as he did.

He opened the bottle, and everyone cheered as the cork popped, and the champagne bubbled over into the tub. The idea of drinking her first champagne with Kim made the evening implausibly magical, and with the warm night air and full moon, the night began to take on a surreal aura.

Danny passed glasses to everyone, and Kim poured the champagne into his guest's stemware. Zia didn't dare make eye contact with Becky, keeping her attention focused solely on Kim.

"A toast," Kim said. "To the prettiest girls at the party!"

Everyone raised their glasses, but as she started to take a sip, Kim stopped Zia's hand and entwined his arm with hers. She looked at Kim, his face only inches from hers, and knew that for the rest of her life she would remember this night. Kim had created the perfect setting – the champagne, the romantic toast – and then the evening breeze and low hanging stars joined in, all conspiring to seduce her.

"Now you can drink," Kim said, leaning toward Zia and taking a sip from his glass. She bent forward, but before her lips could touch the glass, a wall of water showered the couple. The injured finger Zia had so carefully tried to protect was soaked!

"Oh, I am so sorry." Becky's anger simmered just beneath the surface of her forced smile. "I slipped when I stood to toast everyone."

Zia didn't believe her for an instant and wondered if Becky's true intentions were as obvious to everyone else. From the expression on Kim's face, they were.

Zia sat down her glass, which was now as full of hot water as it was champagne. "Excuse me." She motioned to her left hand as she removed it from the wet cover-up. "I need to dry this off."

Kim helped Zia out of the hot tub. "Just go through the kitchen and take the second door to the left," Kim instructed, tossing the contents of his glass into the closest flowerbed.

"Thanks," Zia smiled at Kim, giving Becky a callous glare as she walked toward the back door.

Zia had an uneasy feeling as soon as she stepped inside. She felt out of place walking through Kim's empty house. At least she assumed she was alone because the house seemed eerily vacant.

She walked quickly to the second door and pushed it open. The bathroom was huge and as beautifully decorated as the rest of the house. Zia closed the door behind her and looked around for something with which to dry her finger. There was a small hand towel by the sink, and Zia used it to blot the soggy limb guard. As she pressed, she could feel her new finger inside. It was almost to the end of the guard now!

Zia carefully folded and replaced the towel when she was through. She briefly surveyed her appearance in the mirror, fluffing up her damp hair and biting her lips to give them some needed color.

She opened the door to leave, but as she did, she realized she wasn't looking into the hallway. This was a bedroom. She glanced around, realizing that the door she'd entered through was actually behind her. She placed her fingers back on the handle, preparing to close the door, but as she did, something in the bedroom caught her eye.

It wasn't polite to wander through someone's empty house and she knew it, but the urge was too great. She'd just take a closer look at what drew her attention, and then get out before anyone knew.

Hesitantly, she entered the room and walked toward a set of four watercolor paintings illuminated by accent lights. They were beautiful 16 x 20 inch paintings, and Zia was sure she recognized one. She looked at the bottom right hand corner, and sure enough, there it was - Kim's signature!

This was the cityscape she'd watched him paint in art class the previous year. She smiled at the memory. That was when she'd noticed Kim for the very first time. Zia had sat just behind and to the right of Kim. It gave her the perfect view of his painting - and his profile. She wasn't sure which one she'd found more captivating.

Each day she was more taken with his appearance and the artistry that flowed from his fingers. Most days, she found herself unable to concentrate on her own canvas at all, completely enthralled in watching the movement of Kim's hand as he painted.

As his work progressed, Kim began wearing his hair pulled up in a half ponytail to hold back the long strands that often fell over one eye. His hair was jet black then, not the highlighted sienna he now wore, and Zia loved the Asian male ponytail. Besides affording Kim better concentration, it also allowed Zia to scrutinize his profile even closer.

Her fascination – downright obsession – with Kim became so intense that eventually Zia began skipping the study hall she had before art class, just to come in early and work on her own painting without distraction. In that way, she could discreetly watch Kim as he entered class and settled in at his work area. By then, Zia had memorized his every movement.

She would follow the motion of his long slender fingers as they searched for the perfect brush. He would hold it delicately between his fingers as he worked, and with each stroke, Zia imagined he was making love to the canvas - colors exploding across the fabric with the seeming happiness of having flowed from his hand.

Kim would occasionally lean back and survey what he'd brought to life, and Zia would wait for the meager smile to appear at the corners of his mouth. Then she would know he was satisfied and content.

Exhausted, he would lean back in his chair and remove the hair band, allowing the ponytail to fall away, and his hair to caress his cheeks and neck as it returned to its original style. His back would arch, and he would place one hand on each side of his ribcage, slowly pushing his palms down until they rested on his hips. Finally, he would rise from the seat and slowly remove his smock, hanging it gently on the nail beside his easel.

The routine rarely varied, and everyday Zia watched and waited for his last movement before leaving class – that of leaning over to pick up the holdall he'd casually flung behind his chair. The corner of her eyes secretly followed Kim, hoping he would glance up and notice her. He never did. On neither entering, nor leaving the classroom, did he ever acknowledge that he was aware of her existence.

Zia was still leaning over, taking in every nuance of the painting, remembering the day he'd added this color or drawn that line, when she suddenly felt a presence behind her. Instinctively, she knew it was Kim.

She was going to turn and apologize for entering his bedroom without permission, but before she could, she felt him press his bare chest against her back. He placed both hands on her upper arms, raising them slowly until his open palms circled her shoulders. Kim allowed his hands to close gradually, fondling Zia's skin with a prolonged teasing of his fingertips. He held her so closely that she could feel his heart beating against her back, causing her pulse to race.

"Do you like my paintings?" he purred in her ear.

Zia struggled to answer. "Yes...very much."

Kim removed his right hand and leaned his chin onto her shoulder, the movement causing a seductive shift in position. He pointed to an area on one of the paintings and began describing artificial shadow lines. As he did, Zia could feel the warmth of his breath on her neck, and the vibrations of his voice moving through his chest and into her back.

He continued speaking for several minutes, describing this or that about one of the four paintings, but his words were lost on her. After the first few statements, Zia had stopped listening. Kim's reflection in the paintings' glass frames held her gaze, and her ears and body heard and felt only his inhaling and exhaling.

As his chest moved forward and back, Zia closed her eyes and synchronized her breathing with his. The caress of Kim's breath upon her neck was disarming, and Zia surrendered, allowing her head to tilt back onto his shoulder.

Maybe Becky had been completely right to worry about what might happen on an evening like this. If she'd actually had the chance to consume some champagne, Zia could blame her immediate desires on the alcohol - but she hadn't, and she couldn't. She had nothing and no one to blame but herself for the unspeakable things she found herself wanting to do to Kim, with Kim. And tonight, she didn't feel guilty.

The overhead light suddenly switched on. *Now* she felt guilty! *Very* guilty! In the glaring light, she was ashamed of herself.

"Oh, sorry," Jandi called from the doorway. "Your guests are looking for you. All the seniors want to take a picture together."

"Okay, I'll be right there," Kim answered.

Zia hoped Jandi would extinguish the light, returning their bodies to the shadows, but she exited the room without flipping off the ceiling light or closing the door. With the fluorescent glow overhead, Zia now felt vulnerable and exposed.

If Kim felt the same way, he didn't let it show. "So, which one is your favorite?" he asked. Zia pointed to the cityscape. "And why is that?"

"Because I watched you paint it."

"What?" He sounded honestly surprised.

"I sat behind you in art class last year. I guess I watched you from a distance. I mean, watched you paint it from a distance." Zia hoped her recovery was quick enough that he didn't understand her original meaning.

"You didn't watch me work on it every day though?"

"Yes...I did. I noticed from the very first day how talented you were, and from then on...I watched...from the first stroke to the last stroke." Zia wondered what the difference was between flirting and just saying too much.

Kim moved in closer, but returned his eyes to the canvas. "That's my favorite too," he sounded pleased with her choice.

"I never would have envisioned the Orlando skyline to be so beautiful." Zia stepped back to admire the painting, but Kim leaned over laughing.

"What's so funny?" Zia didn't understand. What had she said?

"That's not Orlando," he continued laughing. "That's Seoul, where my parents were born."

"Oh." Zia felt rattled. "I guess that explains why it looks so much better than O-Town." She tried to shrug off her embarrassing mistake.

"Come on!" Danny and Jinho both appeared at the door, motioning for Kim to follow them. Again - an interruption! This was becoming an annoying pattern.

"Alright, alright," he waved them out of his room. "I gotta get out there, but I want you to have this." Kim removed the painting from his wall.

"Oh, I couldn't. It would ruin your beautiful display." Zia glanced over at the empty spot left by its removal.

"No, I want you to have it. I can't believe anyone would care enough to watch me work on a painting from beginning to end, but *you* did. Please... take it." Zia hesitated for an instant, but then allowed Kim to place the canvas in her carefully upturned hands.

"And maybe one day, you'll get to see Seoul in person," he said, allowing his fingers to brush across hers as she took the painting. "I'll take you to Namsan Tower, and we can take a lock."

"A look?" Zia thought she'd misunderstood.

"No, a lock." Kim gave her a sweet smile, which she returned, but she still had no idea what he meant.

"Now!" Jinho yelled once more from the doorway, causing them both to jump. With an apologizing smile, Kim turned and walked quickly out.

Zia looked down at the painting. She couldn't believe he'd given it to her. She'd spent the better part of her sophomore year watching Kim create it - and now she held the painting in her hands! It was hers!

Still clutching the canvas, Zia exited Kim's room and walked back to the kitchen. Through its bay window, she could see Kim and his senior guests lined up, smiling for the camera. Becky stood next to him, her arm wrapped around his waist. Her other hand was placed on his bare chest - the same chest that had only moments before risen and fallen in unison with Zia's. The same chest whose heart she could feel beating.

As she watched, Kim placed one arm loosely around Becky's shoulder. With the other, he reached up and held the hand she had placed on his chest. Everyone smiled for the picture. Everyone *but* Zia.

She left the house without retrieving her cover-up from the back yard, and walked alone to her car. Outside, she could still hear the laughter flowing from the backyard. She placed Kim's painting in her trunk and slid into the driver's seat, guiding the Scion toward the automatic gate. It opened as she crossed the laser-beamed security.

Zia exited quietly and drove slowly away through the sleepy neighborhood, thinking about Kiel, and feeling confused and guilty once again about what had just happened between her and Kim.

Zia didn't generally use the car's computer when staying in Celebration - there was no need to - but tonight, she felt lonely driving through the dark streets and turned the system on.

"Hello, Adam."

"Allo, darlin'. What may I help ye with?"

"Nothing," Zia let out a deep sigh. "I just wanted to hear a friendly voice."

"Awright, luvy. Rain is forecast for this evenin', so remember yer brolly." His accented speech made Zia smile.

"Thanks, Adam. It's nice to have someone watching out for me."

"Why, I'd be barmy not to fancy a fit bird like you. Yer a right buff crackling, m'dear." Adam slipped into his randy scouse git personality. Translation: Horny guy from Liverpool.

"Don't overdo it Adam."

CHAPTER 15
THE SLEEPOVER

Zia woke up early the next morning feeling victorious in conquering - at least for one evening - her fear of being alone in the dark. Of course, she'd left every single light on all night, including the porch and patio lights. But, she had gone all the way up to the third floor bedroom and slept alone – with her lights off.

Even though she was feeling triumphant in surviving the night alone, Zia was still feeling off balance from the previous evening and spent most of the morning in self-scrutiny. Where Kim was concerned, Zia realized she could lose control as easily as an alcoholic in a liquor store.

While she went about her morning activities, Zia forced Kim from her thoughts and replaced him with daydreams about her alien Romeo. Tonight they would be alone in her bedroom!

With her focus solely on Kiel and the evening ahead, Zia's school day passed in a quick succession of unforgettable events. Only once did she even find herself scanning the hallways for a glimpse of Kim.

The instant she got home from school, Zia walked and fed Bellaboo, making sure the canine was gratified with a new chew toy to ensure no evening interruptions.

At the appropriate time, Zia commanded, "Computer on" and within seconds, Kiel appeared before her. As with the night of their dinner date, he had the computer set in full screen 3-D, creating the illusion that their rooms were seamlessly connected.

With his dining table removed, Zia had a clearer view of Kiel's bedroom. On the far wall, she could see a massive canopy bed, its dark mahogany carved with a draping garland motif that circled all four posts. Slim bombe chests stood on each side. Decorative gold patterns embellished the drawers, and green marble tops glistened under the ceiling lights.

Although Zia was dressed in sleeping attire, Kiel was wearing what appeared to be regular street clothes. Zia's heart sank, expecting a replay of the week's earlier events.

She waited for him to break the news to her that he was off on another trip with his father, but instead Kiel smiled and said, "Hello

Zia. I did not know what to expect at a sleepover, so I am unprepared."

Zia's heart picked up. "You do have the entire evening free then?" She wanted to make certain.

"The entire evening," he answered, with a smile.

"Zero cool! I mean, that's wonderful," Zia reworded her response, knowing Kiel's elucidator wouldn't be able to translate her teenage slang.

"How do we begin?" he asked, and the question made Zia laugh.

"Well, we have to sleep on the floor, so you need one of these." She pointed to her sleeping bag.

"I do not think I have one of those, but I can improvise." Kiel walked to the massive canopy bed and removed the heavy fur blanket that covered it. He pulled it to the screen and placed it next to Zia's drab green sleeping bag, returning to retrieve two ivory colored pillows from the bed.

"Now what?" he asked.

"Well, you need to change into whatever clothes you sleep in," Zia instructed.

"I sleep in nothing."

He looked serious, and Zia froze for an instant before answering. "Well, out of modesty, you'll have to adjust for me." He gave her the usual tilt of his head.

Zia almost wished he'd say he couldn't accommodate her request, but instead he replied with a smile, "Very well, I will find something suitable."

Excusing himself, Kiel walked away from the computer screen and toward what Zia assumed to be his dressing area. From what she could view through the half open door, it appeared as beautifully decorated as his bedroom.

She watched as he entered the room and stepped behind the barrier; however, the dressing area was mirrored on all sides, allowing Zia to still view his reflection. For an instant, and only an instant, Zia lowered her eyes. But it was no use. They seemed to have a will of their own and returned immediately to the image on the screen.

Zia watched with anticipation as Kiel removed his shirt and placed it on a hook just out of her view. She wasn't disappointed. The muscular planes of his chest were sleek and solid.

He was apparently unaware his movements were being watched, but he turned his back to the screen before slowly unbuttoning the top of his pants. Zia's uncorrupted half cautioned, "Look away", but as she momentarily averted her eyes, her unrestrained half demanded, "Look back!" and she turned her eyes again to the mirrored dressing area.

In the glass reflection, Zia could discern that Kiel was now completely undressed, but because of the door's angle, she could glimpse only a bisected view of his body. She felt unsettled by her own pleasure in watching him, but she couldn't - no, she wouldn't - force herself to look away now.

She began at his apex and worked her way down – slowly. From this angle, she could see that his thick, dark hair hung down much further in the back than she'd realized, reaching just above his shoulders.

Even with the partially opened door cutting his anatomy in half, Zia could still see the smooth expanse of his broad shoulders. She continued her lustful scrutiny in his back and followed the elegant curve of his spine into the sleek muscled flesh of his buttocks.

Zia hadn't previously noticed the light umber sheen to his body, and at first glance, she assumed his skin's glow was the result of tanning. She ran her eyes across his torso, but there were no visible tan lines, indicating to Zia that his rich skin color was derived from nothing more that it's own natural radiance.

Kiel had the muscular silhouette of an athlete, with a lean upper body and a powerful lower body. His legs were long and bestial, and the tensile strength of his thighs continued down into his calves, giving him the appearance of an untamed animal.

Zia watched as he bent forward and placed one foot into a pair of what appeared to be satin pajama pants. He pulled them onto his hips and turned around, moving a bit forward and allowing Zia to see his full image in the mirror for the first time. As he turned, the pants fell slightly above his pelvic area.

Zia marveled at the smooth, taught muscles of his abdomen, and then *something* caught her eye. At first, she thought it must be a shadow or a crease in his skin. But no, as Kiel's hands moved to tie the pajamas resting loosely on his hips, Zia realized she hadn't been mistaken in what she'd seen!

He had *two* belly buttons! One positioned just slightly below the other.

Mesmerized by the genetic anomaly, Zia was completely unaware that Kiel had moved into the main dressing area, and was now watching her reflection in the mirror too. She felt her face burn as she moved her gaze from his abdomen to his eyes and realized they were examining her. In any other instant, she would have immediately removed her stare to avoid embarrassment, but with his eyes focused on hers, she found herself unable to look away.

Time stopped.

When it resumed, Zia was cognizant of Kiel's movement toward the screen. He sat down cross-legged on the fur blanket directly across from Zia. "Why do you continue to look at me as you do?" he asked.

Again, Zia felt herself fumbling for some answer other than the truth. She certainly couldn't admit what carnal thoughts had tingled in her brain as she watched him undress.

"Uh…uh…you have two navels!" she blurted out.

Kiel glanced down at his stomach and back at Zia. With a teasing grin, he leaned onto his side and propped up on one elbow, stretching out his long legs on the animal skin blanket. He reached with one hand and seductively pulled his pajama pants down much lower than necessary, allowing Zia to indulge her imagination.

"Do you not have umbilicus?" Kiel questioned her, a light smile on his lips.

She stared at the two depressions in his abdomen and swallowed hard. "No, I don't."

He looked completely surprised. "Were you not born of a mother?" Did you not grow in her womb?" His voice sounded skeptical.

"Yes, I did," Zia replied. "But, I have only one belly...uh...umbilical scar."

"What?" Kiel didn't seem to believe her. "Let me see!" Zia looked around, unsure how to respond. "Please," he begged, and Zia couldn't refuse. She was as much an anomaly to him as he was to her.

"Well, okay." Zia gave in and stood up, demurely removing the robe she had been wearing.

As she let it drop, Kiel returned to an upright position, focused on what she would do next. To show him her single navel, Zia would have to lift the bottom of her already skimpy nightgown, exposing only the panty she wore beneath.

She wasn't worried about that, in fact, she wouldn't mind giving Kiel a preview of coming attractions. What worried Zia was how to conceal the bud guard now that she had no robe pocket in which to hide it. She couldn't continue to keep her left hand placed behind her back without looking awkward.

Kiel looked at her anxiously.

She hesitated only briefly and then relented, pulling the bottom of her nightgown up to expose her abdomen and her single omphalus. His eyes widened, and then rose to meet her stare.

Zia quickly lowered her nightgown and sat back down on the floor, sliding her damaged finger inside the sleeping bag. She looked directly at Kiel. Apparently, his attention had been anywhere but on her injured hand.

"Your race must be very sturdy to require only one umbilical cord from its mother." He shook his head in amazement.

Zia had been thinking the exact opposite. His race must be blessed with their uncommon beauty and stature *because* of their second umbilical cord.

For several minutes, neither spoke, Zia lost in her musings about his unusual anatomy. What else might be different with his physical make up? She suddenly had a frightening - although gleeful thought - but quickly put it out of her mind.

"What do we do next?" Kiel's words broke her errant daydreaming.

"Well," Zia cleared her throat, trying desperately not to fixate on his bare chest. "We usually watch a scary movie."

Kiel tilted his head and smiled at Zia.

"Do you know what that is?" She wasn't sure how to read his facial expression. "I mean, do you watch supernatural...you know...paranormal movies on Taotrue?"

"I know, and we do," Kiel replied.

"Good. I picked one I think you'll like." Zia stood up and carefully maneuvered her damaged finger out of Kiel's view. She was actually beginning to feel pretty confident in her subterfuge.

"Generally, I watch movies on my computer screen," Zia laughed lightly. "But since *you* are *on* my computer, I got an old flat screen for us to use." She pointed to the television she'd retrieved from the back of Oma's closet. She'd brought the antiquated set in earlier, and set it up in a position she hoped would be adequate for them both.

"It has an old DVD player we'll use," Zia said, glancing over and smiling at Kiel.

She inserted the DVD and returned to her place on the sleeping bag, waiting for the movie to begin. She sat just to the side of Kiel and looked over her shoulder, smiling at his image on the wall screen. He returned her smile.

The movie began, and as they watched, Kiel asked numerous questions about the horror feature and Earth movies in general. Zia sensed from his comments that he was enjoying the picture, and she felt satisfied with her selection.

About an hour into the movie, Zia's back began to ache, so she leaned against the wall screen to relieve the pressure. When the film ended and she turned around, she was surprised to see that Kiel had moved his body directly behind hers.

"Oh," she said, with a startled smile. "I didn't realize you were right there."

His 3-D image was so real, so inviting that Zia wanted to throw her arms around his neck. She didn't though. She knew she'd just end up smashing her face against the wall.

"I was pretending you were leaning on my shoulder while we watched the movie," he replied.

She liked that Kiel used that word... pretending. It meant he might be imagining things about her in the same way she imagined things about him.

"What do we do next?" Kiel seemed to be enjoying his first sleepover.

"Well, we girls usually just listen to music and talk until we fall asleep," Zia explained.

"Then, that is what we should do."

Zia smiled and instructed the computer to play selections from one of her favorite erotic instrumentalists. As the music began, she and Kiel slipped beneath the covers, lying with their heads on pillows facing each other. Kiel requested the lights in his room to dim, and Zia followed his lead. The faint glow created a romantic smokiness, but still allowed each to see the others facial features.

The two made small talk for a while, laughing lightly as they did. When Zia felt comfortable enough in the conversation, she asked Kiel the question she'd been holding onto all evening.

"Kiel, do the people of Taotrue use Simulacrums?"

She watched as his eyes shifted to the bottom of the screen. They moved back and forth, obviously reading a translation of her question. He returned his gaze to hers and responded in the positive.

"Then you use Parallax Portals as well?"

Again, his eyes fell to the bottom of the screen, sailing across whatever translation appeared there. He returned his eyes to hers. "Yes, we do."

"Do you think a Simulacrum from Taotrue could reach a Parallax Portal on Earth?" She wondered if the anxiousness in her voice gave away her reason for asking the question.

This time Kiel's eyes didn't lower to read some unseen translation scrolling across his computer's screen. He looked directly at Zia and answered, "Yes. I know for certain it would."

Even though she was in a prone position, the fluttering of her neck's pulse made Zia feel as if she might faint. She closed her lids for a second and then gazed back at the orchid eyes watching her.

"I'll have access to a portal in only a few weeks. Could you...would you... come to the prom...as my date?" Zia waited for his answer, her heart pacing behind her ribcage, threatening to leap from her chest's enclosure like a wild animal.

Kiel adjusted his head on the pillow. "Zia, I do not know what a prom is, but if I can be with you, I will come. You do not need to ask again."

A soft smile began at the corners of Zia's lips and quickly spread across her face.

For the next half hour, she talked of nothing but the prom. She explained to Kiel what a prom was, when it was, what she would wear, what he should wear, when he should arrive, and the most important thing - the sector position of the portal through which he would be entering.

He seemed to feel as lighthearted as Zia as they laughed and planned their prom night together. The mood began elevated, but as fatigue took over, they began to speak fewer and fewer words to each other. Finally, Kiel was silent.

The hush from the computer screen startled Zia into full alertness.

"Kiel, Kiel?" she called softly. The only answer was the faint sound of his deep breathing.

Zia looked longingly at Kiel, lying on his side, one hand under his pillow and the other one resting lightly on the pillow's edge. His dark hair swept across his forehead and fell in raven pools on his snow colored headrest. In a closed position, his panoptic eyes appeared even more elongated, the heavy lashes extending their line.

The fur blanket draped across Kiel's waist had left his upper torso bare, and Zia watched the slow rise and fall of his chest, wanting to reach out and feel the beating of his heart beneath it, to the feel the warmth of his skin. Her body ached as she watched him, unable to act upon her natural desire.

She hesitantly moved a hand from beneath her covers and placed it on the wall screen. She began at his waist and traced the length of his body with her fingers. Kiel moaned and repositioned his head on the pillow, causing Zia to jerk back her hand. She waited several minutes, admiring his strong profile. He was beautiful in sleep.

Zia placed her fingers to her lips and then to his. "Goodnight Kiel. Keep me in your dreams." She dropped her hand to the pillow and closed her eyes.

Within minutes she was asleep, completely unaware that the eyes of the boy opposite her watched throughout the night as she slept.

Chapter 16
PROPINQUITY

Tess's ringing woke Zia with a start. Her body felt so stiff. Why was she lying here on this uncomfortable floor?

Her brain's turnstile suddenly awakened, turning slowly and allowing the previous evening's events to flood through its drowsy gates. She glanced at the wall. The computer screen was off now, and her room felt lonely and abandoned without the extended view into Kiel's bedroom.

The phone rang again and Zia jumped. She frantically unzipped the sleeping bag and rolled out, stumbling to her nightstand to retrieve the device.

"Hello?" she yawned.

Chessie's voice was shallow and listless on the other end. Her mother - Zia's grandmother - was dying, and Chessie had purchased tickets for Zia and Shane to fly to Texas that afternoon. She didn't know if Grandma would still be alive when they arrived, but she wanted them both there anyway.

Zia hung up and glanced around the room. She had so much to do before Shane showed up to drive them to the airport.

First and foremost, she had to find someone to take care of Bellaboo, so she called Zoolynne. Her friend was more than happy to dogsit and drove over immediately to retrieve her houseguest.

As soon as Zoolynne and her canine companion drove away, Zia returned to her room and started throwing jeans and T-shirts into a small carry on suitcase. She wasn't sure how long she'd be in Texas, but her mother had advised she travel light. Zia had just walked into the bathroom to retrieve some toiletries, when she heard the elevator button ding.

"Hey kid," Shane yelled down the hall. "Come on. Gotta get goin' now."

"Coming," Zia called back, tossing everything into her travel bag. She grabbed her purse on the way to the bedroom door, but then stopped abruptly. She dropped both her purse and suitcase and rushed back to the computer screen.

"Computer on," she commanded. "Take me to Kiel Shovarga's dispatch folio."

She brought up the wall screen keyboard and began typing. 'Going out of town for a few days. My grandmother is dying. Will contact you as soon as I return.' Zia was about to hit *send,* but then added, 'Thank you for a wonderful evening.'

Shane was impatiently waiting in his car when she rushed outside. The two rode in silence to Orlando International, and they didn't say much more to each other on the plane ride to Texas, sleeping most of the way.

"Please return your seat backs and tray tables to their upright and locked positions and fasten your seatbelts as we prepare for arrival." The flight attendant's voice roused Zia from her nap, and she raised the window shade to look out at the landscape rising from below. Nothing had changed in west Texas. It was just as flat and desolate as ever.

Zia glanced at Shane, so tall his legs must be cramping in the confined space. He looked as uncomfortable as she felt. Zia fidgeted nervously in her window seat, watching the mesquite bushes and pump jacks creep closer. Thank god she'd escaped this arid wasteland when she was still young. The aerial view was depressing enough without actually being immersed in it. She bet the birds even felt queasy when they flew over and took in the godforsaken view.

Grandma always said the beauty of west Texas was hidden underground – meaning oil. Yes, it was definitely there. Permeating the air with its gaseous smell and making the water undrinkable.

"Welcome to Midessa ya'll." The flight attendant's southern drawl rolled through the cabin like tumbleweeds in a sandstorm.

Zia never could understand why local businesses insisted on referring to the Midland-Odessa area with a mashed up name. Combining the names wasn't going to create a warm camaraderie between the rival cities any more than the Friendship/Unity obelisk the city governments placed halfway between the towns over a hundred years ago. A bride could take her husband's last name, but that didn't insure a happy marriage.

Besides, the people of Odessa and Midland enjoyed being at odds with each other - blue collar versus white collar. That was obvious from the competing signboards the siblings walked past as they exited the plane. One after another, they lauded the crowning achievements of their respective city.

"Odessa, Texas! Home of the Permian Panthers – Sixteen Time State Football Champs."

"Midland, Texas! Hometown of President & Mrs. George W. Bush."

"Visit Odessa – The Real Friday Night Lights – Go Mojo!

The banners continued all the way to the baggage claim area where Chessie was waiting for Zia and Shane. She looked as if she hadn't slept in days. Her usual cover girl face was void of cosmetics, and her hair was a tangled mess held together with a plastic clip.

Chessie gave each of her kids a big hug, and with a forced smile, led them out of the terminal and to the parking lot. Zia followed behind her mother and brother, walking with her eyes on the ground. Seeing her mom this way created a dull ache in her heart. She kept her eyes on her shoes, lulling herself into an anesthetized state with the rhythm of her footsteps.

And then, she saw something that made her heart leap, and she felt happy in that instant!

A horny toad dashed behind the wheel of one of the parked cars, and Zia wasn't going to let him get away. She dropped her bag and fell to her knees, scrambling to catch the blunt nosed lizard.

"AaaHaa!" she squealed with delight as she scooped up the toad in her hands.

Shane stopped and looked at his sister through bewildered eyes. "What the hell are you doing?"

Zia held out her hands. "Look what I caught!"

She knew Shane would be just as excited as she was to see a horny toad again. Not that they were really toads at all, just cold-blooded vertebrates renamed for their froglike appearance.

"Wow. I haven't seen one of these in years." Shane touched the lizard's spiky back, causing it to puff up its rounded body in a defensive pose.

Zia pleaded, "Can we take it with us, mom?"

She hoped her mother would be instantly agreeable. It would save them all a lot of time because Zia was prepared to whine and beg – and refuse to get in the car – until she got her way.

"Alright." Chessie looked at the reptile in her daughter's hands. "But we'll have to let it go before we get to the hospital."

That was fine with Zia. She just wanted to keep him for a little while.

Shane threw their bags in the trunk, and the family piled into Chessie's rented Volvo. They headed away from Midessa International and turned right toward downtown Midland. The cars just behind them turned left, obviously heading to Odessa.

Along the way, Zia stroked the two horns extending from the toad's cranium. She wished she had some gold paint.

Zia glanced at the oil derricks dotting the vista. She watched them fly past the car's window, and her thoughts drifted back to when she was a little girl, growing up in the Permian Basin.

She and her best friend, Hallie, would spend long summer afternoons rummaging through the neighbor's trash cans, "alley hunting" as they preferred to call it. Chessie found her daughter's pastime unsanitary, but Zia knew there were all sorts of treasures waiting to be discovered in someone else's waste bin. And Texas alleys held other exciting secrets too, namely horny toads.

Zia and Hallie would use their magic staffs, which resembled homemade walking sticks, to coax the mysterious creature from behind boards and weeds in the alley's loamy soil. They were careful with their captive prize, protecting it in gently closed fingers as they rushed home to transform the fringe-scaled reptile into the magical being they knew it really was.

The car plodded over bumpy streets, and Zia watched the horned toad bounce up and down in her lap. If Hallie were here, they could recreate the magic of childhood. A gentle dab of gold-leaf paint on the horns of their pet would turn him into a handsome prince, waiting for an eight-year-old princess's kiss to release him from his curse.

"Okay, sunshine. Here we are." Chessie brought the car to a stop by a dusty vacant lot. "Time to release your frog prince," she smiled at Zia in the rearview mirror.

To the uneducated, this dry parcel of land looked like a barren dumping ground. But Zia knew the loose sandy soil, teeming with red ants would be a smorgasbord for her bewitched paramour.

"Goodbye, sweet prince. It was nice to see you again." Zia lowered her hands to the brown dirt, and the lizard scampered away, pursuing an ant as it vanished beneath a Yucca plant. She smiled at the image, remembering that there were things she liked about west Texas.

When they arrived at Midland Memorial, the three walked directly to Grandma's room. Chessie sat down in a chair outside the room and leaned forward, placing both hands across her face. Without looking up, she motioned for Shane and Zia to enter without her.

The siblings looked at each other and then slowly pushed the door open. Oma sat on the bed, cradling her daughter in her arms. Through blood shot eyes, she slowly glanced up at the pair, and Zia felt her throat begin to close.

Neither she, nor Shane moved toward the women, nailed in place by the shock of the picture their features created. Zia hadn't been to visit her grandmother in several years and was unprepared for how much she'd aged. To an outsider, it would have appeared that a daughter was holding her dying mother in her arms - but it wasn't true.

With her face placed against her daughter's, Oma's youthful appearance took on a fallacious look. The counterfactual image of the mother and daughter was too painful, too unnatural for Zia. Her eyes burned, the tears blurring her sight the same way reality blurred the scene before her.

Grandma passed away in her sleep, free of pain according to her doctor. There was no elaborate funeral, only a small graveside service attended by family – just the way Grandma had wanted it.

They returned home on a rainy Monday afternoon. After carrying in their luggage, Shane hugged everyone goodbye and headed back to UCF. Zia stood on the porch and watched until her brother was out of sight. Usually she was happy to see his car's taillights turn the corner, but today she was hoping he'd make a U-turn and head back to the house – and her.

Zoolynne had already dropped off Bellaboo, and Zia patted the little pug on the head as she stepped back inside and walked to the elevator. Her mother and Oma had already gone upstairs, and the house was still and sedate in a very unsettling way.

"Come on, Tooey." Zia held the elevator door so the pup could join her for the ride upstairs.

When she arrived on the third floor, Bellaboo ran ahead to Oma's open door. Zia gave a faint tap to announce her arrival but entered without waiting for an invitation. She had never seen Oma look so distressed. Not even when Opa died did she look this grievous.

"It's not right for a parent to outlive a child," Oma said, as Zia sat down on the bed beside her.

"But people live so much longer now…and it was Grandma's choice not to use rejuvenation products." Zia tried to console her great-grandmother.

Oma walked to the dresser mirror and surveyed her reflection. "Even before this, I was beginning to feel like Dorian Gray." She lowered her eyes.

"Who's that Oma?" The name sounded vaguely familiar. "Oh…I remember the movie," Zia said, quietly.

Oma looked back at the mirror. "Melanie was my only child," she said, staring at her own face.

It was so strange to hear Grandma referred to by her given name…Melanie.

"She was the sweetest little girl in the world," Oma continued. "And I thought she would stay young forever, but before I knew it, she was grown and giving birth to Iden and Duchess."

Zia knew her mother hated being called Duchess, which was why she insisted everyone use her nickname, but Zia loved the sound of it.

Oma returned to the bed and sat down. She let out an agonizing sigh and tears fell from her drooped head into her lap.

"Zia," Oma turned to look at her. "You'll never know how much your mother loves you until you have a child of your own. There's no love stronger than the love between a mother and her child." Zia nodded, not knowing how to answer.

Oma reached over and took a photo from her nightstand. "Melanie was so beautiful."

Zia looked at the picture in shock. She'd never realized it was a photo of Grandma. She had always assumed it was Oma when she was younger…really younger…the first time around.

"I held her in my arms the day she came into this world and took her first breath, and I held her in my arms the day she left this world and took her last." Oma's shoulders began to shake. Zia moved to comfort her, but Oma held her hand out and motioned to the door. "There's someone downstairs who needs you even more than I do."

Her mother! Zia had been so consumed by the image of Oma and Grandma in the hospital, that she'd completely forgotten Chessie had lost her mother as well.

Zia rushed downstairs and entered her mother's room. Chessie was lying on her bed, facing the wall.

"Mom?" Zia called quietly from the doorway. "Mom?" she called again.

The light on Chessie's nightstand was set on dim. Zia walked around the bed and bent down in front of her mother. She was asleep - obviously, deeply asleep.

Zia rose to turn off the light and then saw the role of sleeping stamps lying on the nightstand. She looked back at her mother and placed a hand on her chest to check her breathing. Everything seemed ok. Zia loosened the covers and pulled them over her mother. She turned off the light and walked to the bedroom door, closing it softly behind her.

"Goodnight, Duchess," she whispered.

On her way back upstairs, tess beeped with a message from Zoolynne. She wanted to know if Zia was interested in meeting everyone at the North Village Park to watch the nighttime shuttle launch.

"I'll be there," she messaged back, thankful to get out of the house.

She had forgotten there'd be a launch tonight, even though she and Uncle Iden had discussed it at Grandma's funeral. Zia supposed he was back at the spacecoast by now, preparing for the launch with all the other NASA bigwigs.

She'd wanted desperately to ask him more questions about Kiel and Taotrue when she saw him in person, but his mother's funeral hadn't exactly been the appropriate place.

It was almost dark when Zia left the townhouse, and the street lamps were beginning to switch on. The moon was already visible, swimming in the purple sky.

She headed east, toward the park. Its location in the middle of the boulevard made it one of the best locations in Celebration for watching shuttle launches and skycarriage ascensions - daytime or nighttime.

Just before Zia reached the park, she bumped into Twilah who also lived in North Village. Twilah wasn't exactly the person Zia was hoping to see, but she was walking over to watch the shuttle launch too, so they crossed the street together and strolled toward the picnic tables.

Zoolynne and Gentry were already there, sitting atop one of the tables and chatting up Xander and Axel. Breckin and Chandra stood a few feet away, leaning against the wrought iron fence that circled the swimming pool. Zia wanted to join Zoo and Gen, but they were preoccupied, flirting with the two guys who were obviously enjoying the attention. They didn't even notice Zia.

Zoolynne reached over to stroke Xander's arm, and Zia felt a bolt of jelousy shoot through her chest. She'd never felt that way about her best friend before, but it wasn't fair. Zoolynne could physically touch the guy she was attracted to.

She followed Twilah to the pool fence and joined the others. Zia pressed her back against the wrought iron and looked up at the full moon. The afternoon rain had passed quickly, leaving behind the perfect evening for a launch. The nighttime sky was bright and full of dancing stars, and the reflection of the moon on the pool created a romantic feeling - for those lucky enough to be there with a partner.

"There it goes," yelled Axel, and they all rushed to the center of the park to watch.

It began as a red dot but quickly expanded. The colors burst across the horizon as if an unseen hand had pulled back a curtain and allowed the morning sun to stream in. Out of it appeared a bright white light, moving upward and creating the illusion of two moons in one sky.

Zia fantasized about being onboard a skycarriage traveling to Taotrue to see Kiel. How jealous her friends would be when they discovered that the son of a distant planet's Prime Minister was courting her!

The shuttle continued its climb, its fleeting brilliance leaving a path of gray smoke visible in the circle of light. The vapor trail began to get smaller and smaller until it finally disappeared, leaving the horizon, and Zia's dreams, once again dark. Her flight of fantasy had ended as quickly as the evening launch.

Twilah and Chandra walked back to the picnic tables, where Zoolynne and Gentry were waiting for their dates to rejoin them. Zia and Breckin followed.

Chandra stretched out on one of the long benches, absent-mindedly playing with her French-manicured nails. Twilah sat down next to her friend and crossed her long legs, bouncing one foot as she rummaged through her purse for a flask of vodka.

She pulled out various items in her frantic search – lipstick, condoms, and a half dozen white paper sacks. Twilah was the only person Zia knew who actually carried around airsick bags in her purse. But after any family vacation involving air travel, she'd always return with a new stash. They came in handy for drunken binges and, well…purging binges too.

The sound of a car pulling to a stop at the nearby curb interrupted Twilah's frenetic liquor hunt.

"Hey, Chandy, Twi!" One of the guys called from the front seat.

"Oh, my god. It's those guys we met last night at Old Town!" They had obviously made a good impression on Chandra.

"Come ride around for awhile," the driver called.

"Sure thing," Chandra yelled back, and then turned to Zia. "Come on, come with us. You don't have anything else to do."

"Yeah," agreed Twilah. "It's time for you to grow up and start baggin' some knob."

Could Twilah make what they were about to do sound any more unappealing? The bile that flowed from her mouth never ceased to amaze Zia.

"No, gotta pass." Zia grimaced at the thought of spending an evening with the kinky crew.

"What about you Gen?" Twilah reached over and flicked the gold cross hanging from Gentry's neck. "Jesus died for your sins, so you might as well enjoy them."

"Look, Twilah, just because you don't go to church…" Gentry began, but Twilah interrupted with a giggle.

"Oh, but I do," she smiled. "Didn't you know? I'm a Crystal Methodist!"

"You know I don't appreciate it when you joke like that!" Gentry scowled at Twilah, who raised her hands in a surrendering motion.

"Okay, just kidding…geesh!" Twilah grabbed Chandra by the arm. "Let's get outa here. All this sweetness is gonna give me diabetes."

The two girls sprinted to the waiting car and climbed into the back seat. Zia saw the boy in the passenger side hand Twilah a stamp, which she immediately placed on her tongue.

"Any of you other Celebrats wanna come along?" The driver called.

"No thanks," Zoolyne yelled back.

"Okay, but it's your loss. I'm like Space Mountain. Girls will wait in line for hours just to ride me!" He waved as the car pulled away from the curb.

"What a dung pusher!" Xander had walked up with Axel just in time to hear the last part of the conversation. "I hate all those Lickers!" Xander draped his arm around Zoolynne in a vigilant display.

Axel glided over to Gentry. "Listen, we're heading over to Piper's. You girls wanna join us?" He rested his arm on Gentry's shoulder, twining his fingers through her hair.

"Sure, but can we meet you there?" Gentry smiled coyly at Axel.

"That's fine." He squeezed his arms around Gentry's waist in a playful way. "But hurry!" He gave her a you-know-what-I-mean look and sauntered away with Xander.

Zia had the feeling that when Axel said *you girls*, he didn't mean her. Obviously, the trip to Piper's Alley was for couples only. That's why Gentry asked if they – meaning her and Zoo – could meet them later. She wanted to avoid the embarrassment of driving off and abandoning Zia and Breckin on the sidewalk.

The second Axel's car pulled away, Zoolynne grabbed Zia by the arm. "Xander asked me to the prom tonight!" She tried to talk in a subdued voice, but her excitement forced the words out in a bellow that Zia found immensely annoying.

"That's really great, Zoo." Zia forced a smile.

Now that Zoolynne had a date, she was more than anxious to discuss the prom. "You already know Gen's going with Axel, so what about you two?"

Breckin and Zia looked at each other.

"Well," Breckin hadn't had much to say during the course of the evening, but now that Zoolynne had posed the question, he was full of chatty enthusiasm. "I'm going with Boyd. He's Canadian you know, so he'll be using Way Back's portal." He paused and squeezed his palms together. "He's so scrumptious, I could just die."

"So, come on. Give us some details," Zoolynne pressed. "How'd you meet him?"

"Online," grinned Breckin. "He found me."

"You're such a hopeless romantic." Zoolynne laughed before turning to Zia. "What about you Zizi?" She reached over and gave Zia a slight swat across the knee.

Zoolynne's gesture was supposed to be affectionate, but Zia took it as a slap of sympathy. Zoolynne didn't need to ask the question *just* to include Zia in the conversation. She was Zia's best friend, so if Zia had a date to the prom, Zoolynne should *already* know about it. Zoolynne thought she knew the answer even now - but she didn't.

A sly smile appeared on Zia's lips. "Well, I asked someone I met online to come with me too."

Zia was right about her friend. Her answer not only caused Zoolynne to look surprised, but downright shocked. Only Gentry had suspected that Zia had a guy she was keeping hidden, and now she was anxious to find out who he was.

"Who, who?" Gentry leaned over to Zoolynne. "I just *knew* she was keeping a secret all this time!"

"Well, he doesn't live here. He lives up there." Zia pointed to the north.

"In Orlando?" Breckin asked.

"No." Zia bit the side of her lip and pointed again. "Way up there?"

"Farther than Daytona? He doesn't live in Georgia does he?" Zoolynne was suddenly enjoying the guessing game.

Zia paused, "Well, no."

"Oh shit, don't tell me you invited some kicker from Texas." Zoolynne had a disappointed frown on her face.

"No!" Zia raised and dropped her shoulders. She got up from the picnic bench and stood in front of the group. To make herself perfectly clear, Zia looked directly overhead and pointed in the same direction. "Up there."

At first, there was silence, and then all three burst out laughing. "Oh my goddess, you are so funny!" Breckin leaned forward and poked her in the ribs.

Zia already didn't like condescending knee swats, and now she hated patronizing rib pokes! Her blood was churning, and when she didn't laugh along with her friends, the expressions on their faces suddenly changed.

"You aren't serious are you?" Gentry looked at Zoolynne and Breckin to see if they were in on the joke.

Zia didn't change her expression. "Yes. I am perfectly serious."

"There's no way." Zoolynne gave Zia a strange look.

Zia wasn't sure where to begin, or even *if* to begin. Trying to convince her friends of Kiel's existence was going to be harder than she'd expected, but she *had* to try. Zia didn't want them to think she was nuttier than they obviously already did, so she just started talking…and talking…and talking.

By the time she was through, she'd told them everything about Kiel. And breaking her own discretionary rules, she even told them about the sleep over and his two belly buttons.

When she was done, the four friends sat without speaking. No one said a single, solitary word. Finally, Zia couldn't stand the awkward situation anymore and broke the silence.

"You guys still don't believe me, do you?"

"Of course we do." Zoolynne placed a coddling arm around Zia's shoulder, but her touch was better suited for a child than a peer.

"I can tell you don't!" Zia yanked Zoolynne's arm away. "Do you think I just went crazy overnight?"

"No, but you have been under a lot of stress lately…with your grandmother passing away and…"

"What the hell does that have to do with it?" Zia cut Zoolynne off. "I didn't just meet him yesterday. We've been talking for over a month!"

"Zia, please don't be upset." Gentry tried to calm her down. "But it's just hard to take you seriously."

"Me?" Zia snorted. "Look who's talking about being taken seriously! Someone whose day to day life is summed up in the T-shirts they wear." Zia pointed a shaky finger at Gentry's chest. "Including tonight's!"

She re-read its message: *Glad To See You're Enjoying My Ex Boyfriend. My Parents Always Taught Me To Share My Used Toys With The Less Fortunate.*

Gentry had a nice, new boyfriend, so why did she have to wear a shirt mentioning some worthless, ex piece-of-crap!

Zia was so upset she couldn't even continue talking. She paced back and forth, making huffy grunting sounds in the back of her throat. She'd waited all this time to tell her best friends about Kiel, and *this* was how they repaid her!

"Now, Zia…" Here came Zoo's patronizing tone again. "It's just hard to believe because, well…uh…this guy…"

"His name is Kiel!" Zia snapped.

"Okay, Kiel." Zoolynne continued cautiously. "So he's an alien, but he has Asian features like Kim, he's tall like Kim, he's built like Kim, and he's unavailable… like Kim."

Zia thought she was through, but Zoolynne continued her sermon. "He also has the same initials. Kim Song, Kiel Shovarga - K.S. Coincidence? How can you expect us to believe that you, out of *every* girl on Earth, has an alien lover just waiting to – even before Zoolynne said it, Zia knew the punch line – probe you!"

"Zia," Gentry tried to be gentler. "If he's real, he's not from another planet. You're being played."

If he's real? Did she say *if* he's real? Zia exploded.

"Fuck you both! I'm going home!"

Zia stormed away, but as she walked, she could still hear faint whispers and knew her three friends were discussing what she'd just confided to them.

Halfway down the block, Zia heard someone running behind her and she picked up the pace. Breckin caught up with her anyway and took her by the hand.

"I believe you." He looked his friend deeply in the eyes and tried to smile.

"I hope you really mean that!" Zia turned away from him and continued down the street.

When she got home, Zia could see a large number of uninvited guests milling about under the glaring porch lights – Florida lovebugs. It was lovebug season again, and Zia hated the acidic arthropods. Those irritating black pests, immediately joined with a mate after hatching.

Urban legend had it that the bugs were synthetically created in a University of Florida lab, but Zia didn't believe it. No genetic experiment could go this wrong.

She looked down at the pathetic bugs' drifting movements, the larger bride pulling her small groom around. They reminded Zia of Twilah and Chandra – a couple of fornicating insects scampering in tandem across Celebration.

Zia stepped on one of the bugs, causing it to drag behind its dead, but still connected, mate. For some reason, her action, and the image it created, made Zia feel better.

She stood on the front porch, squashing one after another, until dozens of lovebugs were left single, with nothing but a deceased lover still clinging to their segmented bodies.

Inside, the house was still quiet, and now - thanks to her so-called friends - even more depressing. She felt so degraded, so dejected – and a lot of other adjectives that started with D. Zia could only hope that seeing Kiel's handsome face again would brighten her mood.

She took the elevator to the second floor, stopping to check on her mother. She was relieved to find her still sleeping tranquilly.

Zia trudged up the stairs to the top floor. Oma's door was shut, and no light shone from underneath, so Zia continued down the hall into her own room. Closing the door, Zia walked laboriously to her dressing area.

She looked at herself in the mirror. "I am not crazy!" she yelled at the girl in the glass.

Her hands shook, and she leaned over the bathroom counter to steady herself. After getting a drink of water, Zia shuffled back across her bedroom and slumped into the computer chair.

What if she *was* mad? What if Kiel really was only an invention of her twisted mind? Maybe she had just created a fantasy world where she could have a storybook love. Perhaps if she just admitted that he didn't exist, he would disappear. Her delusions would end. She would be cured.

BULLSHIT!

Zia twirled herself around and faced the wall. "Screen on, computer on."

Tonight there was no waiting. Instantly, she and Kiel were connected. He looked pleased to see her, but there was a glimpse of concern in his blue and red mingled eyes.

"Zia, I am sorry about your grandmother. Is she...."

"No, she passed away," Zia interrupted. "But thank you for caring."

Neither said anything, and Zia pursed her lips until she realized the image was probably very unattractive.

"I, uh..." She paused, but Kiel continued where she'd left off.

"...longed for you."

"Yes, I missed you too." Zia smiled.

She liked the words he used better than her own. *Longed for* sounded so romantic - and much more intimate.

Without the benefit of the wide screen, Zia could only see Kiel's upper torso, but the image was enough. He was wearing a form fitting gray jersey top, and Zia no longer had to fantasize about what crux hid beneath it. Now, she knew.

Tonight Kiel's eyes seemed darker and deeper, and suddenly Zia realized why. A wide black headband circled his head; completely hiding his lavender-tinted hair, save for the V-shaped point in the middle of his forehead. Zia hadn't realized he had a widow's peak. The point in his hairline only added to the power and virility of his unframed face. It was exquisite, alluring beyond words.

Whenever Zia thought she'd finally become accustomed to Kiel's magnificent appearance, she was proven wrong. He continued to become more tempting each time she saw him.

"Zia," he sounded startled. "What is that on your hand?"

Zia couldn't believe she'd been so absent-minded! The limb guard would be coming off in only a few days now. How could she have been so careless as to allow her hand to be exposed?

Even during their sleepover, she'd been cautious, always making certain to keep it covered. She'd just had too many other things on her mind, too many upsets during the evening to pay attention to the guard. Zia looked down at her finger and decided to be honest - or at least as honest as she felt necessary.

"It's nothing serious, just a cut that I have covered until it heals." She raised her hand and wiggled the finger inside the bud guard, thankful that except for the tip, the entire finger was there and visibly moving.

"I am sorry." Kiel looked at Zia's hand, and then back at her. "I hope you are not in too much pain."

"No, no. Not at all. And I get the bandage off next week." She made sure to lessen the severity of the injury by calling the bud guard a bandage.

"I am pleased. I would hate to think of you in physical pain."

Zia elevated her eyes to his. She wondered if he realized the enormity of physical pain she *was* in. She couldn't believe it possible for one person's body to ache so profusely for another, but

Kiel could take away the pain. He could erase it with one touch of his hands.

Whether he felt the same, or simply read it on her face, Kiel slowly raised his right hand and placed it upon his computer screen.

It was no longer necessary to hide her damaged corpus. There was no reason now, and perhaps there never had been. Maybe it never had been necessary to hide her imperfections from a perfect being.

Zia raised her left hand and placed it upon Kiel's. And there, through a creation born of a motherboard, she found what could ease her pain.

Something separable in existence from the body – the touch of love.

CHAPTER 17
THE RETURN OF RILEY

During the next few days, Chessie seemed to be, if not recovering from the death of her mother, at least slowly accepting it. Oma, on the other hand, except for early morning trips to the Resurrection Clinic, remained secluded in her room, worrying both Zia and Chessie.

Several times a day, Zia would stop by her great-grandmother's room to check her condition. Oma always appeared pleased to see Zia, but she wasn't the same – something was different. And then, there was that *smell*. What was it, that peculiar odor? It smelled like formaldehyde, but why would a living, breathing person smell like that? What was going on, what were they doing to her at that clinic? Zia's curiosity increased until it consumed her every thought regarding Oma.

To make matters worse, Zia decided to watch *The Portrait of Dorian Gray* late one night. She couldn't remember the plot and had to understand what Oma meant by saying she felt like the title character.

The movie's story line only upset Zia more. Dorian Gray was a man who never aged, only his life-sized portrait kept hidden away in the attic, placed there so no one would see the hideous features carved into its face by age and sin.

Frightening thoughts slithered through Zia's mind. Was Oma even genuinely alive, or was she being *kept* alive by… Zia didn't want to think about it…or that smell. She knew formaldehyde based solutions were used for embalming. The idea scared Zia, and even walking past Oma's bedroom began to scare her.

By week's end, she no longer stopped by to check on the family's matriarch. The pungent odor seeping from beneath Oma's closed door sickened Zia, and she couldn't enter the room without becoming physically ill. She was frightened and began locking her bedroom door at night.

It was a Thursday afternoon when Zia's fears about her great-grandmother were realized. She was coming home from school, and had just turned onto Castle Gap when she saw the two vehicles speeding toward her down the boulevard. The first was an ambulance, followed closely by an organ donor transport.

Someone had died! Someone whose medical chip indicated they were a registered organ donor. Oma was registered. Zia's hands began to tremble uncontrollably. She hated the sight of a carcass caravan. One transport filled with its newly harvested crop, the other with the still-warm remains of its cultivated fields.

The vehicles sped past her Scion and turned onto Celebration Avenue, their lights flashing an announcement of death and rebirth.

It could be anyone Zia told herself. Besides, she hadn't even seen from which house the transports left. There was probably nothing to worry about. But as she pulled to the curb, Zia saw Shane's car parked out front - and he never made a mid-week appearance. Never! She rushed to the front door and let herself in.

"Hello?" Zia tried to keep her voice light, but inside, a shaking hand twisted the knot in her stomach.

There was no response. Was that a good sign or a bad sign? Maybe she'd just overreacted. Her brother could've driven home midweek simply to check on everyone. A lot had been going on lately, so there was probably a reasonable explanation for his coming by.

Zia almost had herself convinced, but when she walked to the rear of the house and saw Mom and Shane sitting silently on the sofa, she knew there was something very, very wrong. They looked up as Zia entered the den. Shane appeared tense, one arm draped protectively around his mother's shoulder.

Serious lines appeared on Chessie's forehead as she struggled to speak. "It's Oma," she finally got the words out, but it wasn't necessary for her to finish the sentence.

"No! Oh, no!" Zia fell to her knees. "Please, dear god! No!" she screamed. Chessie moved to the floor and took her daughter in her arms.

"God damn it all!" Zia wailed at the top of her lungs, pulling away from her mother and pounding her fists on the rug.

Chessie grabbed Zia by the shoulders and shook her. "Stop this!" She pulled Zia to her chest and held her tightly. "Oma isn't dead! She's been taken to rehab."

Rehab? Rehab was for overprivileged adolescents and narcissistic celebrities, not for her great-grandmother. Zia didn't understand.

"You mean that vulture wagon wasn't here for her?" Chessie looked puzzled by Zia's question. "The organ donor truck that was just on our street!" Zia was emphatic. "You mean it *wasn't* here for Oma?" Chessie gave a faint shake of the head.

"Listen to me." Shane moved from the sofa. He joined his mother and sister on the rug and wrapped his arm around Zia's shoulder.

"That smell…" Zia pressed her face against Shane's chest, and felt him shudder as he continued, "…that odor coming from Oma…it was paraldehyde. It's a drug used to bring alcoholics out of deep comas or delirium tremens."

Zia tried to listen, but she was finding it difficult, if not impossible, to arrange her thoughts. "What's a delirium tremor?" she asked.

"Tremen." Shane corrected her. "It's an acute episode of delirium caused by withdrawal from alcohol."

"You mean Oma was...*is*... an alco..." Zia's words trailed off.

Shane patted his sister softly on the back before resuming his explanation. "She was given paraldehyde to calm the tremens and help her sleep. It's excreted through the lungs, so that's why Oma had the strange smell coming from her."

Shane's answers only created more questions – disturbing questions. Zia looked at her brother. She needed more answers, but the tess in her coat pocket continued to vibrate, distracting her from the discussion at hand.

Her tess had been pulsating non-stop since she entered the house. She'd tried to ignore its demanding call, but the urgency finally forced Zia to retrieve the device from her jacket and address what was so important.

It was Breckin.

Zia hadn't been speaking to him, Zoolynne or Gentry since their encounter at the park, but obviously, he wasn't going to give up on reaching her tonight. Zia flipped to her messages, expecting to see a heartfelt apology. It was about time they all fell on their knees and begged for her forgiveness. But Breckin's words weren't about friendship or forgiveness.

Zia was completely unprepared for what his text said. "Riley is in Piper's Alley. Come now." Tess beeped again. "She's wearing your ring!"

Zia couldn't believe it! The overwhelming sadness she'd felt only moments before turned into a blinding rage, and adrenaline splattered through Zia's veins.

She looked first to Shane. "Riley's in town!" Zia paused to take a deep breath. "And she's wearing my fuckin' ring!"

Shane knew what his sister's next words would be and stood up. Zia lifted herself from the floor and stood beside her brother, turning to look at their mother.

"I'm getting it back," she said. "You wanna come?" She didn't have to ask twice.

"Hell, yes!" Chessie grabbed her purse from the coffee table and motioned toward the garage.

The three ran into and over each other trying to get out the back door, and it would've been a funny scene had their reason for doing so not been so serious. In a rush of confusion, they scrambled to the car and climbed in.

As soon as the doors closed, Chessie slammed her BMW into reverse. Zia flinched, afraid her mother was going to back into the garage door before it was completely up, but somehow Chessie made it safely down the alley and onto Celebration Avenue.

As the BMW flew down the street, Zia sent messages to everyone she knew. Some were already in Piper's Alley, some had seen Riley, and some had not. Those at home and unaware of what was happening texted back to say they'd be heading to Piper's immediately.

When they approached the Celebration Hotel, Chessie slowed down to search for a parking place, but Zia couldn't wait. She bolted from the car, and Shane followed.

They hit the ground running, but even with his six-foot frame, Shane couldn't keep up with his sister. Zia sprinted toward the Piper's Alley crossover. All she could think about was Oma and the beautiful Zia ring she'd given her for her birthday.

Oma had never even had the pleasure of seeing her great-granddaughter wear it, and now - on the same night that she'd been taken to the hospital - that piece-of-shit Riley was in town, and wearing Oma's ring!

Yes, Riley was right in the middle of Celebration. Right where Zia had the friends...and the power! Just the thought of it caused a wicked smile to spread across Zia's face. She felt like a terrier that had just cornered a rat! Riley didn't know it yet, but she'd picked the wrong night to show up.

Everyone in Piper's Alley obviously knew Riley was there and that a confrontation was about to occur, because a loud buzz went up the second Zia entered the alley. She rounded the corner and grabbed the first person she recognized.

"Spotswood!" She held him by his collar. "Where is she?"

"At Cheezy's." He pointed to the end of the street.

Zia turned on her heel, and with every step, the anger inside her swelled. She ran and Spotswood ran after her, both unaware of the large group of teenagers surging behind them down the back street.

Zia rushed to the end of the alley and grabbed Cheezy's screen door, slamming it open with such fierce aggression that she broke one of its hinges. Breckin and Zoolynne were waiting just inside the café.

"Tell me where she is!" Zia demanded, her tone so vicious that Zoolynne could do nothing more than point to the women's restroom, a mere twenty feet from where they stood.

Zia started for the door, but as she did, Riley emerged.

For an instant, Riley looked startled to see Zia, but immediately regained her composure. Zia was roughly half the size and weight of the dancer, and she could tell by Riley's expression that she expected her encounter with Zia to be nothing more than a trivial annoyance.

Riley didn't realize that the dozens of kids lining up behind Zia weren't there just to watch a good fight. They were there to support their friend, but Zia never glanced around. She didn't want or need assistance from anyone. She was too raw from the news about her great-grandmother, and now...to see Oma's gift on Riley's beefy hand made Zia want to eject the contents of her stomach! Riley couldn't even fit the piece of jewelry on her husky ring finger and had slid it onto her pinkie.

"Well," Riley's voice was hard, but her eyes betrayed the apprehension she felt at having Zia confront her head-on. "What do you want?" She hissed.

Zia didn't say a word. Her head tingled, the sensation creeping down her arms and into her hands, which were slowly curling into two fists.

"Nothing to say?" Riley snarled. "Then let *me* ask you a question. How's your little naked finger feeling these days?"

Zia held up her left hand, allowing Riley to see the limb guard she'd been forced to wear while her finger re-grew. "It's feeling pretty strong," she said.

Riley looked at Zia's hand, giving her a snort and a roll of the eyes. Riley began to walk away, but as she did, Zia reached out and grabbed her by the wrist.

"But not as strong as this hand!" Zia's right fist caught Riley directly across the cheek and nose, causing her to collapse on the floor in a pile of blood.

Riley tried to sit up, but as she did, Zia shoved her back down, pulling the ring off her pinkie finger. Riley glared at Zia, blood running down her nose and dripping into her mouth. Zia carefully placed the ring in her pocket and squatted down. She leaned over Riley and grabbed her around the neck, Zia's face only inches from Riley's bloodied profile.

"If you *ever* come back here," Zia warned, "We Celebrats are gonna kill you!"

She released Riley from her grip, causing the girl's head to fall back and hit the floor with a sickening crack. Satisfaction swarmed through Zia as she stared down at Riley, sprawled on the café floor.

Suddenly, everyone at Cheezy Winn's broke into loud cheers and applause. The noise startled Zia. With her focus solely on Riley, Zia had completely blocked out everything else happening around her.

Zia rose to leave, but as she walked to the restaurant door Riley screamed, "I'm pressing assault charges!"

Zia turned, elevated by her classmates roaring yells. "Do it." Zia was surprised to hear her own voice so calm and measured. "There's already a warrant out for your arrest, and I'm sure the cops would love to know where you are, so do it…call them." She turned back around and continued toward the exit.

Zia didn't care how or when Riley left Cheezy's, nor was she waiting around to watch her departure. Zia felt vindicated - she had her ring back, and that was all that mattered.

Zia looked at Shane, leaning against the front door with his arms crossed and a sly smile on his face. His stance and expression reminded her of the day he'd shut off her game room system, but this time, she didn't mind his smug grin. She was actually learning to like this guy…her brother.

As Zia walked through the still cheering crowd, Zoolynne caught her be the arm. "Look," she said, motioning with her head. Zia turned toward the staircase.

Kim and Danny stood on the bottom steps, supporting Riley's two minions. They both had a remarkable set of bruises already forming around their eyes and jaws. Kim nodded to Danny and they let the two thugs drop to the floor. Again, everyone cheered.

Zia's smile turned into a loud, happy laugh. Shane wrapped one arm around his sister's shoulder, but before she allowed him to escort her through the door, she gave Kim a thumbs-up sign and mouthed the words, "Thank you."

He smiled broadly, but instead of returning her thumbs-up gesture, Kim placed a closed fist over his heart and then extended his open palm toward Zia. "You're welcome," he mouthed the words.

CHAPTER 18
BE CAREFUL IT'S MY HEART

"Zia Barrett," the nurse called from the open door.

"Oh yes, that's me." Zia retrieved her purse, following the physician's assistant down the hall to one of the examination rooms.

"I bet you'll be happy to get that limb guard off," she said, motioning Zia into the room.

"I'll be even happier to finally have my finger back!"

"Well, Dr. Markison will be right in, so just have a seat." The nurse smiled, closing the door softly behind her.

Zia crawled onto the examination table. Finally, the guard would be coming off - and just in time too. The prom was only days away now.

Zia felt her finger through the guard and wondered if she'd have a scar where her finger had been...she didn't like to use the word...amputated. If there did turn out to be an ugly scar, she could always cover it with her Zia ring.

"Knock, knock." Dr. Markison peeked around the door before coming in. "How's my patient feeling today?"

"Excited."

"I bet you are." Dr. Markison approached the table and took her hand in his. "Well, let's get that bud guard off and see what we have."

Zia had assumed the guard would just slip off, but the doctor had to do a great deal of tugging before she felt her finger release and slowly slide out. She felt nervous. What would it look like? She shut her eyes while the doctor swabbed the finger with some type of cleaning ointment.

"Okay, take some deep breaths, and open your eyes." The tone of Dr. Markison's voice indicated he was pleased with the results.

Zia opened her eyes and looked down at her finger. There was a very faint line where the new growth had begun, but it looked perfect! Perhaps a shade pinker than her other fingers, but why shouldn't it be? It was a brand new baby that had never seen the sun.

"Try wiggling it," the doctor instructed.

It felt a bit stiff, but after a minute Zia was able to bend it all the way down until it touched her palm. Dr. Markison looked satisfied with her recovery.

"Alrigt then, I'm officially releasing you as my patient." He smiled and walked to the door. "I just need to have the nurse update your medical chip, and you're free to go."

"Thank you *so* much." Zia raised her hand and waved an exaggerated goodbye to the doctor, showing off her new digit.

Within minutes, a young man dressed all in white entered the room. Zia recognized him immediately. He attended the same church as Oma and sang in the choir. Zia always looked for him when she visited with her great-grandmother. He was young and handsome, and certainly more engaging to look at for an hour than the geriatric preacher who moralized from behind his pulpit in one unvaried tone.

Oma was faithful to her little bethel, but Zia secretly renamed it the Church of the Great Ennui, its congregation condemned to eternal boredom.

"On which side is your medical chip implanted?" He smiled at Zia, removing a palm-sized device from his coat pocket.

"My right side." Zia motioned behind her right ear.

"Okay then." The handsome nurse used his fingers to pull back the hair from her face, and pressed the small device to an area between her neck and jaw line.

The combination of his attractive looks and the touch of his hand as it cradled the hair against Zia's neck made her feel uneasy. If only he was an ugly, middle-aged woman. Zia glanced down at his nametag – Shawn Beckitt. That was a nice name. It fit him.

The device beeped and Shawn removed his hand, allowing Zia's hair to fall back across her shoulder.

"How do I know you really implanted my medical records and not someone else's?" she asked.

The young nurse looked up at her, and Zia immediately wished she could recant the rude question. But it didn't seem to faze

Shawn. Maybe he got asked the question on a regular basis, because he just smiled and turned the device so Zia could see her name scrolling across the top – Zia Kathan Barrett.

"That is you, right?" Shawn repeated the words aloud, mispronouncing her middle name. No surprise there - everyone did. Zia couldn't understand why people tried to make it sound like Kathy Ann.

"You have the spelling right, but my middle name rhymes with Nathan."

"Indeed?" The young man turned the device around and laughed lightly as he re-read her name.

"You go to my great-grandmother's church. I've seen you there before." Zia wanted to say something friendly in case Shawn had considered her earlier question bad mannered.

"Oh, really? Who is your great-grandmother?" Shawn's tone was pleasant, but he didn't look up. He was busy typing something on the medical device before returning it to his coat pocket.

"Oma Delancey. I mean, Victoria Delancey." It sounded odd to call Oma by her given name. It made her seem more like a woman and less like a great-grandmother.

"Sure, I know Victoria." Shawn's voice sounded intrigued. "I can't believe Tori's a great-grandmother though."

Oh, no. He used a nickname when referring to Oma! Was it a term of endearment? Had Shawn assumed she was younger than she actually was, or had Oma intentionally led him to believe she was younger for a *particular* reason?

"You didn't...uh...date her, did you?" Zia held her breath.

"No," Shawn answered with a bewildered chuckle, and held up his left hand. "See that ring? I'm married."

Zia let out a sigh of relief. "I'm sorry I asked, but you never know with my great-grandmother. She likes younger men...or at least men who look younger." Zia glanced sideways at the handsome nurse, her eyes betraying what she was wondering.

"I *really* am as young as I look. Twenty-nine next month." He grinned and motioned for Zia to slide off the table.

"Shawn? I mean, sir?" Zia leaned over to retrieve her purse from the floor. "On that subject, do you know what they do to people at the Resurrection Clinic?"

"It's just across the medical annex." Shawn walked to the exam room door and gestured with his open palm for Zia to exit first. "Why don't you stop in and ask them?"

Shawn smiled as Zia passed but wagged a scolding finger. "And don't call me sir. I'm not that old...yet."

When she was back outside and alone in her car, Zia reached into her purse pocket and removed Oma's birthday gift. As she slid the ring on, Zia was surprised at just how smooth and soft her new finger felt.

"This is for you, Victoria Delancey," she spoke to herself in the rearview mirror.

Zia's focus shifted, and behind her reflected image, she could see Florida Hospital where Oma was in rehab. If only she were allowed visitors, Zia could rush over and show Oma how nicely her finger had healed – and how nice the Zia ring looked on her hand.

Zia's gaze continued across the medical sector. Next to the hospital sat the New U Medical Resurrection Clinic, its windowless brick façade benumbing the area like a forsaken tomb.

Zia made a split second decision.

Sliding back out of her car, Zia walked toward the clinic. She was going to find out once and for all what happened to people when they were admitted into its inner sanctum. Zia approached the building's large circular entrance. As she neared, the heavy stone-colored door rolled away, allowing her inside.

Half a dozen men and women sat on uncomfortable looking high backed chairs. The place was eerily quiet except for some soft music floating through the room. No one was talking.

In fact, it appeared everyone was doing their best to avoid being noticed by their neighbor. Patients buried their faces in books and computers, anything to avoid eye contact with the person seated next to them. Apparently, no one wanted to be "outed" as a clinic customer.

Zia walked to the receptionist, respectfully avoiding unwanted eye contact with any of the uncomfortable looking patients sitting on the uncomfortable looking chairs. The beautiful blonde sitting behind the desk slid the glass reception window open and greeted Zia with an approving smile.

"Good afternoon, and may I say, you look fabulous. I don't know who did your previous work, but you look just like a teenager."

"I am a teenager."

The receptionist's smile dropped at Zia's response. "Oh, I'm sorry. What may I help you with then?"

"I'd just like some information."

The receptionist's smile returned. "Wonderful to hear. You're never too young to start staying young."

Zia wasn't really sure what that meant, but the lovely blonde seemed enthusiastic about her job, so Zia continued. "If you don't mind, I'd just like to know what it exactly is you do here. I mean, what do you do to keep people from aging?"

"First, let me introduce myself. My name is Candy." The golden haired receptionist smiled and handed Zia a brochure titled "Rejuvenate Before It's Too Late!"

"Now," asked Candy, "How old do you think I am?"

She looked twenty-five, but since she was asking Zia to estimate her age, she must be much older.

"I dunno. Thirty?" Zia guessed.

"No." Candy smiled widely, obviously pleased with herself. "I am sixty!"

"Wow! You look great." Zia was honestly impressed.

"And it's all thanks to Telomerase…and a little plastic surgery." She gave Zia a big grin and a wink. "I can see you're wondering what that is." Zia nodded, and the receptionist rambled on. Now that Candy was extolling the virtues of Telomerase, there was no shutting her up.

"Telomere shortening is an anti-aging therapy that eliminates age related issues and rejuvenates old, worn out organs." Zia didn't need to ask questions. Candy was more than happy to supply answers.

"The body," Candy continued, "typically contains cells that have twenty three pairs of chromosomes, and at the end of each chromosome is a protective cap called a telomere. Telomeres are cut shorter every time a cell divides, causing the telomere to eventually stop working. They either fall into a suspended state called senescense or die. This process is what wears out cells and contributes to the aging process."

"So, do patients have surgery to repair their telomeres?" Zia asked.

"Oh, no, no. It's much easier than that." Candy was beaming again. "Patients are injected with an enzyme called Telomerase."

She paused to point to the sign above the nurse's station. Zia glanced up at the placard. "Time Erase With TelomErase," it advised.

Candy continued, "When patients are given the enzyme, the signs of aging are reversed, and even tissues that were previously destroyed can be repaired."

"Wow, I wonder if Mom uses this too."

Zia hadn't realized she'd spoken aloud until Candy asked, "Well, how old is your mother?"

"Oh!" Zia looked startled. "She's forty-ish."

"And how old does she look?"

"Forty-ish."

"Well," Candy smiled. "That doesn't mean she isn't taking enzyme injections. She'd still need a little snip-n-sew to maintain outward beauty." Candy winked again. "So, are you here to begin your injections?"

"Me?" Zia looked shocked. "I'm only seventeen."

"Oh dear." Candy looked disappointed. "You still have a year to wait. You can't legally be given Telomerase until you turn eighteen."

Now Zia was really confused. "Pardon me, but why would someone who's still young take enzymes to repair tissue damage that hasn't occurred yet?"

Candy's face lit up at the question, and she launched back into her spiel. "My dear, Telomerase therapy must begin when you're still young and your body is free of living cancer cells. Telomerase reactivation is risky in older adults who have already begun experiencing the health problems which come with age."

"I'm sorry," Zia interrupted. "But I'm still not sure I fully understand. Doctors can cure cancer."

"That's true, but when there is an overpopulating of cells, there is an ever-present risk of cancerous cells developing. That's why reactivating telomeres in aging adults doesn't eliminate the risk for cancer. Reactivation can't remove the senescent cells which already exist in their bodies, and the price tag for a cancer cure is heavy."

Zia looked at the brochure in her hand. That's what it meant by "Rejuvenate Before Its Too Late." Could this explain why grandma had aged as she did? Maybe at some point she'd wanted to receive the age reversal enzyme, but she'd simply waited too long. Her older body already contained too many dead and suspended state cells.

Zia looked at the receptionist. "Thank you very much. I appreciate your explaining this to me."

"Anytime, sweetheart." Candy smiled. "And be sure to come back and see me when you're eighteen and can legally drink from the Fountain of Youth. Remember, you have to be young to stay young."

That evening, the first thing Zia did when she talked to Kiel was show him how nicely her 'cut' finger had healed. The second thing was to show him the Zia ring Oma had given her. She was still explaining the significance of the symbol when he interrupted her.

"Zia?"

"Yes?" The look on his face made her feel apprehensive.

"I must leave tomorrow to travel with my father."

Zia presented a steady exterior, but her insides wobbled. "So...you won't be coming to the prom with me after all?"

"No, no. I will be there, just as I promised!" Kiel flashed a cunning smile. "But while I am traveling, I will not be able to visit with you. I will probably not speak with you again, until I see you...in person."

"But you will be there." Zia closed her eyes in relief. "You will be able to use the portal?"

"Yes, just as I promised you."

"Cross your heart?" Zia couldn't believe such a childish saying slipped out.

Kiel laughed at her question. "What does that mean?"

"Just that you promise it with all your heart."

"Very well then." He folded his arms across the middle of his chest, creating the look of a mummy about to be wrapped for burial.

Now it was Zia's turn to laugh. "No, not like that! Use your finger, and cross your heart like this." She made an X sign over her left breast.

"Does it matter which side I cross?" Kiel was making this much more complicated than it needed to be.

"Well," Zia continued to laugh. "Obviously, you cross the side your heart is on."

The smile left Kiel's face, replaced with a puzzled expression. "I have a heart on both sides. You... do not?"

Zia's smile vanished as well. "No. I only have...one." Zia pointed to her left side.

Apparently, there was much more that was different with Kiel's physical composition from just the two belly buttons.

"Zia," he spoke softly, noticing the sudden sadness in her eyes. "I will never do anything to intentionally hurt you or make you sad, and I will never make you a vow I can not keep." Kiel cleared his throat and leaned forward in his chair.

With a caress across his chest, Kiel's finger traced the outline of a cross. "I promise to always be careful with your heart."

CHAPTER 19
LOVELY ME

Once again, Zia was a celebrity at school. The 'Riley Incident' at Cheezy's had pushed her to the front of the popularity line. Even days after the event, everyone was still gossiping about the confrontation. The single punch Zia delivered to Riley had evolved with each retelling until the current story had the girls in an all-out fistfight, with Zia finally knocking Riley out cold.

At first Zia had enjoyed the attention, but by midweek she was growing weary of all the blather and finger pointing that occurred whenever she entered a room. She'd heard the words *That's the girl I told you about* whispered from more freshman lips than she cared to count.

But there was at least one good thing to come from it. She, Zoolynne and Gentry were finally speaking again. There was no mention of Kiel by name, nor was there any acknowledgement that her friends had changed their minds about his existence, but at least

they were conceding that Zia's prom date would be arriving by
Simulacrum.

At noon, the trio discussed prom plans over an unappetizing
lunch in the school cafeteria. "Nothing tastes good today. Even the
coffee tastes jotty!" Zia held the cup away from her mouth.
Zoolynne looked at the container in Zia's hand and realized the limb
guard was gone.

"My god! Your new finger!" she squealed.

Zia glanced cautiously around the cafeteria. She hoped her friend
hadn't spoken so loudly that those sitting nearby heard. It would just
cause the whispering and pointing to start up again.

"Why didn't you tell us?" Zoolynne couldn't believe it.

"I just wanted to see how long it'd take you to notice." Zia
smiled mischievously.

"Well, it looks great." Zoo reached over and held her hand.

Gentry leaned in for a closer look. "How does it feel?"

"Good." Zia shrugged. "Just like the old one."

"Well, it's about time you get a manicure." Zoolynne rubbed her
thumb across Zia's rough cuticles. "In fact, why don't we all get a
manicure after our hair appointments Saturday? Gotta look perfect
for the prom."

Zia liked Zoolynne's idea. It was nice to have her best friend
back.

The remainder of the week drug by so slowly that Zia felt like she was trapped in some sort of time warp. The evenings seemed endless without Kiel to chat with after dinner. Her mom was working third shift at the hotel, and with Oma still absent, the house seemed like a big empty shell. Bellaboo had become Zia's only nighttime companion.

And the solitary evenings gave Zia way too much time to worry about Kiel and various *what ifs*. What if his father decided to extend their trip? Had Kiel even told his father about her? What if he didn't have permission to use a portal, or to meet some girl from another planet?

Why hadn't she asked Kiel these questions? If she knew the answers, she might feel more secure about his arrival on Saturday night, but she hadn't asked - and now it was too late.

Prom day finally arrived, and Zia was up early, already feeling the beginnings of nail-biting jitters. The Sand Castle Hotel had called Chessie in to cover the shift of a sick staff member, and Zia desperately needed to talk to someone. She paced nervously around the kitchen, finally ascending the staircase and walking down the hall to Oma's bedroom.

It was the first time she'd been inside the room since Oma went into rehab. Zia cautiously opened the door and took a deep breath as she entered the space. Thank god, the smell of formaldehyde had evaporated.

She walked across the room and retrieved the music box from her great-grandmother's dresser. Zia sat at the foot of Oma's bed and opened the lid, trying to remember the song's lyrics. She was so consumed in her own thoughts she didn't hear Shane come up the stairs.

"Boo!" He peeked around the doorframe.

"Oh crap!" Zia slammed the lid shut. "You scared me!"

"Sorry," he smiled. "I just drove over to see your new finger."

"I know." Zia's grin went up on one side. "And have mom do your laundry. Well, she's not home, so you'll have to do it yourself."

Shane walked over to the bed and plunked down beside his sister. "Okay, you got me on that one, but let me see the new body part anyway." Zia raised her hand.

"Looks good, kiddo." He turned her hand over, checking out both sides. "Oma's ring looks good too. You missing her a lot?"

"Yeah. I guess that's why I'm just sitting here." Zia looked around the room. "Oma was the one person I could always talk to, and I thought she'd always be here for me." Zia twisted the ring on her finger. "But, I was being selfish. I guess Oma had her own problems too…she just cured them in a different way."

"Well, can I help?" Shane actually looked sincere.

Two months ago, Zia wouldn't have dreamed of confiding anything to her brother, but somewhere along the way their relationship began to morph into something different, so she decided to give him a chance.

"Seeing that you're all I've got at the moment, maybe you can," she said.

Shane smiled at her answer. "Okay, shoot." Being a last-ditch confidante didn't seem to bother him.

"Well, my prom date is using a Parallax Portal, and I'm worried that his Simulacrum might not be able to travel the long distance."

"Is that it?" Shane looked disappointed she didn't have a bigger problem. "That's a stupid thing to worry about. A Simulacrum can travel anywhere in the world. Where's he coming from anyway?"

"Taotrue."

Shane furrowed his brow, trying to remember his geography. "Is that somewhere in Alaska?"

"Yeah, somewhere like that." Zia could tell it would only complicate matters if she were to be completely honest with her brother.

"You know what?" Zia rotated sideways on the bed, facing Shane. "Just give me one of those grandmotherly sounding pieces of advice, and we'll let it go at that."

"Hmmm." Shane thought for a while. "Don't be so busy looking for your favorite dish that you forget to enjoy the buffet." He gave Zia a big smile, apparently pleased with his patriarchal observation on life.

"What the heck is that supposed to mean?" Zia had expected more from her brother.

"I'm not sure, but I thought it sounded like something Oma would say."

"Well, actually," Zia thought for a second, "I guess it does sound like her. But maybe you should give me some advice that isn't quite so grandmotherly." Zia suggested.

"Okay." Shane squinted one eye and looked at the ceiling. "How about this? Sug Pung, Do Ung." Zia looked at her brother with a blank expression. "It's Swedish for 'Suck balls, Die young,'" he explained.

"Geeze, thanks Shane. I'm not some guy in a locker room, you know." Zia decided to try a different approach. "Maybe you could just give me some advice using your own words."

"I've already forgotten what it is you need advice about." Shane was hopeless.

"I don't know…" Zia stared at the music box in her lap. "Just life in general, I suppose. Sometimes I feel like I'm all alone…like living shouldn't be this hard."

"Listen, kiddo." Shane placed his arm around Zia's shoulder. "We're all following the same yellow brick road, chasing the same white rabbit, down the same goddam hole."

Zia looked at her brother curiously. It was an odd comment, but Zia actually understood it. Everyone struggled through life, not just her.

"I never thought I'd say this Shane, but thanks!" Zia was already feeling better – much better. His blunt analysis was like a slap across the face during a fit of hysteria.

"I gotta meet Zoo and Gen in a few minutes to get our hair done, but will you be here when I get back?" Zia hoped he would be. Having her brother in the house made her feel better.

"Probably not, but kid...I mean Zia...have fun tonight." Shane smiled at his younger sibling, and she smiled back.

"I will." Zia got up from the bed and walked to the door.

"But, listen," he warned. "Be a good girl."

"I promise." She smiled over her shoulder as she exited the room.

Shane called after her. "I mean it!"

The grin on Zia's face couldn't have expanded any further. It was ridiculously comforting to know that her brother was genuinely concerned about her...uh, chastity. But, come on! Her date was a Simulacrum after all. Honestly, how much purity could he legitimately take from her? Hmmm...another new idea to ponder and worry about. If you had sex with a Simulacrum were you technically still a virgin? Thought overload!

Zoolynne and Gentry were waiting outside the hair salon when Zia pulled up. The parking lot was packed. Every Cinderella in Celebration was at the Lovely Me salon, all waiting for their appointed Fairy Godmother to transform them before the ball.

"Welcome to Lovely Me," the recorded voice trilled as the friends entered the parlor. Two dozen chairs lined the back of the shop, and giggling girls shuffled everywhere.

"Hello, my darling," Gio called to Zia from the front counter.

He'd been styling Zia's hair for four years, and she still wasn't sure if he knew her real name. Gio called everyone darling. Either he loved that particular term of affection, or it was easier than remembering hundreds of client's names.

"Come with me, darling." Gio motioned to Zia, and she followed him to the washbasins in the far back.

After a quick shampoo and conditioning, they returned to Gio's station, and he began to towel dry her hair. That was when Zia heard the ear-splitting voice, its nauseatingly artificial twaddle coming from the chair beside her.

Oh dear god, not Becky!

Zia could only hope Becky was so self-absorbed with her own reflection that she didn't notice who was sitting on either side.

"So, my darling, who are you going to the prom with?" asked Gio.

Zia swallowed and tried to answer in the quietest voice possible. "Well, he doesn't live here. He's using the portal."

The words had no sooner left her lips than Becky's voice rose by several decibels. "Oh, this hairdo looks wonderful," she gushed to her stylist. "I'm going to put cherry blossom baby's breath in it when I get home. The color will just match the rose corsage Kim is getting for me."

Zia choked when she heard Kim's name, but Becky continued to speak in the amplified voice, her enthusiasm way overboard.

"I feel *so* sorry for any poor girl not going to the prom with a Breather. Those Simulacrum dates have to end when the dance is over, and we all know the best part of prom night happens *after* the dance!" She finished with an irritatingly high-pitched giggle.

Thankfully, Gio turned on the blow dryer, drowning out any remaining drivel spilling from Becky's mouth. Zia stared straight ahead, pretending not to notice the flurry of activity swarming around her. She watched Becky intently out of the corner of her eye, and let out a sigh of relief when she paid her hairdresser and left the salon.

Gio smiled at his Rapunzel as he turned off the blow dryer. "Now, my darling, what wonderful things are we going to do with these long, golden tresses?"

"Well," Zia looked around the salon. Every single girl had some version of the same style – an updo. Even her mother had worn the identical upswept hairdo in her prom photo twenty-five years earlier. Zia removed the pink transmitter from her purse, and held up a picture of her Grecian gown for Gio to see.

"Say no more." Gio whirled Zia's chair around, running his fingers through her hair. "When I'm finished, you'll be a goddess worshiped by all!"

If it had been anyone else uttering those words, Zia would've known they were nothing more than empty promises, but Gio was different. He really was the shaman of the salon, waving his comb and curling iron like a magic wand.

If he promised he'd turn her into a goddess, he would.

And he did.

When Gio swiveled her chair back toward the mirror and Zia saw her reflection, she was convinced he really could work magic. In a line of carbon copy hairstyles, Zia's was completely different.

Her long blonde hair was caught up high in a Grecian style held by a jeweled clasp, her face outlined with loose French braids that wrapped around the sides and joined in the back. Gio's goddess interpretation enhanced all the facial features usually hidden behind her straight hair and shaggy bangs.

Zia wasn't sure she even recognized the girl with the swanlike neck staring back at her from the looking glass. The features of the girl in the mirror were startlingly feminine, her hair serving to frame, not cover her delicate face. Zia blinked, and the girl blinked back, her large emerald eyes set like precious stones in the snowy hollows of her fair complexion.

Zia had become Cinderella.

That evening, Zia took her time getting ready. The sun was down and the house was empty, but Zia wasn't afraid to be alone anymore.

Chessie had called to say she'd be home as soon as possible, but Zia told her mother not to rush - and not to worry if Zia was already gone when she got in. Zia would be just fine riding with her friends in the limo Xander and Axel had hired for the evening.

And besides, Zia consoled her mother, since she didn't have a date escorting her to the prom, Chessie wasn't missing out on witnessing one of those momentous events in a young girl's life.

Zia had been deliberately vague with details about Kiel, telling her mom only that he would be using Way Back's portal. Chessie had been surprised Zia wasn't attending the prom with a Breather, but didn't seem upset. Zia figured it was probably because she'd have less to worry about if her daughter's date was an asexual Simulacrum.

Zia twirled in front of the dressing room mirror, admiring her reflection. "How do I look?" she asked Bellaboo, comfortably positioned on the bed's fleecy pillows. Bellaboo raised her head, and wagged her tail in approval.

"Why, thank you." Zia grinned at her new roommate.

With Oma away, the dog had decided to bunk in Zia's room. She welcomed the company, and Bellaboo seemed content with her new accommodations. She rolled lazily over on one side, apparently exhausted from her wardrobe critique. Zia laughed at the pug. She looked like a Tootsie Roll with legs.

Still smiling at her pet's cocoa candied likeness, Zia raised her eyes from the sleeping pooch and let them settle on the painting hanging over her bed – Kim's painting. A pang of sadness clawed through her chest, and she turned around before it could take deeper hold.

Just then, the doorbell sounded. Zia lifted her eyes to the ceiling and pressed her palms together as if in prayer. "Thank you, sweet savior," she said.

Zia grabbed her purse and headed downstairs to the entry hall. She gave her white satin gown a final once-over in the vestibule mirror, and satisfied with her appearance, opened the door. Breckin stood alone on the front porch, wearing a white full dress tuxedo with tails.

"All I can say is wow!" Zia greeted him with an impressed nod of the head.

"I was just about to say the same thing about you." Breckin took Zia's hand, spinning her around to admire the entire gown. "Well, we may not be going as dates to this prom, but aint no couple gonna look more excellin' than we are when we make our entrance!"

"That's true," Zia agreed with a laugh. "We are *far superior* to everyone else." She and Breckin giggled at her use of Spotswood's favorite line.

Zia glanced around her friend at the waiting limo parked by the curb.

"I told the others to wait outside because I wanted to escort you myself." Breck smiled at Zia. "And I'm glad I did, because I was the first to glimpse your unimaginable beauty this evening."

"Oh stop it," Zia jokingly scolded him. "But…thank you."

Breckin placed one hand across his waist and the other behind his back. He bowed low, his head dropping below Zia's midriff.

"My lady, your carriage awaits."

FINAL CHAPTER
NIGHTS IN WHITE SATIN

Arriving unescorted to her Junior-Senior Prom wasn't exactly the way Zia had envisioned this special night should begin.

She leaned over to look out the limo window. The twilight sky was purple, the color she'd come to associate with Kiel. Just ahead Zia could see the brightly colored buildings of Downtown Disney - the white tent of Cirque de Soleil, the rusted water tower at House of Blues, the glittering marquee outside the AMC theatre, and the bright searchlights of Pleasure Island criss-crossing just behind them.

"Wow, valet service!" Zoolynne watched the rushing about of top-hatted parking attendants as their limo pulled to the curb next to Planet Hollywood.

Bodies covered every square inch of Downtown Disney, and even exiting the vehicle would have been a challenge if not for the valets blocking the area.

"Onward comrades!" Xander gave Zoolynne a gentle push out the limo door and joined her on the sidewalk. Gentry and Axel scooted out next, followed by Zia and Breckin.

A group of platinum-haired senior girls strolled by, each with an adoring, slobbering jock on her arm. They slowed down to size up the newly arrived competition, but picked up their pace after a few seconds.

"Guess we didn't look like much of a threat," Gentry whispered to Zia

"I guess not," she answered.

Zia was more concerned with the large assembly of students pouring into the area than some brain-bleached bimbos. Between the locals, tourists and prom-goers, Disney's West Side was almost non-navigable. Zia was wondering which direction they should take when Axel decided to appoint himself leader, and with a sure-fire plan of attack, led his group forward.

"Go toward the light," he told them as they fought their way through the crowd.

After pushing through a group of mouse-eared conventioneers, there was a break in the conflux of jostling bodies, and the friends stopped to take a breath and gaze at the solar powered lights beckoning them toward the Hyperian Wharf and Pleasure Island.

"All the extra strobe lights look great, huh Zia?" Breckin circled his arm through hers.

"Uh...yes." Zia glanced around. "It really does."

Everything did look better tonight. She'd never seen Downtown Disney quite so bright, so teeming with exuberant personalities. But even in the midst of all these people, Zia had never felt so all alone.

"Look," Axel pointed.

A red carpet extended out from Pleasure Island's bridge. The entire area was roped off and a flashing signboard placed near the crossover announced "Special Event Tonight – Invitation Required."

"I can't believe they closed down the whole place just for us," Gentry squealed. "I feel so important."

Zia felt more apprehensive than excited about what the evening might bring, but Kiel had made her a promise. He said he'd be there…so he would. He had even crossed *both* of his hearts. No more worrying, Zia told herself. That was it…done…finished…at least for a while.

The friends shuffled toward the bridge, the girls sneaking glimpses at who-was-with-who and what dress so-and-so was wearing. They'd need to remember all the details, so they could rehash them at school Monday morning. Even in her anxious state, Zia knew that rule.

After handing their prom invitations to a security guard at the P.I. entrance, the golden rope lowered, and the companions marched inside. Free from the disorderly throng opposite the braided barrier, the friends crossed comfortably over the bridge and into the outdoor courtyard.

A large number of prom-goers strolled back and forth, laughing and taking pictures with the costumed stilt walkers hired for the evening's entertainment. Belly dancers performed a seductive dance on a nearby stage, and Axel and Xander paused briefly to admire their gyrations.

An elaborate photo area had been set up near Way Back's entrance, one side for couples and one side for individuals. Zia and Breckin watched as their friends posed for photos, but neither of them made a move toward the singles only side. The sign above the photo area might as well have said, "Losers stand here!"

"Maybe we'll have another chance for photos inside." Breckin looked hopeful.

"Yeah, maybe." Zia tried to lift the corners of her mouth. And maybe her date would show up.

After the couples finished taking pictures, Xander and Axel suggested the friends return to watch the belly dancers. It was only right to take advantage of the free entertainment according to Axel, but Breckin didn't agree. His desire to be one of the first guests waiting at the Parallax Portal forced the group to continue.

Secretly, Zia was thankful Breckin was the one rushing everybody toward Way Back's and saving her the embarrassment of having to do it herself. Moreover, she was sure Zoo and Gen were thankful too - but for different reasons.

As they approached Way Back's, Zia spotted Mr. Petty standing with several other chaperones at the entrance, only, unlike them; he was dressed in accordance with the evening's affair.

The prissy pedagogue had taken the Bohemian attire seriously, his frame bedecked in an elaborate Sultan costume. He stood with a closed fist on each hip, his body draped in a black tunic with heavy saffron robes and a gold sash. A shiny maroon turban, embellished with a large jade crystal, rested on his head.

"I never saw *that* outfit in the school's costume department!" Breckin looked at Zia with a raised eyebrow.

Zia returned his look with a crooked grin. "He probably bought it just for this special occasion."

"Welcome to my harem," Mr. Petty ushered the friends inside the club.

They looked at each other and suppressed a laugh. Zia still wasn't sure whether Cicero Petty kept a male or female genie in his lamp at home – maybe he had one of each.

When they entered the venue, the girlfriends let out a collective gasp as they surveyed the lobby. Even though Zia knew the prom theme was Arabian Nights, the magnificent fusion of visual treats caught her unprepared.

Beaded curtain canopies graced the area, inviting guests in with their intoxicating design, and crystal pendant lanterns flickered from the ceiling, softly lighting the lobby corridor. The friends followed the illuminated pathway to the nightclub's dance hall.

"Wow, the prom committee did a damn good job! Even I'm impressed." Axel turned to appraise the room, pulling Gentry in a circle as he did. "Except for the stage, this place doesn't even look like Way Back's."

Everyone agreed with his assessment. The entire club was a vibrant color palette filled with iridescent chiffon gazebos, glimmering mesh columns, and curtained arches of fabrics in jacquard and sateen. Authentic looking Moroccan hassocks lined the walls, giving students various places to sit and visit.

The tables at the far end of the room beckoned with black velvet cloths and embroidered silver tassels. Tall glass jars filled with flickering fireflies graced each tabletop, and as soon as she spotted them, Zoolynne had to have one of the romantic niches. She insisted the couples claim one before they were all taken, and Xander relented, following her to the far end of the room.

In a polite gesture, Breckin and Zia excused themselves so Gentry and Axel could join the other couple, but secretly, they were anxious to get moving in the direction of the portal. It was located on the far wall next to the stage, and there were already a fair number of students waiting in the area.

As they approached, Laverne Lavendusky appeared and announced that in mere moments, the surrounding student's dates would begin coming through the portal.

Zia and Breckin looked at each other and squeezed hands in anticipation of what was about to happen. Ms. Lavendusky switched on the portal, and immediately, shadowy images appeared and began walking forward into the venue.

Zia peered over shoulders and heads, craning her neck to look at the faces of those entering. It made her feel uncomfortable, as if she was at the Orlando airport waiting for her bags at luggage claim.

After twenty minutes, most of the waiting teenagers' dates arrived, and the united couples wandered off to join the other students.

Suddenly, Breckin threw both hands to his mouth. "Oh my goddess, there he is!"

Zia looked at the young man exiting the portal. He was almost a foot taller than her friend, with broad shoulders and long silky blonde hair.

"Doesn't he look handsome?" Breckin gushed.

"He does Breck, but remember so do you." Zia smiled at her friend.

"I'll introduce you later..." Breckin rushed forward to meet his date.

Zia briefly watched them embrace before returning her eyes to the portal. Very few figures were emerging now. Only about a dozen students remained in the waiting area with Zia.

She felt the butterflies beginning to move in her stomach, but tried to steady herself. "He said he'd come, he said he'd come. And he will, he will," Zia kept repeating the words in her head.

She watched as a shadowy figure appeared, obviously a male, and very tall. Zia moved quickly toward the portal, but a female dressed in all pink rushed past her and embraced the figure as he entered the light. Zia's heart fell.

She waited another fifteen minutes. The first band had already taken the stage, and Way Back's was more crowded and noisy than ever. By this time, only Zia and two other girls remained in the portal area. They smiled sheepishly at each other without speaking, each girl hoping she wouldn't be the last one waiting.

Time seemed to have slipped into slow motion, but when Zia finally risked a glance at her watch, she realized that another half hour had passed. Why had she looked at the time? That one glance caused everything to reverse. Now, time began to accelerate, and it was moving much too quickly. Song after song played, and with them, moments Zia could never recapture.

She glanced around and realized that one of the two girls waiting with her had left. Now it was just Zia and one other pathetic teenage girl, the two of them waiting for dates that might, or might not, show up.

She wasn't sure why, but after a while Zia became obsessed with watching the young woman. The girl wasn't ugly, but she wasn't attractive. She was somewhere between run-of-the-mill and better-than-nothing. Dark freckles covered her face and arms, her hair pulled high on her head in a too tight bun. She wore a powder blue dress with a simple A-line design, which unfortunately accentuated her small bust line and wide hips.

The girl looked sad. Under other circumstances, Zia would have rushed to place an arm around the girl's shoulder to comfort her...but not tonight. Tonight she and Zia were in the same place.

Twenty more minutes passed. The girls gave faint smiles to each other. Zia couldn't believe this was how she was going to spend her entire prom - standing alone on the fringes with some strange girl, obviously stood up at the last minute.

Zia comforted herself with the knowledge that the dates of everyone else using the portal had arrived from North America - or if not that - at least planet Earth! She was the only one waiting for a date to arrive from across the universe. The thought made her feel better for a moment.

While Zia watched, the freckle faced girls head bowed, and her shoulders began to rise and fall as she sobbed. She turned to leave, but Ms. Lavendusky rushed to her side, placing a compassionate arm around her waist. Zia could tell that Ms. Lavendusky was consoling the girl, but she couldn't hear the words.

Zia backed a good distance away from the portal, not wanting the same exhibition of sympathy lavished on her in front of everyone.

Ms. Lavendusky didn't notice Zia waiting in the shadows, and returned to her post at the portal's entrance. But she was no longer watching for guests to arrive. She'd redirected her attention to the performing artists long ago.

Zia's concentration, however, was still on the portal, and her eyes were riveted to the machine when Zoolynne, Gentry and their dates approached.

"I'm sorry." Zoolynne gave her friend a hug and a sad smile.

Gentry leaned over and squeezed Zia's hand. "Me too."

"Thank you, but you don't have to say that. He'll be here." Zia barely glanced at her friends.

She simply couldn't remove her gaze from the portal, and besides, she didn't want anyone feeling sorry for her – she could take care of that herself. They'd never believed Kiel was going to come anyway, she knew that.

"Ya'll go on and have fun. I'll find you later." Zia made a shooing motion with the back of her hand and gave her friends a hurried smile.

The couples reluctantly returned to the dance floor and Zia returned her eyes to Ms. Lavendusky. She was standing at the portal's entrance, clapping along to the music.

Zia hadn't checked the time in some while and glanced quickly at her watch. No! It couldn't be! It was exactly eleven p.m. – the dance would end at midnight. She looked back down at the timepiece and her body began to sink.

Frenzy swam around Zia, threatening to drown her in a pool of hysteria if she didn't fight her way to the surface. Zia struggled to suck air into her lungs, reminding herself to take deep breaths. She could handle this.

There was a reason he wasn't here. All she had to do was think rationally. Kiel *could* have been mistaken. Maybe a Simulicrum from Taotrue couldn't transmit through a portal on Earth. There was a logical explanation for his not coming. Wasn't there? If she'd only been able to talk to Kiel during the last few days, she wouldn't have the nagging feeling of rejection with which she now had to contend.

Or…what if he was already here? Maybe she'd somehow missed Kiel as he passed through the portal, and he was walking aimlessly through the club looking for her.

Or…maybe he'd come through the portal, and she hadn't noticed him because he was really no more than two inches tall! How could she really know his actual size - she'd only seen him through a computer screen. Oh my god, that was it! There was going to be some awful Twilight Zone twist of fate when they finally met, something to prevent them from ever consummating their love for one another.

"Oh, shut up, shut up," Zia whispered to herself. She had to get her imagination under control…but still…she hoped no one had stepped on him.

She was near enough to the portal that Kiel would see her if he did finally emerge, so Zia pulled herself back into reality and forced her attention elsewhere.

In the far shadows, she noticed Twilah and Chandra for the first time. They were with some guys Zia didn't recognize. Where did they go to school again? Twi had told her all about them during chemistry lab, but Zia hadn't really been listening. Were they from Dr. Phillips? Yes, that sounded right. That's where Twilah said they went to school.

They were nice looking from what Zia could tell, and they were obviously out for a good time – just like all of Twi and Chandy's guys. Zia squinted for a better look. It appeared as if Twilah was trying to sit on her date's lap – something that would've been much easier to do had he not been standing up.

Zia moved her eyes to the rows of tables outlining the back wall. She couldn't believe it! Spotswood had a date with poor Annie from Musical Theatre, but poor Annie looked like she was enjoying herself.

Spotswood gallantly pulled out her chair and then rushed to the nearby bar. He quickly returned with a drink and placed it carefully in Annie's hands. Even shy, simple Annie was having more fun than she was.

Again, Zia redirected her attention - this time to the band. She hadn't enjoyed any of the artists who'd performed. Her own noisy thoughts had drummed their singing from her ears. She tried to focus on the stage, but through the dancers, she saw a figure clad all in black gliding toward her.

His hands rested casually in the pockets of his jacket, and his stride was self-assured. Even his silhouette was aggressively confident. A few feet from her, his face came into the light. Kim had never looked more handsome, his tall frame draped in a masculine cut translucent black tuxedo jacket. As he passed under the flickering lanterns, his coat shimmered with metallic vertical stripes.

Oh, dear god, no! Zia lowered her eyes and glanced to one side, hoping Kim hadn't noticed her standing alone. Maybe he'd just walk on past. Strange that she'd want him to do such a thing, but she did. She *really* did.

Zia simply couldn't endure the embarrassment, and began desperately pleading, praying, and petitioning God to show her some mercy.

He didn't.

Kim stopped directly in front of her.

She couldn't look at him and continued to stare at the floor, pretending to be deep in thought. Maybe if Kim thought she was enthralled with some unseen object on the ground, he'd go away.

No luck. He moved closer.

From the corner of her downcast eyes, she watched Kim and prayed he didn't notice her panicked breathing. With her head still hanging, he gently placed his forefinger under Zia's chin, and raised her lowered face, forcing her to make direct eye contact.

"I have never seen anyone as beautiful as you are tonight." Kim moved his hand to the side of Zia's face, gently stroking her cheek with the backs of his fingers.

"Thank you." Zia's vision turned misty, and she blinked back the tears she swore she wouldn't cry.

"The prom's almost over." Kim continued to caress her cheek. "We'd have never left the dance floor if I'd been your date." He leaned closer to make his meaning clearer. "I wouldn't have wanted you out of my arms."

As he did, Zia pushed his hand away. "Do you mean you actually thought of me?" The words leapt from her mouth before she had time to consider what she was saying. "Why didn't you invite me then?"

Kim stepped back, looking shaken by her outburst. "Do you think I just saw you for the first time tonight? That I've never noticed you before?" He sounded hurt. "I...I wanted to ask you out the night I saw you in the club...and then at my graduation party...but you vanished. You ran away from me."

He couldn't be more wrong.

"I didn't run away. I just...got out of the way...so you could be with Becky." Zia's lip trembled.

"What do you mean *be* with Becky?"

"I saw you taking pictures...she had her hand on your chest...and you reached up to hold it." The quiver in Zia's voice punctuated her battered ego.

"You should have stayed around to watch then. I reached up to remove it!"

She couldn't believe what he was saying, what his words meant. It meant Zia - not Kim - had sabotaged the remainder of their evening. Once again, Zia had allowed herself to slip into her comic book alter ego, Anxiety Girl, able to jump to the wrong conclusion in a single bound.

She nervously shifted her weight from one foot to the other, preparing to go into an emotional tailspin.

"And even after that, I still wanted to invite you to the prom...but by then it was too late." Kim glanced around before continuing. "I heard you were coming with someone from...from..."

"Out of town," Zia finished Kim's sentence.

What had he heard, that she was coming with ET? What had Zoo and Gen told everyone? She looked at him closely, searching for a clue.

Kim stared back at Zia, and, she began to relax. She had no choice. Whenever he blinked, the incline of his eyes created the illusion of a comfortable hammock, calmly swaying in the breeze.

But it wasn't just the pendulum swing of Kim's eyes that gently rocked Zia back into a temperate setting. There was something else. Something she couldn't see. What was it about him that he could do this to her all the time?

Kim gulped hard, the Adam's apple bobbing up and down in his throat. "This isn't what I wanted to happen. I'm sorry about tonight and about..." He stopped and extended his hand. "May I?"

Zia willingly relented, placing her hand in his. Kim hadn't done or said anything wrong. She was the one who'd been way out of line and she felt humiliated, but there was nothing she could do about it now. Zia swallowed her embarrassment and forced a smile, allowing Kim to lead her to the dance floor, his warm touch melting away any icy acrimony still coursing through her body.

As they thread their way through the crowd, Kim entwined his fingers with Zia's, their wrists pressed together so she could feel the drumming of his pulse. It seemed to be beating as quickly as hers.

When they reached the center of the dance floor, Kim slipped his right hand gently around Zia's waist and pulled her to him. At least she'd have this one dance as a remembrance of her prom. She placed her left hand on his shoulder, and they slowly drifted with the music.

With each step, Kim's embrace tightened seductively, the gesture causing the rest of the dancers and the room around Zia to evaporate. They swirled alone across a starless sky, pulled into their own secret vortex. Why couldn't *this* have been her prom? This one perfect dance stretched across the entire evening.

When the music ended, Kim's body remained pressed to Zia, locked with hers in a prison of regret. She made no effort to pull away. Kim gently reached up to caress the hand resting on his shoulder, and his fingers brushed across the Zia ring.

He pulled her hand back, his voice suddenly alive with excitement. "Zia! Your finger's healed!" Kim clasped her hand in his.

"Yes, it is." Zia looked down at her hand, cradled in Kim's, remembering the night of the incident - the night he came to her rescue.

Kim placed his thumb on top of Zia's ring and slowly moved it from side to side. "So this is what you lost your finger for." He studied the piece of jewelry while suggestively massaging her palm with his fingers.

Kim lifted Zia's hand to his mouth, and against her will, she inhaled deeply. He gently brushed his lips across her knuckles and then slowly turned Zia's hand over. He seductively kissed her palm, gently closing her fingers as if to hold in his kiss.

"This is for you to take with you...always," he whispered.

"For...always?" Zia whispered back.

"Do you remember when I told you that one day we would take a lock to the Namsan Tower in Seoul? Did you ever figure out what I meant?"

Zia shook her head, wishing now that she had put the question to her computer. Obviously, it meant something more than what she had thought.

"Couples ride the cable cars up to the tower's viewing deck," Kim explained, still gently holding her closed hand between his. "They write their names on a lock and place it on the gate surrounding the area. They're called lover's locks because they symbolize the couple's promise that they will never separate."

Zia couldn't believe what Kim was saying to her. What it all meant...or could have meant.

He looked deeply into her eyes, and Zia looked back, but she wasn't careful. Her introspection extended too far. She must have fallen into the recesses of his gaze because there was a sudden bright flash.

"This will make a fantastic picture for the yearbook!"

Zia recognized the voice. It was Katie Crane, one of the yearbook editors. Suddenly, Zia was transported back to the dance floor, pulled out of the chasm of Kim's eyes by the camera flash.

"You two make a really cute pair," Katie commented before leaving to take a picture of another couple.

Zia turned again to Kim, but before she could fall back under his spell, she heard another voice.

"There you are!" It was Becky.

"Excuse me if I cut in." She glared at Zia. "But I'd like to dance with my date." Becky's tone wasn't its usual high-pitched chirp. This time it was low, ominous – and threatening. "Come on!" She locked her arm through Kim's and began elbowing her way through the crowd, her lips pressed together in an angry line.

Kim reluctantly followed, but after a few steps, he pulled away and turned back to look at Zia, his eyes connected to hers by the thin thread of their fleeting moment on the dance floor. She stood paralyzed, not moving from the spot in which Kim had left her.

Seconds passed and then Becky placed a commanding arm around Kim's shoulder, forcing him to follow her into the mob, a wall of dancers closing in behind them.

And just like that - he was gone.

Zia slowly pivoted and walked back to the dance floor's edge. She stopped and glanced down, realizing she still carried her hand in a gently closed position as if holding something fragile. Softly, she opened her fingers and looked at her empty palm.

It didn't matter what words Kim had spoken to her, or the way he'd looked at her on the dance floor. She stood alone. A solitary silhouette watching the world from the sidelines, living her life through second hand smoke instead of first hand inhale, and always going home alone and lonely.

The room - the world - closed in on Zia, and she shut her eyes, stealing a long, deep breath. The thick air inside the dance hall filled her nostrils. It smelled of musk, and she exhaled. The air flitted sluggishly from her lungs, and Zia wondered why she should even bother to continue inhaling. What was important enough for her to take the next breath?

And then, she heard it.

It was *his* voice!

Familiar, but somehow changed. Recognizable, but completely new and unbelievably arousing in its cadence and resonance.

"Zia," he said. "I am here."

She felt his hands on her shoulders, and with his fingertips, he slowly turned her body to face his. Was this real? Could it be?

But there he stood. Kiel.

Kiel Shovarga, from the planet Taotrue.

Kiel Shovarga, who had traveled across a galaxy - a universe - to be with Zia.

In that instant, everything changed! The sadness of the evening evaporated. The melancholy tune coming from the band suddenly sounded joyful. The heart Zia had only moments before wished to stop beating could now *not* stop beating; it's pulsing so strong she could hear its rhythm in her ears.

She knew it was only Kiel's whole image transported through a Simulacrum, but...it was Kiel! He was standing beside her and staring into her eyes. Zia didn't speak or move, her eyes locked on his, afraid that if she looked away he might vanish.

This was the moment – the instant when they saw each other for the first time. Not as images on a screen, but as real, living beings.

He gave her a long appraising look. Was he disappointed? She worried as she searched his face. He moved her body away from his and held her at arms length, his visual examination continuing down her body.

With his eyes removed from hers, Zia scrambled to refocus on what was happening, to assure herself it wasn't all a dream.

Kiel towered above her, and Zia found his physical perfection unbalancing. The ravishing black hair she'd so admired was now only inches from her face. It was even darker and thicker than she'd expected, its purple hue enhanced by the dance floor lights.

He wore a tight fitting satin ivory suit sporting a gold trimmed Mandarin collar. Amethyst gems ran the length of his chest, and the jacket's hemline fell just below his narrow hips.

Zia's first impression was that - as silly as it sounded - he looked like a prince. Yes, that was it! That was what he looked like! He was beautiful, almost godlike. His appearance set him apart from everyone else at the prom – male or female.

Kiel returned his attention to Zia's face and she quickly met his gaze. Those eyes! Those violet eyes! They were more piercing than Zia could have prepared for. They burned like candles, only candles flickered, and with these, the flames shot straight up and out.

They seemed to dive beneath her cornea, delving into her thoughts, her very marrow. Zia felt transparent, as if he could see right into her. Could he read her mind? She immediately dropped her eyes at the thought, and as she did, she felt his hands leave her shoulders.

Was this it? Well, she could certainly understand his disenchantment with her appearance. She was sure he'd expected something more from the Earther he'd come to know through a computer screen.

But then, just when she was certain of his dissatisfaction, she felt his open hand press firmly against her middle back and the other hand move to cradle the nape of her neck. He pulled her closer, and Zia raised her eyes to meet his.

Gently, he pressed his body to Zia, his lips finding hers and caressing them with a touch that was tender yet feverishly determined. His strength held her upright, but she felt herself slipping as she welcomed the soft pressure of his lips on hers. His kiss was stirring, and Zia felt a feral craving come to life and pump violently through every artery in her body.

She hoped his kiss would never end, but he gently released her from his arms, allowing her head to rest against his chest. Neither spoke a word until Kiel broke the silence.

"Zia, I was worried I would not make it in time to be with you tonight. Arriving here took longer than I expected."

She wondered what had happened. A thousand questions rolled through Zia's mind, but the tone of his voice kept her hypnotized. Was it the language translator Kiel wore on his collar that made his words flow so thick and rich, or was this really his *natural* voice?

"Kiel," someone whispered. "I can't believe you're here."

Who was talking? Zia didn't recognize her own voice. It sounded so meek, so timid. She needed to say something else, something more, but her thoughts floated in circles. What she really wanted was to ask Kiel to kiss her again, but he stepped back to survey his surroundings before she had the chance.

"So, this is a prom." He glanced around the room.

Zia followed his gaze, observing the place through new eyes. Somehow, it all looked different. "Yes, this is it," she smiled.

Suddenly, the movement of her classmates turned into an erotic ballet. The club's blue spotlights shone down, creating the illusion that the partners moving in unison were melting into one. Everything was wonderfully upside down. Zia glanced up at Kiel.

"Why did it take you so long to get here?" she asked. I didn't think you were coming."

"Zia, my dear sweet Zia." He cradled the side of her face in his hand. "So many things prevented my earlier arrival, but I cannot speak of those now. I am here with you, but our time is short. It will end soon."

Kiel reached into his pocket and retrieved a small black box. "I believe I promised you a birthday present."

He turned it toward Zia, and lifted the lid. Inside was a delicate silver necklace. On its chain hung a star encrusted with stones that sparkled more brilliantly than any diamond Zia had ever seen. She ran her fingers across the glistening jewels and looked up at Kiel.

"It's beautiful," she punctuated the last word with a smile, and he looked pleased.

Kiel carefully removed the necklace and fastened it around Zia's neck. "Now, whenever you gaze at a far away star, you will think of me… and know I am waiting for you to be with me." He had barely gotten the words out of his mouth when a loud voice interrupted.

"Thank you students for attending this year's prom." Principal Lidwine's voice boomeranged through the club. "This will be the last dance."

Immediately, students began to crowd the dance floor, pressed together for the final slow dance of the night. Principal Lidwine introduced the last band of the evening, and they began to play.

Nights in white satin never reaching the end
Letters I've written never meaning to send.

This was an unfamiliar song, one Zia had never heard, and yet she found it haunting. The melody was full of sorrow, but there was a romance hidden under the sadness of the lyrics.

Gazing at people, some hand in hand
Just what I'm going through, they can't understand.

Kiel watched as couples swirled before them, and Zia wondered if the young people on Taotrue danced in the same fashion as the ones on Earth. He returned the black box to his pocket and turned to Zia.

"I would very much like to dance with you." Kiel extended his hand.

Well, she would soon find out if a slow dance was a slow dance no matter what solar system you came from. Zia smiled and placed her hand in Kiel's, his fingers curling around her own. He squeezed her hand softly, and slid his arm around her waist as they walked to the dance floor.

Zia's mind raced as they passed between her classmates' sweaty, writhing bodies. There were things she wanted to ask Kiel. Things…but she couldn't remember what they were. What was it she wanted to say to him now that they shared the same space? What was it she wanted to ask?

They stood in the middle of the club, Kiel looking down at Zia, his head tilted to one side, his eyes searching her face. She looked up at Kiel and suddenly knew the answer, the solution in his eyes. Her questions could be answered without a single word, no conversation necessary. They had done enough talking over the computer. She wanted to do those things you couldn't do through a computer screen.

Kiel reached out to Zia and held her tightly, his hands stroking her neck and back as their bodies swayed to the music. As they danced, Kiel explored her body with not only his mouth and hands, but also his hips. Zia touched him in return, unembarrassed and unaware that her friends stood only a few feet away, unknowing that the fervor of their intimacy was so impassioned that it was met with envy by those who observed it.

Zia never saw Zoolynne and Gentry's pleasantly surprised expressions or Chandra and Twilah's envious looks, and she never saw Kim and Becky who stood motionless near the stage. She never felt Kim's eyes silently follow her and Kiel as they drifted across the dance floor.

Beauty I'd always missed with these eyes before
Just what the truth is I can't say anymore.

"Goodnight students," Principal Lidwine spoke again. "Please begin exiting the dance hall now." The song continued, but the rocking of the dancers stopped.

Zia and Kiel stood motionless, but watched as the Breathers walked hand in hand toward the general exit. The couples laughed and talked excitedly, knowing that the end of the dance didn't necessarily mean the end of the evening. They could still look forward to a continued evening of drinking, drugging, sex, romance - whatever they desired. They had tonight, tomorrow, and the next day to spend together - or not - depending on their moods.

Zia turned Kiel toward the Parallax Portal, where a different view greeted them.

Breathe deep, the gathering gloom
Watch lights fade from every room.

Couples huddled in dark corners, groping, grasping at their last moments together. Those heading toward the portal walked closer than did those leaving by the general exit. They held each other tighter - hanging on for as long as they could - and Zia pressed her head to Kiel's chest as they fell in line with the others.

They were now close enough to the portal to see those exiting. As the partners stepped through the machine, a silver shimmer surrounded each couple, creating a glittering silhouette. The effect was beautiful, but Zia watched in horror as the silhouette changed from two to one, and a single shadow walked alone from the portal into the gloaming beyond the exit doors.

"Oh, no, no," she pleaded, clinging to Kiel's arm.

Sounds of sobs and wailing filled the air, as one after another, Zia watched two enter the portal and exit as only one. Only a few yards ahead Zia could see Breckin and his date step through the swirling egress. They were downcast, holding each other until the final moment. There was a momentary shimmer, causing a silvery outline of the pair, and then, darkness. A faint light reemerged, and Breckin's solitary figure walked away into the night.

Impassioned lovers wrestle as one
Lonely man cries for love, and has none.

Zia had dreamed of feeling like Cinderella on prom night, and now she did. With every step, the clock inched closer to striking midnight, but it wasn't her gown that would return to rags or her coach that would return to its pumpkin form - it was her prince. He would simply disappear.

They were upon the portal. Zia turned to Kiel and grabbed him around the waist, kissing him deeply and passionately.

"Keep moving," warned Ms. Lavendusky.

They stepped forward. Zia had never held so firmly nor clung so desperately to anything as she now did Kiel's hand, her grip so tight that her fingertips went numb. With the other hand, she held the star necklace around her neck, knowing it too would disappear when they stepped through the exit.

Cold-hearted orb that rules the night, removes the colors from our sight

Red is gray and yellow white, but we decide which is right

....and which is an illusion.

The words scalded Zia's ears. She cursed its author, demanding for the song to end, and then - it came so quickly.

The shuffle from the people behind pushed Zia and Kiel into the portal. Zia looked for the last time at Kiel's face, instinctively closing her eyes as the glow from the astral gateway began to swirl around her.

On the other side, the night sky appeared stark and black, and even the moon seemed cold and unforgiving. Zia still held her right hand to her throat, but as she released her grip, she felt something fall against her neck. Frantically, she reached back up and felt its outline with her fingers. The star necklace still hung around her neck! How was this possible?

She stumbled forward, pushed by those exiting the portal behind her.

But after only a few steps, Zia's body unexpectedly jerked backward. At first she didn't consider why her body had reacted as it did, but then, suddenly, Zia realized her left hand wasn't empty!

She held something in it, something firm, yet smooth to the touch. Without warning, it moved and Zia jumped, yet she didn't dare turn her head to look at what had caused the movement. Her whole body trembled, but even in her panic Zia forced herself to regain composure.

"Breathe," she told herself, and then Zia slowly, cautiously turned her head.

Zia couldn't believe what she beheld in the moonlight. But there, in the alley behind Way Back's, was what had created the movement between her fingers.

Placed there, in the orb's soft glow was...Kiel!

He stood at Zia's side, still clutching her hand. Zia looked at his face, bathed by the moon's halcyon stream, his hair's wine colored highlights blowing softly in the warm Florida breeze. He was real! He was alive and breathing! He was standing beside her, and...Oh, dear god. Zia's composure crumbled, and she collapsed in Kiel's arms.

"Zia, do not be upset," he spoke softly, stroking her hair. "It is me, the real me. When I told you I was traveling with my father, I was not being dishonest with you." Kiel leaned his head to one side, checking to see if Zia understood his words.

"But, bu…" Zia couldn't complete the sentence. Her breathing was rapid and deep, and she struggled to find her voice. "Wh…why didn't you tell me earlier that it was really you?"

"Would you have believed me?"

"I think so…why wouldn't I…probably…I'm…not sure." She looked at the smile forming at the corners of Kiel's lips, and realized she was beginning to grin as well. "But, if you didn't come through the portal, how did you get here?" she asked. "In a skycarriage?"

"Well, no. Not exactly that way either, not in the way you imagine." Kiel laughed. Leaning close to her ear, he whispered, "But, your Uncle Iden said to tell you hello."

"What?" Zia's head snapped back, and Kiel's smile increased until it spread across his entire face and extended into his eyes. Zia opened her mouth to ask another question, but Kiel placed a finger over her lips and gently shook his head, indicating that a full explanation wasn't necessary now.

Zia remained still, and Kiel reached out to her, softly placing one hand on each side of her hips. She looked at the young man standing across from her. He was alive and - just as important - anatomically correct, give or take an extra component here and there! She felt an electricity surge through her body at the realization, any remaining willpower giving way to his luring touch.

His hands moved with an enticing sexuality along the outline of her body, passing briefly over her waist and up to her rib cage. They slipped provocatively along the outside of her breasts before coming to rest on the crevasse of her cleavage.

Was anyone watching them, Zia wondered? She could look around…she could check…if she could focus, but she couldn't. She felt dizzy.

Zia's head tipped backward and Kiel leaned into her, cushioning her back with his open hands. His lips lay upon one side of her collarbone, sweeping lightly to the other. She dug her fingers into the muscled planes of Kiel's back, and his mouth parted slightly, allowing her to feel the sensation of his tongue as his kiss continued onto her shoulder and into her neckline. His warm breath tickled her earlobe, and she shuttered as he removed his lips, his face moving back to focus on the crest of her expression.

She smiled lasciviously and pulled Kiel into the shadows of the darkened alley. To hell with anyone who could see them now - anyone who might still be watching!

Zia pressed her body to his and could feel his heart – no, hearts – throbbing furiously. She slipped her hand beneath his jacket, and placed an open palm over his left breast, feeling the pulsing beneath the contours of bone and sinew. Her hand slid across his bare chest, and there, beneath the corded muscles of his right breast, beat *another* heart. It was true! Her own heart pounded with excitement, and she pulled him closer. Three hearts rhythmically beating as one.

Zia lifted her face to Kiel, and he impulsively moved his hands to the back of her long, slender neck, extending his open fingers up and into her hair. Desperately, desirously he clenched the tresses, pulling Zia's face toward his and pressing his lips to hers.

Feverish, his mouth opened and the passion within him spilled over into Zia, his kiss quickening and caressing her soul. She let go and surrendered, allowing herself to fall into a soft and secure place within his arms.

How any of this was possible, she didn't know… and she didn't care.

Not now, anyway.

Not tonight.

WATCH THE SKIES
FOR THE SEQUEL TO

ZIA

LANDING 2012

ABOUT THE AUTHOR

TERRY LOVETT was born Teresa Anderson and grew up in the oil fields of West Texas. She attended Texas A&M University where she majored in mass communications. During her junior year, the family moved to the Land of Enchantment where she was crowned Miss New Mexico and competed in the Miss America Pageant. After college, she married and returned to Texas but in 2003, as a newly single parent, she relocated her family to Celebration, Florida. She became a Fantasyland cast member and worked in Walt Disney World's Magic Kingdom until 2010. Today, she is once again a resident of the Lone Star State, but will always consider The Sunshine State her second home.

Made in the USA
Charleston, SC
14 May 2011